'There is a matter on ~~...~~ ~~...~~ ~~...~~ ~~...~~erable
assistance to me ~~...~~ ~~...~~other.
'*Was* there a R~~...~~ ~~...~~ my
father's mother, ~~...~~ ~~...~~nate
marriage?'

'Lord, how shoul~~...~~ ~~...~~ Lady Frederick replied
brusquely. 'I never paid the least heed to your father's
family. Why do you wish to know?'

Mr Ranleigh shrugged. 'Because Miss Daingerfield-
Nelson informs me that her name is not Daingerfield-
Nelson, but Hadley, and that her grandfather was a
cousin of my grandmother.'

Lady Frederick snorted. 'A pretty tale! And she took
you in with it? She *must* be a beauty—and a sharp one
to boot.'

Mr Ranleigh allowed his abstracted gaze to rest on one
highly polished boot. 'No, she is not a beauty,' he said
critically. 'Neither has she taken me in. Nevertheless I
am very much inclined to believe that she was speaking
the truth. And if she is indeed a Hadley—'

'Speaking the truth!' Lady Frederick repeated scornfully.
'A common creature from the theatre connected with a
Duchess of Belfour? What makes you think she is?
Good Heavens, Robert, anyone could make such a
claim!'

Also by Clare Darcy in *Star*:

GEORGINA
LYDIA
ALLEGRA
VICTOIRE
LADY PAMELA

CECILY

Clare Darcy

Star
A STAR BOOK
published by
the Paperback Division of
W. H. ALLEN & Co. Ltd.

A Star Book
Published in Tandem in 1976 by Tandem Publishing Ltd
This edition reprinted 1978, 1980, 1981
by the Paperback Division of
W. H. Allen & Co. Ltd
A Howard and Wyndham Company
44 Hill Street, London W1X 8LB

First published in Great Britain by
Allan Wingate (Publishers) Ltd, 1975
Originally published in the United States
by Walker and Company, 1972

Printed in Great Britain by
The Anchor Press Ltd,
Tiptree, Essex

ISBN 0 352 302216

To Lois Dwight Cole

CHAPTER ONE

The curtain was about to fall on the second act when Mr. Ranleigh arrived at the theatre—a piece of indifference which Lady Comerford, who had invited him to make one of the party in her box that evening, was inclined to regard not so much with indignation as with despair. She should have known what to expect, she told herself bitterly, for she had more than once been warned by Mr. Ranleigh's outspoken mother, Lady Frederick Ranleigh, that not even a young lady so much sought after as Miss Comerford would be likely to induce her son to alter the habits that had for years defeated the efforts of the wiliest of matchmaking mamas.

'Not,' Lady Frederick had added, 'that I should not be excessively happy to see him settle at last, but when a man has reached the age of two-and-thirty without falling into any of the *dozens* of traps that have been laid for him, it is of no use to expect him to marry until he has made up his own mind in cold blood to take the step.'

All of which meant, Lady Comerford thought with doleful candour, surveying Mr. Ranleigh's tall, impeccably attired figure as he bowed over her hand, that Robert Ranleigh was handsome, immensely wealthy, agreeable—if one were prepared to overlook a certain autocratic brusqueness in his manner, and a sometimes uncomfortable ironical expression in his grey eyes—and related to half the best families in England, in addition to being the acknowledged Nonpareil in those sporting pursuits on which gentlemen seemed to set such store. It was obvious that he might have his pick of the young ladies on the

5

Matrimonial Mart; all she could allege, in justification of her own hopes, was the fact that he had seemed to seek her Gussie's company somewhat more frequently since Gussie had let him see, with a freedom of conduct which her mama deplored, that she was very fond of *his*.

But he had recently declined a week's shooting at Comerford, though he must have known that Gussie would be present, and had pledged himself merely to 'look in' on them at the theatre this evening—a vague promise which he apparently considered committed him to no more than that, for he remained in the Comerford box only until the end of the ensuing act, and then went off to engage in conversation with his cousin, Lord Portandrew, and a group of the latter's friends.

He was greeted by these gentlemen with a great deal of enthusiasm, and, after having been complimented by one on a new hunter which had performed to advantage with the Quorn the week preceding, was invited by his cousin to give his opinion of a young actress appearing in a minor role in the play.

'Miss Daingerfield-Nelson,' Lord Portandrew pronounced reverently. 'Tell me, Robert—*have* you ever seen such a deuced enchanting creature? I mean to say, those eyes . . .!'

Mr. Ranleigh, after considering for a moment, inquired if the young woman who had taken his cousin's fancy was the one who resembled a startled fawn, and who had very nearly driven the leading lady into an apoplexy, at a dramatic crisis in the latter's affairs during the act just past, by forgetting her lines completely.

'No, really!' Lord Portandrew protested. 'I don't mean to say she can *act*! Wouldn't expect her to—not a girl with a face like that! Dash it, she don't look like she ought to be out of the schoolroom!'

Mr. Ranleigh said that perhaps it would be as well if she were not. He was regarding his cousin's longtailed coat, with its extravagantly padded shoulders and nipped-in waist, with an expression of frank revulsion, which prompted his lordship to inquire with asperity why the deuce he was looking at him like that.

'Just because you don't care to cut a dash yourself,' said his lordship, 'there's no need for you to look down your nose at someone who does. If you want *my* opinion, Robert, that rig of yours is too sober by half.'

As Mr. Ranleigh's exquisitely cut coat of blue superfine, worn with a plain white waistcoat from which no more than one fob descended, and with a single pearl set in the folds of his snowy neckcloth, was known to have excited the admiration even of such a connoisseur of fashion as the Prince Regent, Lord Portandrew was interrupted at this point by several voices, all reminding him rudely that if he were endowed with the Nonpareil's fine figure and broad shoulders there would be no need for his tailor to seek to give him consequence by the use of buckram wadding and buttons as large as crown-pieces. Lord Portandrew, who was not egotistically inclined, accepted this set-down in good part, remarking equably that he had no intention of entering the lists with his cousin sartorially or in any other way.

'Wouldn't do me any good if I did,' he said simply. 'Look at Gussie Comerford now—hasn't taken her eyes off him since he left their box. Do you know I tried all last season to fix my interest with that girl? Fact! Came dashed close to offering for her, but I knew it wouldn't answer. Deuced embarrassing if every time one's cousin walked into the room one's wife forgot one was alive.'

Sir Harry Brackenridge, a tall gentleman with hair of an odd brassy-yellow colour, whose air and style of dress proclaimed him to be a buck of the first head, remarked languidly that he rather fancied Miss Comerford's prediction for Mr. Ranleigh was not a fair test of the matter.

'The fact is,' he said, 'the fair Gussie and her mama have an eye out for a great fortune, dear boy. I'm afraid Robert would be no more favoured than the rest of us if he weren't so disgustingly rich.'

'Well, I don't know *that*,' Lord Portandrew said obstinately. 'All I *do* know is that he has only to raise a finger and females come running.' He nodded toward the stage, where the curtain was about to rise. 'Take Miss Daingerfield-Nelson,' he said. 'Here the lot of us have been trying all week, one after the other, to get her to take supper with us after the play. But ten to one, if Robert sent round *his* card with a word of invitation scrawled on it, he'd be able to walk off with her on his arm this very evening.'

Sir Harry's brows rose. 'Care to venture money on that, Tony?' he inquired. 'Lay you a monkey he couldn't bring it off.'

'Done!' said Lord Portandrew, with a happy disregard for the fact that it was scarcely in his power to carry out the terms of the wager, since this must depend entirely upon his cousin's willingness to oblige him by making the test.

The rising of the curtain at that point put an end to any further discussion of the matter, for Lord Portandrew settled down at once to a careful scrutiny of the stage, anxious to miss no single moment during which its boards might be graced with the presence of Miss Daingerfield-Nelson.

These moments, unfortunately for his lordship, were few, for the young lady's part was a very brief one, involving in this act no more than her appearance on stage in a group of relatives of the heroine to whom a will was to be read. She spoke the few lines allotted to her quite creditably, however, in a clear, though slightly hurried, voice, and—what was more important to her admirers—afforded them meanwhile an excellent view of a pair of enormous eyes under the fashionable coiffure *à la Tite* in which her dark locks had been dressed, and of a slender figure set off to admiration by a high-waisted tamboured muslin gown.

Mr. Ranleigh, raising his quizzing-glass to observe more closely the young woman who had roused such interest among his friends, was not inclined, however, to revise his earlier opinion of her. He found her lamentably lacking in presence, and while acknowledging the effect of those great eyes, still felt that one might as well fall into raptures over an engaging colt. Obviously the chit *did* belong in the schoolroom, and what she was doing on a London stage—bidding fair, by her

8

very novelty, to become the newest rage among a set of bored young Tulips of the *Ton*—he could not well imagine. His lips twisted in a wry smile. Plainly the girl was gently bred, but it would be wonderful if, after a few months or years of finding half the bucks in London at her feet, she did not end as little better than Haymarket-ware. She had neither experience nor—as her very presence on that stage betokened—protectors, and, without talent to make her way in the theatre, her fall must be as rapid as her rise.

Perhaps he half-expected that the hasty wager concluded between his cousin and Sir Harry Brackenridge at the rising of the curtain might be forgotten by its fall at the end of the act; but such was not the case. Sir Harry, whose long-nourished envy of the position occupied by the Nonpareil in Corinthian circles had recently been intensified—almost, his friends considered, to the point of obsession—by the twin humiliations of a resounding defeat in a London-to-Newmarket curricle race and Mr. Ranleigh's easy success with one of the most brilliant of the West-End comets, whose favours Sir Harry himself was known to have coveted, reverted to the matter at once. He said provocatively that if Ranleigh did not care to venture his prestige on the trial he would consider Lord Portandrew's stake forfeit.

This was enough for Lord Portandrew, who promptly asserted that of course his cousin would stand buff.

'Give me one of your cards, Robert,' he demanded. 'I'll write the message . . .'

'Under *my* eyes, I hope,' Brackenridge intervened. 'A simple invitation to supper it must be—no mysteries to intrigue her with the idea that there is any more than that in it for her.'

'Oh, very well!' Lord Portandrew said. He held out his hand. 'Now, Robert, don't throw a rub in the way!' he adjured him. 'Let me have your card-case.'

Mr. Ranleigh did not move to oblige him. 'You'll be gapped, you know, Tony,' he remarked calmly. 'The girl is obviously not town-bred. If she was not to be moved by an invitation from an Earl, she will certainly not be tempted by one from a mere "Honourable." '

'Gammon!' his cousin replied. 'Wherever she comes from, she'll have heard of *you*. Be a good fellow now, Robert, and give me one of your cards!'

Mr. Ranleigh, who was not known as a persuadable man, might have resisted this entreaty also had not several gentlemen in the company shown a tendency to fall into warm contention over the matter. This appeared to decide him, and, taking out his card-case, he handed one of the cards it contained to his cousin, at the same time rising and remarking that he really must return to the Comerfords' box.

'But if she accepts . . .?' Lord Portandrew expostulated, attempting to detain him.

'My dear boy, she won't!' Mr. Ranleigh said lazily, and strolled off.

He remained in the Comerford box for the remainder of the evening, dismissing the matter of Miss Daingerfield-Nelson from his mind—not quite successfully, however, for it did perforce occur to him once more when that young lady appeared again on the stage and immediately began to subject the Comerford box to an artless scrutiny. She showed no interest in the several ladies there, and gave the merest glance to Lord Comerford and to Gussie's latest flirt, a dashing captain in Life Guardsman's uniform who sat just behind her. Obviously it was Mr. Ranleigh who was the object of her attention, and if he had any notion that it was curiosity alone that was prompting the examination it was dispelled when an attendant's discreet tap on the door of the box at the end of the evening heralded the arrival of a missive bearing his name.

Mr. Ranleigh, unfolding the tiny slip of paper, read the following simple message, penned in a schoolgirl's round, careful hand: 'Miss Daingerfield-Nelson accepts with pleasure Mr. Ranleigh's kind invitation to supper this evening.'

Mr. Ranleigh's plans for the evening had assuredly not included a tête-à-tête supper with a young lady half his age, his taste notoriously running to females of riper years and experience. But there was nothing to do but to resign himself to fulfilling the engagement that had been made in his name, and accordingly, after saying good night to the Comerfords, he strolled round to the Greenroom, where he found Lord Portandrew, Sir Harry Brackenridge, and several other of the gentlemen who had been privy to the wager already gathered, some of them in conversation with the players who had been entertaining them a short while before. These gentlemen, indeed, although they were never heard to enter into knowledgeable discussions on the decline of the theatre since the days of Garrick and Siddons, or on the comparative merits of the Hamlets of Kemble and Kean, were connoisseurs of the theatre in their own way, their attention being chiefly directed toward the younger female members of the various companies. They were at home not only in the Greenrooms of Drury Lane and Covent Garden, but also in those of the less fashionable London theatres, and were to be found with equal frequency in the narrow pink room behind the stage at the Opera House, where they might observe the dancers practising their steps before the long pier-glass mirror and choose a new *chère-amie* with the same careful attention they displayed in the selection of an enamelled snuff-box or other expensive article of *virtu*.

Mr. Ranleigh, glancing about the Greenroom as he entered, observed at once that Miss Daingerfield-Nelson was not among the brightly gowned, berouged young women whose trilling laughter and quick, flirtatious movements gave colour and brilliance to the predominantly male scene. Brackenridge noted his questing glance and said, with a malicious smile, 'So she didn't come up to scratch and you have decided to see what personal persuasion can do. Is that it, Robert?'

Mr. Ranleigh put up his brows. 'Not at all,' he said. 'Owing to your curt busy tongue, Harry, I find myself under the necessity of escorting a schoolroom chit to supper—something to which I assure you I am not looking forward.' He added, beckoning an attendant to him, 'By the bye, you had best pay Tony that five hundred you owe him.'

Lord Portandrew uttered a triumphant: 'Aha! Told you so, dear boy! Never pays to lay your blunt against Robert; he comes through every time!'

'Indeed!' Brackenridge said, dispassionately. 'May I see the evidence, Robert?'

'I daresay it—or should I say *she*?—will put in an appearance presently,' Mr. Ranleigh remarked, as the attendant, to whom he had uttered a brief sentence or two, hurried off. He frowned slightly at his cousin, who was showing an unsportsmanlike tendency to crow over his vanquished opponent. 'Do try to contain your raptures, Tony,' he said. 'You are far too mature to be flying into alt over a chit's blue eyes!'

'They ain't blue,' Lord Portandrew corrected him. 'Grey. Nearly black in certain lights. See if I'm not right.' He added hopefully, 'You'll introduce me, of course? Might put in a good word for me during supper, as well—tell her what a good fellow I am, generous as Midas, charming manners . . .'

Mr. Ranleigh sighed. 'You're sure you wouldn't like to take her off my hands tonight?' he asked, and then broke off as a tall, dapper individual, who had figured in the playbill as *Lord Hetherton*—Mr. *Jillson*, came into the room and purposefully approached him.

'Mr. Ranleigh?' Mr. Jillson, who appeared, as far as one could tell under the disguise of his make-up, to be about forty years of age, exuded a jaunty assurance that showed not the slightest embarrassment at the necessity of addressing himself to what he would undoubtedly have characterised as a group of bang-up swells. He was, in point of fact, already a familiar figure to most of them, for he and his wife, a buxom Titian-haired Irish actress some five years his junior, had appeared over the past dozen years in any number of productions at various London houses, the gentleman having assumed with equal success such diverse roles as those of Aspic, the parasite, in *Education*; the would-be seducer, Sir Charles Cropland, in *The Poor Gentleman*; and Lord Belmour, the dull gallant in *The School for Friends*. 'Jillson is the name, sir—as you see, a humble member of the troupe that has just had the honour of entertaining you. I have a matter of some delicacy to discuss with you; if you would care to step aside with me for a moment . . .'

'What's this?' Brackenridge interposed. 'If it's about Miss Daingerfield-Nelson, there's no need to draw him off; we all know about that supper engagement. Or do we?' he added, looking at Mr. Jillson's thoughtful face. '*Is* there such an engagement, or is there not? Speak up, man! There's a matter of five hundred pounds riding on this!'

Mr. Jillson looked shrewdly from Sir Harry to Mr. Ranleigh, as if he were endeavouring to decide which of several possible answers it would be most to his advantage to return. Temporising, he said at last, 'In a manner of speaking, my dear sir, there *is* an engagement—and in a manner of speaking, there is not.'

Lord Portandrew frowned. 'What does that mean?' he demanded. 'Damme, if Robert says there *is* an engagement . . .'

'Let us say there *was* one,' Mr. Jillson emended his statement, his hesitation apparently overcome by the wrathful expression in his lordship's eyes. 'No need to fly up into the boughs, my dear sir; naturally I have no intention of impugning Mr. Ranleigh's word! However, the fact of the matter is that the young lady is not her own mistress. She is unfortunately under the care of a Female Dragon—if I may use such an unflattering term to describe a lady of the first respectability— who accompanies her to the theatre each evening, and who is highly opposed to Miss Daingerfield-Nelson's accepting invitations from gentlemen personally unknown to her.' He withdrew a folded slip of paper from his pocket and handed it to Mr. Ranleigh. 'Miss Daingerfield-Nelson,' he said, 'has already left the theatre, I regret to say, but before she did so she directed me to see that this note reached your hands.'

Mr. Ranleigh, receiving the paper, unfolded it and scanned its contents. 'I am *desperately* sorry,' the same round schoolgirl hand informed him—this time, however, with marked signs of haste, 'but it is quite impossible for me to meet you tonight. Would you be so kind as to come to the Running Boar at eleven tomorrow morning? I am *most* anxious to speak with you.' Squeezed into a corner there was added, handsomely: 'If convenient.'

Mr. Ranleigh, whose impassivity in the face of extraordinary social situations was famous, betrayed no signs of perturbation to his audience, but he was conscious of the inward stirring of an emotion halfway between exasperation and amusement. He was not accustomed to being cavalierly commanded by school-room misses to appear at unfashionable inns at an hour at which he had customarily not left his bedchamber, and his first impulse was to request Mr. Jillson to inform Miss Daingerfield-Nelson that he would not be able to keep the rendezvous she had appointed.

But no more than a moment's thought was required to make him decide against this course. He had not the slightest interest in the girl, but it did not suit him to see Brackenridge triumph. He therefore said calmly to Mr. Jillson, as he pocketed the note, 'You may tell Miss Daingerfield-Nelson that I shall keep the appointment.'

'*What* appointment?' Lord Portandrew demanded, his countenance lightening. 'Do you mean she didn't simply cry off, after all?'

'Not at all,' Mr. Ranleigh replied. 'I have it on her own authority that she is extremely anxious to see me at another time, if convenient,' he added scrupulously.

'Let me see the note, Robert,' Brackenridge suggested, with a rather mocking grin.

Mr. Ranleigh's eyes narrowed slightly. 'Oh no,' he said softly. 'I have no notion what *your* ideas are on the proper treatment of a lady's private correspondence, but my own assuredly do not include passing it about among my acquaintance.'

'Damme,' Lord Portandrew put in warmly once more, 'if Robert says it's so . . .'

'It *is* so, naturally,' Mr. Ranleigh concluded it for him, resignedly. 'Yes, we know, Tony—but you really must allow Harry to keep his stake until he is quite convinced that he has lost it. Supper, you said, I believe, Tony, so supper it assuredly

14

shall be, even though the Female Dragon must be included in the invitation.'

He nodded to the company and strolled from the room, leaving Mr. Jillson, who had been attending closely to the conversation, to prognosticate comfortingly to Sir Harry that, if the wager lay as it appeared to him, he would certainly come out the winner.

'Not a doubt of it,' he declared. 'I need scarcely tell you gentlemen that in Miss Daingerfield-Nelson you see a young lady of quality, who has been educated in the most genteel style, and who, I may inform you, has hitherto resided in the strictest retirement in the country. She is, if I may take the liberty of phrasing it so, a protégée of mine, and I have great expectations of her success on the boards. But I do *not* think,' he went on, with a smile which Lord Portandrew described later as 'dashed self-satisfied,' 'that she will accept Mr. Ranleigh's invitation. In fact, if I did not consider it unfair to take advantage of my superior knowledge of the situation, I should lay a little wager on that myself!'

CHAPTER TWO

The hour lacked some minutes of noon on the following day when Mr. Ranleigh's curricle, drawn by a pair of match-bays that were, as Lord Portandrew had enviously phrased it, 'complete to a shade,' turned into the yard of the Running Boar in a raw November drizzle. It had required some ingenuity of inquiry for him to find out its whereabouts, for it was not among the hostelries usually frequented by the members of the more important London theatrical companies. He had eventually discovered it in the vicinity of Seven Dials, in a neighbourhood so unremittingly squalid that he was pleasantly surprised to see that the Boar itself appeared to be a reasonably respectable house. It even boasted an ostler who, appearing at the sound of carriage wheels, stood gazing with an incredulity amounting almost to awe at the high-couraged pair and elegant sporting vehicle which Sivil, Mr. Ranleigh's groom, was now jealously guarding from any attempt on his part to take into his charge.

Obviously neither the ostler, standing scratching his head behind Mr. Ranleigh as the latter walked leisurely into the tap-room of the inn, nor the assorted jarveys, labourers, and watermen who witnessed his entrance into their snuggery could conceive what business a Corinthian of his cut might have at the Running Boar. But Miss Daingerfield-Nelson's name, when he inquired for her of the tapster, appeared to bring enlightenment to that worthy, at least.

He said doubtfully, however, that he was not sure whether the young lady would care to receive a caller—a statement that was immediately endorsed by a female voice, speaking in refined but decidedly waspish accents and apparently emanating from the passage outside. Mr. Ranleigh, turning, saw a small, erect, elderly lady, in a serviceable pelisse and a flat-crowned bonnet that might have been in the mode a dozen years before, standing just outside the taproom door, regarding him from a pair of remarkably spirited blue eyes.

'May I request that you step into the passage, sir?' she addressed him acidly, her gaze sweeping over him in a comprehensive glance that seemed to sum up his entire appearance, from his gleaming top-boots to the bedford crop that severely restrained a tendency of his crisp fair hair to curl, and cast it into the outer darkness of her disapproval. 'It may suit *your* notions of propriety to bandy my niece's name about in a common taproom, but I can assure you that it does not suit mine!'

Mr. Ranleigh, who could not remember the last time he had been taxed with faulty manners—an occurrence probably dating back to schoolroom days—began to perceive that his pursuit of the elusive Miss Daingerfield-Nelson was to prove the source of more than one new experience for him. However, he stepped out into the passage with an unmoved countenance, and assured the lady—in whom he had no difficulty in recognising Mr. Jillson's 'Female Dragon'—that it was at Miss Daingerfield-Nelson's own request that he was inquiring for her here.

'I don't believe it!' the lady said flatly, and, placing both hands inside the small muff she was carrying, stood confronting him as if she dared him to prove her wrong.

Mr. Ranleigh, aware that any efforts along this line would lay him open to an accusation of having the bad manners to contradict a lady, gave her the faint smile with which he had charmed dozens of far more experienced females into exchanging indignation for complaisance. It appeared to melt her for a moment, but she immediately jerked herself back into antipathy.

'And don't think you can cozen me into letting you see my niece with one of your smiles!' she said. 'Let me tell you, sir, that that child is *not* a light female, though she *is* at the moment obliged to appear upon the stage!'

'Madam, I assure you that I have not the slightest notion that she is,' Mr. Ranleigh said, with perfect truthfulness.

But at this point he was interrupted by a feminine voice that struck with some familiarity on his ear, proceeding from somewhere over his head.

'Mr. Ranleigh!' He glanced up to see Miss Daingerfield-Nelson herself peering at him over the bannisters at the top of the staircase. 'Oh, do come up!' she exclaimed cordially. 'It is so *very* good of you to come—though indeed I wish you might have arrived sooner!'

'Cecily!' the elderly woman interposed, looking up at her with an incredulous expression on her face. 'What in the *world* has come over you? You will go back to your room immediately! *I* shall deal with this gentleman!'

Miss Daingerfield-Nelson sighed. 'Oh dear, Aunt, I was *sure* you would not understand,' she said. 'That is why I didn't wish you to know until after . . . But there is no use talking of that now. Do please bring Mr. Ranleigh up, for I *must* speak with him, and I don't suppose you had rather I did it in the passage.'

The elderly lady gasped, and looked at Mr. Ranleigh to see what effect this forward speech had had upon him. As he seemed not at all shocked, however, she gathered the remnants of her own composure and remarked with dignity, 'I am afraid, sir, that my niece has quite taken leave of her senses. However, she is right about one thing, at least: it will not do to continue this conversation here!'

She thereupon turned about and marched up the stairs, giving Mr. Ranleigh tacit permission to follow her if he chose.

He was not at all certain that he was wise to do so, but by this time his curiosity was thoroughly aroused, and follow her he did. At the top of the staircase he came face to face with Miss Daingerfield-Nelson. She wore a shabby round gown of blue kerseymere, made up high to the throat, with neither frills nor lace, and, with her dark locks ruthlessly confined by a ribbon, looked even more disarmingly youthful than the elegantly attired young lady he had seen the night before at the theatre. She gave him her hand with a mixture of shyness and enthusiasm and said in a rush, 'How do you do? I am so very glad to meet you at last, for I've known about you forever, though I should never have dared to call myself to your notice if you had not expressed the wish to make *my* acquaintance. You see, my name isn't *really* Daingerfield-Nelson; it's Hadley, and—that is, we're related, you know!'

Mr. Ranleigh, finding a situation at last that refused to submit to being encountered with an air of polite boredom, frowned and said, 'Oh, my God!' rather bitterly.

Miss Hadley looked taken aback. 'I—I beg your pardon!' she faltered. A vivid flush suddenly overspread her face. 'Oh! I see! You aren't pleased—of course you're not! But *pray* don't be angry until you've heard me out. I don't intend to ask you for financial assistance; truly I don't! It's only—you see, we have always lived in the country and we don't know *anyone*,' she floundered on desperately, 'and you must know so many people, all of them of the *first* respectability . . .'

Mr. Ranleigh, whose sense of humour had betrayed him into abandoning a proper indignation on more than one occasion, found that it was doing so again.

'Oh, not *all* of the first respectability, I'm afraid,' he murmured, a gleam of amusement entering his eyes.

Miss Hadley checked, looked at him dolefully, and was encouraged to give a small chuckle herself.

'No, I expect they are not,' she conceded, 'for Corinthians *do* go to such places as Cribb's Parlour—do they not?—and to watch pugilistic exhibitions and cock-fights and things of that sort, where the company is probably not at all *comme il faut . . .*'

'Cecily,' her aunt interrupted, scandalised, 'you will oblige me by discontinuing this extremely improper conversation immediately! If Mr. Ranleigh is indeed related to you, he will certainly take a very odd notion of your upbringing if you speak to him in such a fashion!' She looked up at Mr. Ranleigh pertinaciously. '*Are* you connected with the Hadleys, sir?' she demanded. 'If you are not, you had much better go about your business at once.'

It occurred to Mr. Ranleigh that this was an excellent piece of advice, but, somewhat to his own surprise, he found that he was not about to take it. It might have been reluctance to see Lord Portandrew lose his stake that decided him, or, again, it might have been the imploring look in Miss Hadley's eyes. He merely remarked, therefore, that he believed he could satisfy her on that point—a statement which impelled Miss Hadley to say triumphantly that she had known it was so from the start.

She promptly led the way into a small and excessively ill-furnished parlour and, having made her aunt known to him as Miss Dowie, invited him to sit down. She and Miss Dowie then placed themselves opposite, the latter perched stiffly on the very edge of her chair, as if she were prepared to bounce up at the slightest hint of impropriety and sweep Mr. Ranleigh from the room.

Miss Hadley, however, at once began the conversation on a subject of which even the highest stickler would have found it difficult to disapprove. She said, with a rapidity which showed how familiar she was with her facts. 'Your grandmother was born Mary Hadley—was she not? She married Lord Henry Ranleigh, the second son of the Third Duke of Belfour, who later became the *Fifth* Duke when his brother Alfred, the *Fourth* Duke, died without issue. And *my* grandfather was Robert Hadley, whose father and Mary Hadley's father were brothers, so that Robert and Mary were cousins, you see.' She looked at him anxiously. 'Of course it is a very distant relationship,' she said conscientiously, 'but I am sure you will find Robert—my grandfather—if you look on your grandmother's family tree. He married very much against the wishes of his family, I am afraid, so that they quite cut him off—but that doesn't alter the relationship, does it?'

'Not if it exists,' Mr. Ranleigh agreed. He was rapidly reviewing Miss Hadley's genealogical history in his mind; it was accurate enough as far as his own family was concerned, but, beyond the vaguest of memories of some errant relative of his paternal grandmother who was said to have married the daughter of a City merchant and drunk himself into an early grave, he had no recollection of ever having heard of a Robert Hadley. He regarded Miss Hadley coolly. 'Even supposing that you are correct in assuming that it *does* exist,' he said, 'I do not quite gather what it is that you wish me to do?'

Miss Hadley, quelled by this unencouraging inquiry, swallowed visibly and said in a small voice, 'Only—if you would be kind enough to recommend me to some—some respectable family of your acquaintance that is in need of a governess? You see, it is necessary for me to earn my own living, and it is excessively uncomfortable for me to do so on the stage.'

'*Is* it?' Mr. Ranleigh asked, raising his brows—a piece of cold-blooded scepticism that brought Miss Dowie, bristling, into the fray.

'I should think, sir,' she said with asperity, 'that any gentleman worthy of the name could perceive at a glance that this child does not belong in the theatre!'

'Then I wonder that you should allow her to appear there,' Mr. Ranleigh remarked calmly.

To his surprise, tears sprang into Miss Dowie's blue eyes, but she blinked them away swiftly, saying to him with a fierceness which quite belied her diminutive form, 'Do you think I should do so, sir, if there were any other way to keep a roof over her head? Yes, it has come to that with us—but there is no reason, of course, why that should interest *you*. *You* have come merely to amuse yourself by tempting this child into a life that she is as far above as your own sister is, if you have one. But let me give you my word, sir, that *that* you will not succeed in doing, as long as there is breath left in my body!'

Mr. Ranleigh, finding himself cast in the role of heartless seducer by one lady, and of charitable patron by the other, found it expedient to clarify the situation. He therefore explained that his presence at the Running Boar was due merely to an imprudent wager made by a young kinsman of his, and assured Miss Dowie that his interest in her niece did not extend beyond escorting her to supper on a single occasion. This explanation

21

did not mollify Miss Dowie, but, somewhat to his surprise, Miss Hadleigh herself greeted it with every appearance of relief.

'Oh, I am so glad!' she said. 'It makes it so very much more comfortable, you see, if you are not interested in me in *that* way. Not,' she added frankly, 'that I ever really believed you were, for my neck is too long and my mouth far too wide, and you are, of course, accustomed to the company of the most beautiful ladies of the *haut ton* . . .' She noted Mr. Ranleigh's rather startled look and added kindly, 'It says so constantly in the society journals, you know. Naturally we did not subscribe to them ourselves, but Mrs. Ackling was *very* fond of them and took them all, and she let me borrow them regularly.'

'And who,' he inquired, fascinated by this disclosure, 'is Mrs. Ackling?'

'Was,' she corrected him regretfully. 'She died last spring, you see, just before Papa did. Well, she was a neighbour of ours in Hampshire—in fact, the *only* neighbour who ever called on us, for, in spite of being a *very* high stickler herself, she did not seem to mind Papa's Unfortunate Habits as much as the others did.'

Miss Dowie sniffed, and said that, in *her* opinion, the only reason Mrs. Ackling had called at the Grange had been to poke her nose into business that was no affair of hers.

'Telling me that I ought to remove the child from Hadley's influence and take her to my brother Timothy's!' she said. '*That* would be moving from the skillet into the fire, indeed!'

Mr. Ranleigh was strongly aware that, by remaining where he was, he was being irresistibly drawn into the personal affairs of a pair of females of whose very existence he had been happily ignorant four-and-twenty hours previously; yet he made no move to depart.

'That may well be, ma'am,' he said to Miss Dowie, 'but it still appears to me that it would be more suitable for you to place your niece under your brother's protection than to allow her to appear in the theatre.'

Miss Dowie received this speech with a slight compression of the lips and a distinctly militant expression.

'Your reasoning, sir,' she remarked witheringly, 'is quite correct, except for one circumstance. You are not, I take it, acquainted with my brother, Sir Timothy Dowie?'

'I have not that honour,' Mr. Ranleigh acknowledged.

'Then pray do not be making foolish suggestions about my placing my niece under his care,' Miss Dowie snapped. 'The man is a Monster, sir! He has made it quite plain that he will do nothing for the child—and even if he would,' she added, with dark inconsistency, 'her reputation and morals would certainly be in greater danger under *his* roof than they are under this.'

Mr. Ranleigh looked inquiringly at Miss Hadley, who shrugged her shoulders slightly and said that she had met her uncle only twice, so that she could not say that she knew him well.

'But I daresay it would do no good if we were to appeal to him,' she said, 'for he wrote Aunt an excessively disagreeable letter when Papa died, and said he expected Papa had been able to leave us enough to live on, and if he had not, she need not think *he* was able to do anything for us. And that is the last we have heard from him.'

'But, my good child, if he is your uncle and nearest of kin,' Mr. Ranleigh said reasonably, 'surely he will not leave you to face the world without a penny when he is made aware of the true state of your affairs. I should certainly advise you to write to him at once, or to visit him if he is town.'

Miss Dowie shuddered. 'Nothing,' she said, 'would induce me to enter That Man's door,' and then utterly destroyed the high drama of this pronouncement by adding prosaically, 'Besides, he wouldn't let me in. We quarrelled on the occasion of Cecily's mama's death, when I left Dowie House to go to live under my brother-in-law's roof and undertake the child's rearing, and we have not been upon terms since. In fact, his conduct—morally speaking—has been such in recent years that I have found it necessary to sever the connexion altogether.'

Mr. Ranleigh, in his unaccustomed role of family adviser, was about to utter a pithy homily on the absurdity of maintaining a personal feud when one's bread-and-butter was at stake, when there was a jaunty tattoo upon the door and Mr. Jillson walked into the room.

'Ah! Mr. Ranleigh!' he remarked, observing that gentleman with a benign air. 'Our genial host told me I should find you here. Ladies—your obedient servant!'

Seen in the muddy daylight filtering through the unwashed windows, and in a costume consisting of a very short blue jacket and a pair of yellow pantaloons that bagged visibly at the knees, it was apparent that the elegance that had invested Mr. Jillson the evening before had been exclusively theatrical in nature. His air of assurance, however, was unimpaired. Finding himself regarded by Miss Hadley with frank dislike, and by her aunt with a disapproval so marked that it would have made a more sensitive man quail, he looked with bland equanimity at Mr. Ranleigh and remarked, 'I scarcely expected to find you honouring this humble roof with your presence, sir. But I perceive that you are a gentleman of more than usual persistence of character, and that once you have made up your mind to something, you are not easily baulked of your purpose. May I inquire how you have succeeded in your errand?'

'You may not,' Mr. Ranleigh replied, with equal equanimity. 'May I, however, inquire of *you*, sir, whether it is your practice to intrude uninvited upon a private conversation in a lady's parlour?'

'Not at all,' Mr. Jillson protested affably. 'You mistake the situation, my dear sir. I stand—if I may say so—in the role of protector to these two friendless females, and as such—'

Miss Dowie, interrupting indignantly at this point, requested to know what reason he had to believe that the loan of the paltry sum of fifteen pounds gave him any such pretensions.

'You are an impudent coxcomb, sir!' she said. 'Have the goodness to leave this room at once!'

Mr. Jillson bowed. 'Your wish, dear lady, is my command. May I remind you, however, that *my* interest in Miss—er— Daingerfield-Nelson is quite without ulterior motives, beyond the praiseworthy one of earning an honest livelihood for us

24

both?—an advantage I believe I have over Mr. Ranleigh and the other gentlemen moving in the exalted circles customarily favoured with his presence.'

Miss Dowie gave him a glance of loathing. 'Oh, go away and stop your blathering, man!' she said unceremoniously. 'And *do* give over calling my niece by that ridiculous name! Dainger-field-Nelson! Of all the shabby-genteel monstrosities to foist upon her!'

Mr. Jillson, who had apparently become inured to Miss Dowie's frankness in the course of his dealings with her, bowed and implied that he would be very happy to take himself off if he might have the privilege of a word in private with Mr. Ranleigh. This brought Miss Hadley into the argument.

'Oh, no!' she protested. 'Mr. Ranleigh is not going yet!' She cast him a hopeful glance. 'You *won't* go—will you?' she begged. 'Not before I am able to put before you how *easily* you could assist us . . .'

Mr. Ranleigh rose. 'I fear I must,' he said.

'Oh, no!' Miss Hadley exclaimed again, in dismay. 'Indeed, I have told you the truth, sir; we do not at all wish to hang on your sleeve, but a mere recommendation could mean *so* much . . .'

'I shall look into the matter,' Mr. Ranleigh said noncommittally. 'May I bid you good morning, Miss Hadley—Miss Dowie? Mr.—Jillson, is it? If you are quite ready . . .'

Mr. Jillson, impelled out of the room by no more than the flicker of a glance from Mr. Ranleigh's cool eyes, found himself, in the space of five seconds, standing in the passage outside with the door closed behind him. Mr. Ranleigh faced him, waiting.

'Yes?' he said unencouragingly.

Mr. Jillson's air of assurance faltered slightly under that cold, steady gaze. He recovered himself and said, 'My dear sir, surely there is no need to be in such a hurry! Perhaps over a glass of ale . . .'

'If you have something to say to me, you had best say it at once,' Mr. Ranleigh said curtly. 'What is it?'

'Why, I . . .' Mr. Jillson came aground again, then plucked up and said impudently, 'You're in a tearing hurry, ain't you? Well, I'll put it to you straight, then. The fact is, you're looking for no more than a bit of fun, but it's bread-and-butter to *me*, you see! The chit will be worth a fortune, once she's learned her way about a bit—but *not* if she has her head turned by such as you. You know as well as I do what will become of her if she's taken up by your lot before she's had the chance to make a name for herself.'

'And what,' Mr. Ranleigh asked directly, 'will become of her under your protection, Jillson?'

Mr. Jillson described an airy gesture which appeared to encompass infinite space. 'The world, my dear sir,' he said, 'will be at her feet! Even now I am coaching her in the leading female role in *The Beaux' Stratagem*, a part ideally suited to her talents, with which I expect to establish her firmly upon the London stage. Then, let us say, a dozen years on that stage under my aegis—for I shall, of course, in due time form my own company as a setting for her talents. During this period she will reign as the toast of the metropolis—after which I shall retire to a life of well-earned ease, while she marries whichever of her noble suitors has the plumpest purse and the least dislike to bringing an actress into the family.'

'A pretty picture,' Mr. Ranleigh said dryly, beginning to descend the stairs. 'You surprise me, Jillson. I had not suspected you of such romantic dreams.'

'Not in the least, sir!' Mr. Jillson said, following him. 'I assure you it all lies in the realm of sober reality. You have seen the young lady herself, and you will admit that there is something about her—something surpassing beauty; I might almost say surpassing charm—which instantly appeals to the male heart. She cannot fail, if properly managed—a matter to which I intend to devote the considerable store of experience I have gained in twenty years upon the boards.'

He was following close behind Mr. Ranleigh, and was slightly disconcerted, as he reached the foot of the stairs, when that gentleman suddenly halted and turned about, facing him.

'Tell me, Jillson—exactly where did you come upon her?' he demanded.

Mr. Jillson, having no time to reflect, was surprised into speaking the truth.

'As a matter of fact, in Southampton,' he said, 'where the theatrical company which was at the moment enjoying the benefit of my own and Mrs. Jillson's talents was playing at the New Theatre in French Street. I made her acquaintance at the hostelry in which she and Miss Dowie had been obliged to seek refuge after having been turned out of their lamentably higher mortgaged home following the death of the young lady's father, and was able to be of some slight assistance to them in certain financial embarrassments having to do with paying their shot at the inn.' He added cautiously, 'Why do you want to know?'

'The merest curiosity,' Mr. Ranleigh said briefly and, without lingering for any further conversation, walked out the front door and summoned his curricle.

CHAPTER THREE

Mr. Ranleigh drove immediately to his house in Mount Street, where he found his mother, Lady Frederick, entertaining Lady Comerford and Miss Augusta Comerford in the Crimson Saloon. When he entered this apartment he found the two elder ladies seated together on a handsome satinwood sofa, enjoying a confidential gossip on the recent marriages of the three Royal Dukes of Kent, Cambridge, and Clarence. Miss Comerford, a dark and opulent beauty whose oval green eyes were reputed to have broken a score of hearts during her two London seasons, was seated opposite.

Lady Frederick, an imposing dowager of sixty, wore a purple-beribboned cap and a rather remarkable yellow gown with a point lace ruff, for she had a dislike, she was accustomed to saying, of the niminy-piminy colours of the modern vogue. She regarded her son with an air of hauteur that successfully concealed her fondness for him, and remarked to him, in her richly regal voice, 'So you've come in—have you? To what am I to attribute this honour, pray?' She turned to Lady Comerford. 'You do not know, Letitia,' she informed her acidly, 'how fortunate you are to have only daughters. At least you may keep *them* about when you have need of them. Now it does *me* no more good to come to town than if I was to remain at Hillcourt, for if Robert is not in Leicestershire when I am here he is at Newmarket, and if he's not there he's on the Continent. As for Hillcourt, it might fall into ruin if it weren't for me, for he never goes near the place when he can help it.'

Mr. Ranleigh, exchanging greetings with Lady Comerford

and Gussie, strolled up to his mother, possessed himself of her hand, and kissed it lightly.

'What has happened to put you in such a bad skin, ma'am?' he inquired, smiling down at her. 'More royal marriages? I thought I caught Clarence's name as I came in the door.'

'Nothing of the sort,' Lady Frederick said roundly. 'If that parcel of middle-aged fools want to make cakes of themselves with their German brides—and I am sure Kent's, at least, was chosen for him because her previous marriage had already proven her a good breeder—that is entirely their affair.' She gave a short bark of laughter. 'Lord! There is Clarence with ten bastards already,' she said, 'but I daresay he is played out by this time. What a pity it is that he couldn't have married his actress! *That* would have put an end to all this scurrying about for an heir to the throne!'

'Louisa! Really! Before Gussie . . .!' Lady Comerford protested feebly.

'Pooh!' said Lady Frederick. 'Gussie's not one to put on Bath-miss airs. *She* knows the time of day a great deal better than you do, Letitia.'

Gussie indeed seemed quite unperturbed by her hostess's frank speech. She was giving her attention to Mr. Ranleigh, who came over to sit beside her; there was a note of half-teasing pleasure in her voice as she spoke to him.

'Indeed, I told Mama that we ought not to call in Mount Street today,' she said. 'I was afraid we had already put your civility to too great a test last evening at the theatre, when you would no doubt much rather have been paying court to Miss Daingerfield-Nelson than sitting tamely in our box.'

'Good God, has that tale made the rounds already?' he asked without discomposure. 'I daresay you had the whole of it, then—that I was pitchforked into the business trying to save Tony's groats?'

Lady Frederick demanded at this point to be told what it was they were talking of, and was given a highly coloured version of the previous night's events by Miss Comerford—a piece of frankness that was greeted by her mama with a scandalised request to know where she had heard such an extremely improper story.

'From Brackenridge, of course,' Gussie said. She turned again to Mr. Ranleigh. 'You must know,' she said, 'that he, of all people, will lose no opportunity to spread the tale of your discomfiture. Your only recourse will be in parading the Daingerfield-Nelson chit on your arm before the eyes of the town. I daresay that is not *quite* beyond your powers of persuasion?'

Mr. Ranleigh gave her a light answer and turned the conversation to another topic; but when Lady Comerford and her daughter had departed some few minutes later and he was left alone with his mother, he returned to the subject of Miss Daingerfield-Nelson at once.

'There is a matter on which you can be of considerable assistance to me,' he remarked. '*Was* there a Robert Hadley who was cousin to my father's mother, and who made a rather unfortunate marriage?'

Lady Frederick stared at him. 'Lord, how should I know?' she replied brusquely. 'I never paid the least heed to your father's family. Fools or rascals, every one of 'em, except Frederick—and he may have been one, too, only he was such a handsome rogue no one ever found him out! Why do you wish to know?'

Mr. Ranleigh shrugged. 'Because I seem to have discovered his granddaughter. I saw Miss Daingerfield-Nelson this morning, and she informs me that her name is not Daingerfield-Nelson, but Hadley, and that her grandfather was a cousin to my grandmother.'

Lady Frederick snorted. 'A pretty tale! And she took *you* in with it? She *must* be a beauty—and a sharp one, to boot.'

Mr. Ranleigh disposed his long limbs comfortably in a chair, crossing one leg over the other and allowing his abstracted gaze to rest on the highly polished boot that adorned it.

'No, she is not a beauty,' he said critically. 'Neither has she taken me in. Nevertheless, I am much inclined to believe that she was speaking the truth.'

Lady Frederick's dark eyes took on a scornful expression. 'Speaking the truth!' she repeated. 'A common creature from the theatre connected with a Duchess of Belfour? Lord, Robert, you are talking like a flat, and *that* is something I never thought to hear! You, with all *your* experience . . .'

He smiled slightly. 'My experience, my dear, is something which you are presumed to know nothing about!' he said. 'Are you trying to scandalise me, as you did poor Lady Comerford?'

'Oh—Letitia!' she said impatiently. 'Of course I know all about your petticoat affairs—or as much as I want to, at any rate. But it's time you were thinking of settling down, all the same. If you'll take my advice, you'll offer for Gussie Comerford. The family's a good one, she's handsome enough, and I daresay she'd lead you a lively enough dance that you wouldn't have time for your bits of muslin. Not,' she added tartly, 'that *my* opinion will carry any weight with you. Who is this hussy you're dangling after now?—besides being related to Mary Hadley, of course.'

Mr. Ranleigh said, a slight smile gleaming in his grey eyes, 'You are wrong on all points, ma'am. I do value your opinion: it is precisely what I am seeking now. And the girl is far from being a hussy; on the contrary, she is extremely young and innocent, and quite out of her depth in the company in which she finds herself at present. Neither am I "dangling after her"; schoolroom chits are hardly in my line. But if she is indeed a Hadley . . .'

'What makes you think she is?' Lady Frederick demanded. 'Good heavens, Robert, anyone could make such a claim!'

'Exactly,' he agreed. 'However, her aunt, who is obviously a lady, in spite of being a Tartar of the first order, supports her claim, and gives herself out as being the sister of one Sir Timothy Dowie. You would not, I expect, happen to be acquainted with him?'

Lady Frederick's brows came together in a slight frown. 'Dowie?' she said. 'No, I am not, but I've heard the name. My brother Albion knew him in his salad days, I fancy. A shocking loose-screw, if I remember correctly—the sort of person Albion *would* know. But that was years and years ago—thirty at least, I should think. If this is the same man, he should be almost sixty now.'

'As Miss Dowie seems to be near that age herself, that would be very probable,' Mr. Ranleigh agreed. 'At any rate, from what I can gather, he seems to have turned a very cold shoulder to his niece when her father died some months ago—so cold that Miss Dowie was impelled to accept the assistance of a chance-met actor named Jillson in placing the girl on the stage.'

Lady Frederick, who in spite of the harshness of her tongue, was well known for her autocratic and eccentric charities, began to find the conversation of interest. However, she only said severely, 'Nonsense! It sounds to me very much as if you had been dipping into lending-library novels—an occupation which I find particularly revolting in a man. I daresay *you* have been cast in the role of Lord Bountiful in this sentimental drama?'

'If you mean that the girl is hoping to obtain financial assistance from me, she assures me that she is not,' Mr. Ranleigh said. 'She *has* given me to understand, however, that she would appreciate a recommendation to a family of the—er—first respectability which finds itself in need of a governess.'

Lady Frederick surveyed him grimly. 'Coming it much too strong, my boy!' she said pungently. 'Hire a governess off the London stage! You cannot suppose I shall believe that she actually proposed *that* to you!'

'I assure you, she did, however,' Mr. Ranleigh reiterated, smiling slightly. 'I told you she was very young and very, very green.'

'If that is so, it appears to me that it is that aunt of hers who should be seeking employment, not the child!'

'Yes, that has occurred to me, too,' Mr. Ranleigh admitted. 'But if I am any judge, Miss Dowie is past the age to be readily employed to look after young children. She might hope to become some elderly lady's *dame de compagnie*, but I doubt that she would be able to hold such a position long. She lacks,' he explained, a reminiscent gleam in his eye, 'a certain tact.'

Lady Frederick said unsympathetically that at least that might be more tolerable than Henrietta Wixom's behaviour, which was so extremely tactful that you might tell her the moon was made of green cheese without her making bold to differ with you; but apparently her mind at that moment was on neither Miss Dowie nor the distant kinswoman who served as her own companion. There was a faraway expression in her eyes, and after a few moments she announced firmly that Sir Timothy—if the peculiar tale she had just attended to were true—should certainly be induced to do something for his relations.

'Exactly what I have been thinking, ma'am,' Mr. Ranleigh agreed, a muscle quivering at the corner of his mouth.

His mother looked at him suspiciously. 'I daresay you have been leading up to this all along,' she said. 'Now, tell me—why should you interest yourself in this chit? You say she ain't no beauty and you ain't dangling after her, but I've yet to see you stirring a step out of your way for girls who are far more closely connected with you than *this* one claims to be—that brood of Belfour's, for example.'

'Ah, but my cousin Belfour's daughters are not in the hands of a seedy rascal who considers them in the light of salable merchandise,' Mr. Ranleigh remarked. 'I find I have a certain dislike to seeing anyone of my blood in that position. She has, by the bye, an odd look of that Reynolds portrait of my grandmother in the Ivory Saloon at Hillcourt—the same slender neck and enormous eyes . . .'

Lady Frederick said, 'Humph!' and then, grudgingly, 'I expect something must be done. Of course the Hadleys were merely Country people, and I doubt that the old Duke—your great-grandfather—could have countenanced your grandfather's marriage into that family if there had been any expectation at the time that he would inherit the title. Still there's good blood there—some of the oldest in England. It won't do to have it dragged in the mud. You had best go to see Albion. He may be able to tell you where Sir Timothy Dowie is to be found.'

As a matter of fact, Mr. Albion Wymberly, when Mr. Ranleigh ran him to earth at White's a short time later, was quite willing and able to be helpful along this line. Mr. Wymberly, a gentleman of an extreme rotundity which had been agree-ably nourished over some fifty-odd years on the delicacies pre-pared by his own and his carefully chosen friends' French cooks, was somewhat surprised to find himself the object of his nephew's attention, and took advantage of the opportunity to inquire whether it would be convenient for him to make him a small loan.

Mr. Ranleigh took out his pocketbook. 'How much?' he asked resignedly.

Mr. Wymberly looked injured. 'Only a miserable pony. *You*'ll never miss it. I'll tell you what, my boy, if you're going to be as damned tactless as this when a man makes a civil request of you, you'll soon find yourself looking for friends.'

Mr. Ranleigh gave him a rather twisted smile. 'Oh, no, I think not—so long as I contrive not to wake up a pauper some morning,' he said. 'Having now satisfied *your* request, Albion, I'll ask you to satisfy mine. Are you acquainted with a Sir Timothy Dowie?'

'Dowie?' Mr. Wymberly repeated. 'Why, yes. Ran into him only yesterday—and a more repulsive sight I must say I never laid eyes on. His cravat, dear boy! Greasy—positively greasy! And he was used to be rather dapper-dog thirty years ago.'

'What's his family?' Mr. Ranleigh asked. 'Or don't you know that?'

'Of course I know,' said Mr. Wymberly, affronted once more, for he was something of an amateur of genealogy. 'Hampshire people—never distinguished, though the baronetcy dates back to Elizabeth.'

'Money?'

'Oh, no—a competence merely. He was a great gamester in the old days, and ran through the better part of his estate. Still has the place in Hampshire, though, I believe.' Mr. Wymberly regarded his nephew with suddenly suspicious eyes. 'If you're running some sort of rig that involves Tim Dowie, let me tell you, you're better out of it,' he said. 'The way I understand it, he's turned into a damned squeeze-farthing these days, with a taste for taking a man to law for damages if he

34

so much as sends him a crooked look. Best keep out of his path, my boy!'

'Oh, he'd find me an ill bird for plucking,' Mr. Ranleigh said indifferently. 'You can tell me one thing more about him if you are able, though. Had he a sister who married a man named Hadley?'

'Hadley? No, I don't know that—though he did have sisters, if I remember rightly. But Hadley was your grandmother's name...'

'Exactly,' Mr. Ranleigh said. 'And she had, if I am correctly informed, a cousin named Robert, who seems to have contracted an ill-advised marriage.'

'Daughter of a Cit,' Mr. Wymberly corroborated promptly. 'Before my time, of course, but I remember my father mentioning it. Dashed silly thing to do—the girl wasn't even plump in the pocket. Why do you want to know?'

Ranleigh rose. 'I doubt that my reasons would be of interest to you,' he said. 'Might I trouble you for Sir Timothy's direction, if you know it?'

'Always used to put up at Limmer's—but look here, Robert, I'm serious!' Mr. Wymberly said urgently. 'Take my advice and stay clear of him. Good God, if there *is* a connexion, you'll get nothing from acknowledging it but the pleasure of finding yourself with a set of dirty dishes on your hands.'

'Yes, I rather fear you are right,' Mr. Ranleigh agreed imperturbably, and took his departure, leaving Mr. Wymberly—who was well acquainted with his nephew's notorious lack of interest in family ramifications—with his mouth acock behind him.

CHAPTER FOUR

Inquiry at Limmer's Hotel brought the information that Sir Timothy Dowie was not at present among its guests. A knowledgeable clerk, however, was able to tell Mr. Ranleigh that he had been seen there within the past day or two, and had been heard to let fall a statement to the effect that he was staying at a house in Upper Wimpole Street that had been lent him by its owner. Mr. Ranleigh, who had several engagements for the day, none of them in the vicinity of Upper Wimpole Street, looked less than pleased on hearing this, but he was not in the mood to be diverted from his purpose. Driving back to Mount Street and remaining there only long enough to dispatch several messages, he proceeded on at once to beard Sir Timothy Dowie in his borrowed den.

He ran his quarry to earth in a respectable but melancholy-looking house, seated at a table in a small back room with a miserable fire guttering in the grate. As the remainder of the house, its furniture muffled in holland covers, was as chill as a tomb, Mr. Ranleigh was not surprised to find his host wrapped in a greatcoat, and began to wish he had not surrendered his own to the bleary-looking individual who had opened the front door to him.

Sir Timothy, whose old-fashioned garrick allowed only a half-bald head, a grizzled red face, and a somewhat stooped figure to be discerned in the half-light coming through the heavily draped windows, gave him an unwelcoming glance as he walked into the room.

'Ranleigh,' he said, without rising. 'I don't know any Ranleighs. One of the Belfour connexion, I expect. Above *my* touch. What the devil d'ye want with me?'

Mr. Ranleigh, finding that he was not invited to seat himself —an omission which might have been explained by the fact that all the chairs in the room, other than that occupied by Sir Timothy himself, were encumbered by piles of papers and ledgers—unhurriedly removed an untidy heap of documents from one and sat down.

'No, we have not had the pleasure of a previous meeting, I believe,' he said, in an unruffled tone. 'If my information is correct, however, we have a mutual connexion, and it is on this subject that I came to speak to you. You have, I believe, a niece named Cecily Hadley?'

Sir Timothy's brows shot up. 'Hadley? Ay, my sister Grisell's brat—but what the devil has that to do with you?' He checked suddenly. 'Wait now!' he commanded. 'Wait! There was some Ranleigh connexion there, after all; I remember the silly wench's boasting of it when she married Hadley. But what's it to do with you? If ye're the man I take ye to be, ye've better things to do than to be wasting your time over me *or* my niece.'

'You are quite correct. I have,' Mr. Ranleigh assured him. 'It has been brought to my attention, however, that your niece— owing to her reduced circumstances since her father's death— has been obliged to support herself by appearing upon the London stage. I daresay the matter has *not* been brought to *your* attention, which would account for your not having come forward to offer her your assistance.'

Sir Timothy stared at him for a moment, and then broke into a crack of laughter.

'The stage?' he repeated. 'Not *my* niece. You must be raving, man! Why, she's naught but a half-grown chit with her hair in a tangle and her finger stuck in her mouth; nobody'ud pay a farthing to look at her!'

'You have not, I take it,' Mr. Ranleigh remarked, 'seen her lately. Let me assure you that the picture you have drawn is at present a quite inaccurate one.'

'It is, is it?' A look of comprehension crept into Sir

37

Timothy's eyes. 'Ah, so that's the way of it—is it?' he said, giving Mr. Ranleigh a leer and a wink. 'Growed to be a woman —has she?—and now the dogs are after her. Well, what's that to you, my buck? Don't want to marry her—do ye? Because I gi'e ye fair warning—not a penny of *my* coin will ye see settled on her.'

'Thank you, that is a matter that is not of the slightest interest to me,' Mr. Ranleigh said. 'I met Miss Hadley for the first time only this morning, and my one concern is to see her removed from her present entirely unsuitable situation to the protection of some relative.'

Sir Timothy looked at him doubtfully. 'Ah, well—if that's so . . .' he said, and then continued grudgingly, 'Well, I daresay there's no reason she shouldn't go down to Hampshire—though, mind you, I shan't stand the nonsense for any new gowns and kickshaws! If she wants to lead a plain country life and make herself useful, I'll not close my door on her, for poor Grisell's sake. I expect Hadley had something to leave her—eh? They say the Grange was mortgaged, but there must have been a bit left.'

'As I understand it—nothing,' Mr. Ranleigh said bluntly.

Sir Timothy's face flushed with annoyance. 'Ay, that 'ud be Rob Hadley!' he said bitterly. 'Drink and game every groat of it away, and then leave *me* with his brat to feed and house.'

He would have gone on, but he was interrupted at this point by the opening of the door and the unceremonious appearance upon the scene of a buxom middle-aged female in a pelisse of magenta velvet and a bonnet to match, its high poke lined with a pink silk which contrasted boldly with the carroty curls beneath it. Advancing into the room with hand outstretched, she said briskly to Sir Timothy, 'Well, I'm off now, ducky. You must give me some brass for my shopping, as you promised.' She broke off to gaze in some surprise at Mr. Ranleigh and, obviously impressed by the sporting neckcloth, gleaming top-boots, and exquisitely fitted coat that proclaimed the out-and-out Corinthian, to exclaim, 'Eh, now, who's this?'

'None of your affair, my dear,' Sir Timothy said, not mincing words. He opened a drawer in the table at which he sat and extracted a number of coins, counted them out carefully, reflected, replaced one in the drawer, and closed the drawer again. Before the intruder could take the coins from him, however, he had once more changed his mind and drawn back again. 'Nay,' he said hastily, 'ye won't need so much as *that*,' and, reopening the drawer, dropped in another of the coins and handed the remainder to her.

'A-ah, ye're a clutch-fisted old rascal!' she remarked disparagingly. 'Ye said I was to have new clothes when we came up to town, but it's as much as I've been able to do to set a joint on the table and keep coals enough in the house to save us from freezing to death, on the ready I've had from you. But I'll gi'e ye fair warning, Sir Timothy—*this* lot goes on my back, if we go supperless to bed!'

Sir Timothy, who seemed not in the least embarrassed either by her appearance or by her conversation, made her a spirited rejoinder, to which she replied in kind, and she thereupon flounced out of the room.

'My housekeeper, Mrs. Cassaday,' Sir Timothy pronounced imperturbably, as soon as the door had closed behind her. 'A greedy bitch—but they're all alike, ain't they? I'll send her packing one of these days: see if I don't!'

'I should rather hope you might,' Mr. Ranleigh said dryly, 'if it is your intention to take your niece and your sister under your roof. I am persuaded that she and Miss Dowie would not deal in the least.'

'What's that? My sister?' Sir Timothy looked up sharply, with a sudden frown. 'Who the devil said anything about my sister? Damme, I wouldn't let that meddlesome old brimstone inside my door if it was to save her from perdition!'

Mr. Ranleigh's brows went up. 'You must pardon my ignorance, sir,' he said. 'I was not aware that Miss Dowie had independent means.'

'Means? She hasn't a groat. But that's none of *my* affair,' Sir Timothy said callously. 'Hadley was the one should ha' provided for her; she saved him the expense of a housekeeper a matter o' fifteen years. And now she means to come begging to me, does she? Well, you may tell her she'll get nothing out of *my* pocket.'

Mr. Ranleigh, who had not taken Miss Dowie's fierce account of the terms on which she stood with her brother quite at face value, began to perceive that that lady might not, after all, have been indulging in exaggeration. He was not ordinarily accounted a persuasive man, having been fortunate enough to stand all his life on terms with the world where his will was bowed to without argument; but he now swallowed down an inclination to tell Sir Timothy exactly what he thought of his lack of proper family feeling and made an attempt instead to bring him to reason by more diplomatic means.

His efforts were in vain. As a matter of fact, Sir Timothy, instead of abandoning his opposition, showed alarming signs of being about to fly into a towering rage, and at last told his visitor rudely that if he had such a deal of sympathy for Miss Dowie he had best open his own purse to assist her.

'I'll ha' the girl but I won't ha' her, and that's flat!' he said, fulminatingly.

'That is well said, sir,' Mr. Ranleigh retorted blightingly, controlling his own temper with an effort. 'But surely you must be aware that Miss Hadley will not consider abandoning her aunt without some provision being made for her. Even *my* brief acquaintance with her has made me quite certain of that.'

'Then let the two of 'em starve together and be damned to 'em,' Sir Timothy said, 'for I won't ha' Mab Dowie under my roof! It's a hard thing, at any rate, that a man who's never married must be saddled with another man's brat! I'm not a rich man, Mr. Ranleigh, and I've had to learn not to waste my substance. Ye say the girl's on the stage—well, it ain't what I'd choose for her, but I'll wager she'll not need to stay there long.' He cast a shrewd glance at Mr. Ranleigh from under his brows. 'Eh, my lad? When a buck of your cut goes out of his way to look after a chit he's only just met, I fancy she must ha' turned out a handsomer piece of goods than I'd ha' bargained for, so ten to one there'll be some young sprig wanting to put a ring on her finger before she's many months older.'

Mr. Ranleigh, hearing his host fall into these complacent reflexions, realised that he had indeed been wasting his time in attempting to persuade him of his family obligations, and rose abruptly.

'Allow me to tell you, sir, that I consider your attitude unfeeling to the highest degree,' he said scathingly, 'but I see that you will not be moved by my opinion, so I shall take my leave of you.'

'Ay, do that!' Sir Timothy said cordially. 'I'm a busy man, with no time to waste; why, I've an action coming up against my neighbour Kirkstall, ye see, and I mustn't stay on in town too long, neither, or there'll be the devil to pay in Hampshire, for they'll go on down there like I was rich as Golden Ball if I ain't there to put a stop to it. You wouldn't believe what my bill for candles was last quarter, and as for coals . . . !'

Mr. Ranleigh cut short these observations by striding from the room and letting himself out the front door. Sivil, who had been walking the bays up and down before the house, saw from a single glance at his master's hard grey eyes that his mood was an unpropitious one, and hastened to take his place beside him as he sprang into the curricle and took the reins. Sivil was a small, spare man who had been in the late Lord Frederick's employ when his present master was still a boy, and there was puzzlement now in his mind: whatever it was that had had Mr. Robert chasing about town all day in the unlikeliest neighbourhoods, it did not seem to him that it was something that had given him any degree of satisfaction.

He was quite right: his master was in a state of wrathful frustration that was decidedly rare in his experience. There was nothing that he could do to compel Sir Timothy to act as he should in regard to his niece, which meant, it appeared, that the girl must continue to remain under Jillson's aegis.

But at the remembrance of that gentleman's impudently smiling face Mr. Ranleigh's mouth tightened. He had no interest in Miss Hadley beyond the brief compassion he might have felt for any gently bred girl hustled into the rough world of the theatre without suitable protection, but, as he had informed Lady Frederick earlier in the day, it did not suit him to see anyone of his blood in such a position.

He repeated this observation to her a short time later, when, having driven back to Mount Street, he found her again in the Crimson Saloon about to go upstairs to place herself in the hands of her dresser. Yielding, however, to her son's request for five minutes' private conversation with her, she sent the meek Mrs. Wixom, her *dame de compagnie*, from the room, and listened in surprise and disapproval to the brief account he gave her of Sir Timothy's obduracy.

'This is monstrous! *Quite* unheard-of!' she pronounced, when he had concluded. 'But I do not at all see why you have come to *me* with the story. There is nothing that can be done for the girl, now that she has ruined herself by appearing publicly upon the stage. Do you know I have had Anthony here twice since you went out, *demanding* to see you about that ridiculous wager? He seems quite taken with the girl, which will be most disturbing to poor Almeria, for she has been trying to interest him in Woodstone's eldest, and you know there is no earthly use in talking to him of marriage when he has one of his fancies on the brain.'

Mr. Ranleigh said uncompromisingly, 'I am not interested in Tony's fancies, ma'am. What I am interested in is in getting the chit out of Jillson's hands. He does not intend ill to her, I believe, but, if I am any judge of character, he is one of those talented, improvident rogues who never quite attain success in their profession, and he will have no scruples in making use of her in any way that will help him to feather his own nest. I have been considering the matter, and it seems to me that the girl's own idea may serve her best. If she could be placed in some respectable family as a governess . . .'

'A governess!' Lady Frederick regarded her son incredulously. 'When she has been exhibiting herself on the London stage!'

'She has been exhibiting herself there only for the space of a week or so, and under an assumed name,' Mr. Ranleigh said impatiently. 'That will stop immediately, of course. You will take her and Miss Dowie down to Hillcourt when you go there on Friday, and I have no doubt that in a short time, if you will make inquiries among your friends, you will be able to find respectable employment for her in a quiet country household where her London exploits will not come into question. Possibly also for Miss Dowie ...'

He checked, observing that Lady Frederick was regarding him with a look of astonishment, not unmixed with asperity.

'I perceive,' she uttered, with awful calm, 'that you have worked the matter out to your entire satisfaction, Robert. You have miscalculated in only one respect—and that is that I have no desire whatsoever to invite this young woman to stay at Hillcourt.'

For a moment two pairs of very autocratic eyes—one a hard grey, the other dark and brilliant—challenged each other. Then Mr. Ranleigh gave a sudden laugh.

'Very well!' he acknowledged. 'I should have consulted you before laying my plans, ma'am. Let us say that all I shall ask you to do now is to see the girl, and to judge whether you wish her to remain in her present situation. If she does, I believe I can guarantee that within a year she will have been ruined in good earnest, whether she remains with Jillson or is taken up by any one of half a dozen who have the fancy to make her the latest craze—Brackenridge, or Lovett, or Tony ...'

'Anthony!' Lady Frederick snorted. 'He is more of an old woman than I am. If *he* is all she has to fear, her virtue is as safe as mine. And what, pray—if I *do* invite her to Hillcourt— am I to say to anyone who meets her there and recognises her as a young woman whom they have seen upon the stage? It is all very well for you to tell me that she is appearing under an assumed name; people are not blind! And I suppose we can hardly shave her head to change her appearance ...'

'Of course not,' Mr. Ranleigh said, with renewed impatience. 'It won't be necessary. She will probably not be at Hillcourt longer than a few weeks, and she need not go into company at all while she is there. And if she should happen to be seen by somebody who believes he recognises her as Miss Daingerfield-Nelson, you do not require *me* to tell you that you are quite capable of freezing any impertinent comments with a few well-chosen words on the unaccountability of chance resemblances.'

Lady Frederick's face relaxed in a frosty smile. 'No, you abominable boy, I do not!' she said. 'I wish it were as easy to give *you* a set-down, for you are sadly in want of one. You are growing as highhanded as a Turk—quite insufferable!' She rose from the winged armchair in which she had been sitting. 'I must go up now,' she said. 'I dine at the Comerfords', and then go on to Carlton House—a most boring affair, I fear it will be, for Prinny is in one of his melancholy moods, which is the reason for my being asked, I daresay. He says I remind him of the old days, when Frederick was alive.'

'But you will do as I ask in the matter of Miss Hadley, ma'am?' Mr. Ranleigh said, refusing to be put off by this change of subject.

Lady Frederick looked at him with some acerbity. 'Is that a question or a command?' she demanded. 'No, never mind answering me; I'm quite aware that you are capable of turning a graceful phrase when you like, but you will still expect to have your own way.' Mr. Ranleigh, smiling, took her hand and pressed it lightly to his lips. 'Oh, go along with you!' Lady Frederick said tartly. 'Very well, then—I shall see the girl. You may tell her that she may call here tomorrow.'

Mr. Ranleigh, recalling his interview with Miss Dowie, shook his head, a glint of amusement in his eyes.

'I believe, my dear, that we shall do better to call upon her, instead,' he said. 'I may, you see, have prevailed upon you to see *her*, but I am not at all certain that—highhanded as you may think me—I should be able to prevail upon Miss Dowie to allow her niece to come here to see you!'

CHAPTER FIVE

Early on the following afternoon the ostler at the Running Boar had, for the second time in two days, the privilege of beholding a fashionable turnout—this one an elegant barouche with a pair of spanking chestnuts between the shafts—draw up before the door of the inn which employed his services. The lady who was handed down from it by the Corinthian the ostler had seen the morning before wore a lilac velvet pelisse and a fashionably high-crowned bonnet, and favoured her surroundings with a glance of such comprehensive disapproval before she swept inside that Ben Ostler, as he later confessed, was 'fair knocked into horse-nails,' giving it as his opinion that the old Queen herself could not have held herself any higher.

Lady Frederick, whose opinion of the entire House of Hanover was extremely low, would scarcely have been flattered by this comparison; nor was she propitiated by the obsequious courtesies rendered her by the Running Boar's landlady when she perceived her entering her door.

'My good woman,' she informed her in her piercing voice, 'you would occupy yourself far more fittingly in sweeping the dirt from your floors than in bowing and scraping to me in this ridiculous manner!' She turned to her son. 'If I *must* go up those horridly steep—and, I am certain, quite unsafe—stairs, you must give me your arm, Robert!' she declared. 'Really, it is reprehensible for people to live under such conditions, when a little energy is all that is required!'

Mr. Ranleigh, perceiving that she was rapidly attracting an audience consisting of every employee on the premises, to say nothing of the inmates of the taproom, escorted her up the stairs with a smile of some amusement, which still lingered on his lips when he knocked at the door of the room in which he had had his conversation with Miss Hadley and Miss Dowie, the previous morning. It was opened by Miss Dowie, who gazed in some surprise at the imperious dame confronting her.

'You will be Miss Dowie, I expect?' Lady Frederick said, without ceremony. 'May we come in? My son tells me that he met you yesterday and that your niece has some tale of being connected with my late husband's family.'

Mr. Ranleigh, endeavouring to counter the effect of this un-propitious beginning, accomplished a more orthodox intro-duction once he and Lady Frederick had been admitted into the little parlour, but he was too late: Miss Dowie's hackles had already risen. She said stiffly, when she had invited her two visitors to seat themselves, 'I hope you have not come here under the misapprehension that I wished to see you, my lady. It was not with *my* approval that my niece agreed to have any communi-cation with Mr. Ranleigh.'

'Hoity-toity!' Lady Frederick said. 'You need not get up on your high ropes with me, Miss Dowie. It appears to me that you are sadly in need of assistance from someone who has your niece's best interests in view, and *that* I have come prepared to offer you. Where is the girl?' she inquired.

'She is resting,' Miss Dowie said defiantly. 'The theatre, my lady, requires late hours, and I do not intend to see her health undermined by constant keeping of them at her age.'

Lady Frederick nodded her approval. 'Very commendable,' she said, 'May I inquire how old your niece is, Miss Dowie?'

'She is turned eighteen.'

'That is indeed too young for a constant indulgence in late hours. However, the fact of the matter is that, if she is who she claims to be, she has no business being on the stage at all. Perhaps you would favour me with a history of her parentage, Miss Dowie? Or you may be able to produce some family documents that would confirm her story?'

'I could, but I shan't!' Miss Dowie snapped, her eyes spark-

46

ling dangerously. 'Not unless *you*, ma'am, are willing to produce *your* credentials to prove to me that you are what you say *you* are!' She rose from her chair. 'I believe this has gone quite far enough,' she said. 'I did not seek your help, ma'am, and I have no idea of being insulted by you under my own roof, poor as that roof may be! May I bid you good day?'

'No, you may not,' Lady Frederick said imperturbably. 'You are quite right to be angry; so should I be if I were in your place. But I will tell you to your head that you are a fool if you allow that to weigh with you. If your situation is indeed as desperate as my son informs me it is, you should be grateful for any attempt, no matter how ungraciously offered, to assist you.'

Miss Dowie seemed slightly mollified by her guest's frank characterisation of her own conduct, and appeared to be on the point of making some milder rejoinder when the door leading into the adjoining chamber was opened and Cecily herself came into the room. At sight of the visitors she checked.

'Mr. Ranleigh!' she exclaimed. 'Oh, I did not know that it was you!'

'I have brought my mother to see you,' Mr. Ranleigh explained, rising. He turned to Lady Frederick. 'May I present Miss Hadley to you, ma'am?' he said.

Lady Frederick surveyed Miss Hadley in a single eagle glance that took in her outmoded frock, her beautifully erect figure, and the entire lack of anything resembling artifice in her appearance. The result seemed to satisfy her, for she said, 'Come here, child,' and indicated to her son that he should place a chair for Cecily beside her. Upon his complying, Cecily obediently sat down, looking at her ladyship rather wonderingly. Lady Frederick, in her customary imperious manner, tilted up her chin the better to survey her face, and, having completed her inspection, remarked decisively, 'You are quite right, Robert; she has certainly the look of your grandmother Hadley. A disgraceful business, this! How came you to be in such straits, my dear? Did your father make *no* provision for you?'

'I am afraid, ma'am, he was very—very deeply in debt during the last years of his life,' Cecily stammered.

Miss Dowie, who had also sat down again, interpolated at this point, 'If you must know, ma'am, he had a pair of Nasty Habits—gaming and drinking. Well, they have been the ruin of wealthier men than he was! The long and short of it is that when he died everything went—house, land, furniture, the very jewellery that should have come to my pet. We were left with the clothes on our backs and little more. But *that*,' she added, 'is no concern of yours, my lady. I have told Cecily plainly that she has no claim on Mr. Ranleigh, nor has she any more on you.' She sent a glance of marked disfavour at Mr. Ranleigh, who had been content to watch the proceedings thus far with an air of detached but somewhat unholy amusement. 'Not,' she said tartly, 'that he hasn't brought it on himself. If he had not tried to lure her into pursuits which no virtuous young lady . . .'

'Nonsense!' said Lady Frederick. 'I expect he has explained to you that the whole affair was simply the result of a foolish wager. My son has a great many faults, Miss Dowie, but I can assure you that seducing schoolroom misses is not one of them.'

'Thank you!' Mr. Ranleigh said sardonically.

Cecily regarded him with interest, caught the gleam in his eyes and was encouraged to inquire whether he would lose a great deal of money by her flight from his invitation.

'Not at all,' he said. 'It is my cousin who laid the wager— not I.'

'And a pretty wager it was!' Miss Dowie said. 'Your friends may think very highly of you, Mr. Ranleigh, to expect that you would succeed where the lot of them had failed, but let me tell you that in *my* day a gentleman who would lend himself to such a game would be thought no better than an impudent coxcomb.'

Lady Frederick, who unexpectedly appeared to find this sally to her liking, said with satisfaction, 'Ha! You have caught it this time, Robert—and quite rightly, too. However,' she went on, to Miss Dowie, 'that has nothing whatever to say to your predicament. I will tell you flatly that I believe my son is quite right in his opinion that your niece must instantly be removed from the situation in which she now finds herself. Indeed, I wonder that you should ever have permitted her to enter it!'

'I assure you, ma'am,' Miss Dowie said, 'that it is not my wish to see her in it! I had hoped that she might be able to find employment as an instructress of the young in some respectable household on her father's death, in which case I should have gone into lodgings near her and taken up whatever occupation might have come to my hand, whether it was giving lessons or trimming hats. But our inquiries in Hampshire were quite unsuccessful, and we soon found ourselves in such straits that we were obliged to accept Mr. Jillson's offer to bring us to London.'

'Well, I do think,' Lady Frederick said candidly, 'that you might have considered that you were likely to fall into some such predicament before you quarrelled with your brother—not that it appears to me, from what my son tells me, that his roof would be one under which a modest young female might properly be placed.'

Miss Dowie sat up straighter, looking at Mr. Ranleigh. 'I thought you told me you was not acquainted with my brother!' she accused him.

'At the time, that was quite correct,' he informed her, gravely. 'However, on yesterday I had the pleasure of making not only his acquaintance, but also—Mrs. Cassaday's, I believe it is?'

'Aha!' Miss Dowie said, nodding martially. 'So he has carried that creature up to town with him, has he? As much as I should deplore such a connexion, I have told him to his head that if he won't get rid of the woman he ought to marry her—but it would be too much, I daresay, to expect him to do either.'

'Yes, I believe so,' Mr. Ranleigh acknowledged. 'I will do him the justice to say that he *did* offer your niece a home, ma'am, rather reluctantly, and most pointedly excluding any possibility that he would do the same for you. But that arrangement appeared to me, in view of Mrs. Cassaday's situation and— may I say?—your brother's own character, scarcely a satisfactory one.'

'You may say what you please,' Miss Dowie handsomely allowed. 'The man is a Monster, as I have told you before.'

'In that case,' Lady Frederick said briskly, 'you must, I believe, place yourself in our hands, Miss Dowie,' and she thereupon proceeded to lay before her the scheme her son had unfolded to her the day before.

Miss Dowie and Cecily heard the plans that had been made for them with equal astonishment, but with widely differing sentiments. Miss Dowie appeared to be dealing darkly with the notion that a lady as obviously unconventional as Lady Frederick, and as indisputably a member of those tonnish circles whose moral principles she held in high suspicion, might be lending herself to the furtherance of some deep-laid design of her son's on Cecily's virtue. On the other hand, Cecily was gazing at Mr. Ranleigh with a flush of gratitude on her face— an emotion which prompted her to exclaim to him impulsively, 'Oh, I *don't* know how I am to thank you—and when I had been thinking such horrid things about you, too, after you went away yesterday without a word! It all goes to prove, I daresay, that Aunt is right when she says one should *never* judge by appearances!'

Mr. Ranleigh, though unaccustomed to the idea that his appearance might be such as to prejudice any young lady against him, accepted this rather backhanded compliment without visible perturbation, merely remarking that he hoped they might consider the matter settled then. He added that, if the two ladies would be in readiness to leave London on the following morning, his travelling-chaise would call for them at nine.

But this statement again brought Miss Dowie's suspicions to the fore.

'Travel to Sussex in *your* company, sir?' she inquired, her face plainly betraying her mistrust.

'By no means,' Mr. Ranleigh said. 'I do not go down to Hillcourt at present. However, as my mother is travelling with her companion and her maid, it will be a more comfortable arrangement, I believe, if you and your niece make use of my chaise.'

Miss Dowie could find no fault with this, but she had one more rub to throw in the way—the matter, she confessed, with a rather truculent lift of the chin that showed how much against the grain it went with her to mention it, of the fifteen pounds Mr. Jillson had lent them.

'It has been impossible for us to repay the whole of it as yet,' she said, 'and I do not see how we can go off while we are still in his debt . . .'

Mr. Ranleigh, in a matter-of-fact tone, assured her that nothing could be simpler than for him to advance her a sufficient sum to allow her to satisfy Mr. Jillson's claim before she left London, advising her, by the way, to place the money in trustworthy hands for delivery to him *after* her departure, so that that gentleman's active curiosity would not be aroused as to the source of her sudden affluence. His failure to suggest anything so repugnant to her independent nature as the notion that this new debt need not be repaid did much to raise her opinion of him, but she kept her expressions of gratitude meagre until, upon his opening the door as he and Lady Frederick rose to take their leave, Jillson was discovered lounging outside in the passage. This transparent piece of surveillance cast her at once on Mr. Ranleigh's side as he undertook, with a few pithy words that quickly erased the genial smile from Jillson's face, to send the interloper about his business.

'I vow I shall be so glad to be rid of that creeping rascal that I would almost put myself under the devil's protection to do so!' she declared—and thereupon informed Mr. Ranleigh with the greatest cordiality that she and Cecily would certainly be ready to leave at the time appointed.

Mr. Ranleigh, having escorted his mother back to Mount Street—a journey enlivened by her handsome acknowledgement that he had acted quite properly, for once in his life, by undertaking to remove a gently bred child from the influence of such a rogue as Jillson—repaired, with some relief at having

51

disposed of the matter of Miss Cecily Hadley, to White's. Here he was at once accosted by Lord Portandrew.

'The very man I wanted to see!' his lordship declared, dragging him upstairs to the card-room. 'Made a regular nuisance of myself yesterday, calling at Mount Street—but, deuce take it, I want to know what you've done about my wager!'

'Done?' Mr. Ranleigh said calmly. 'Nothing at all. You will have to pay, Tony. I warned you not to lay your blunt on me.'

'Yes, but—but . . .!' his lordship sputtered indignantly. 'You said she'd appointed you a meeting! Didn't you go?'

'Oh yes, I went,' Mr. Ranleigh replied. 'But that fellow Jillson was quite right, you know. The girl is very well guarded. If I were you, I should give the whole thing up.'

'Give—it—up!' His lordship sent him an incredulous stare. 'Dash it all, Robert, I can't do that! I'm in love with her!'

Mr. Ranleigh grinned slightly. 'Coming it a bit too strong, Tony!' he said. 'You've said the same thing at least half a dozen times before.'

'Yes, but this is *different*!' Lord Portandrew said, revolted by his cousin's lack of perception. 'I *must* manage to meet her, one way or the other!' He looked darkly at Mr. Ranleigh. 'It's *my* opinion you're hiding something from me,' he said. '*I* know that smug look of yours. You've probably come to an understanding with her yourself and now you want *me* to step out of the picture. Well, I won't do it, Robert, and that's flat! She may have been dazzled by your reputation, but when she comes to know us both she's bound to realise that *I*'m the one with the sincere, generous, and affectionate nature . . .'

Mr. Ranleigh grinned again. 'Will you *stop* making a cake of yourself, Tony?' he begged. 'I have come to no "understanding" with Miss Daingerfield-Nelson, nor have I the slightest desire to do so.'

'Well, you might make the attempt, at any rate!' Lord Portandrew argued inconsistently. 'Deuce take it, we shall have Brackenridge crowing over us this month to come. Pretty figures we shall cut! I expect you know he's spread the story all over town already?'

'Oh, yes. Gussie Comerford told me,' Mr. Ranleigh said, quite unmoved.

'Well, I must say I never thought you would be so poor-spirited as to let it be said that Brackenridge had cut you out!' his lordship said. 'Because he will, you know! He'd do anything to get the better of you, and he'll be more than ever determined to if you admit you've failed. What's more, he'll succeed. See if he don't!'

'Oh, I rather doubt that,' Mr. Ranleigh said carelessly.

But his volatile kinsman, his mind already diverted into new channels, interrupted any further reassurances by remarking abruptly, 'By the bye, if you won't make a push to help me win *that* wager, you might with another. *Are* you going to offer for Gussie Comerford? I can get two to one here that you ain't.'

Mr. Ranleigh looked a trifle startled. 'Good God, are they laying bets on *that*?' he asked.

'Why, yes! I thought you knew. Your mother's been puffing the match, and I must say I thought myself you were going to come up to scratch this time.' His lordship looked at Mr. Ranleigh somewhat severely. 'You've been more than a little particular in your attentions to her, you know!'

Mr. Ranleigh, conscious that the matter was a sore point with his cousin, whose unsuccessful pursuit of Miss Comerford during the season just past had been notorious, returned a soothing answer and turned the subject—a ruse that served very well, as the topic he chose was the possibility of his agreeing to sell his lordship a pair of chestnuts much coveted by him.

But it was not so easy for him to dismiss the matter from his own mind. There was a slight, thoughtful frown between his brows as he left the club a few minutes later. He had no great wish to marry, but he was conscious that he had reached a period in his life at which it would be natural for him to do so. The debutantes of a dozen seasons having failed to do more than bore him with their compliant manners and eager smiles, he supposed he might do worse than to offer for Gussie Comerford, who—in addition to possessing birth and beauty—

had a lack of conventionality which made her company less insipid than that of most of her contemporaries.

And since, he concluded the argument in her favour ironically, he was past the age at which a man is green enough to look for romance, what odds did it make that he was not in love with her nor she with him? Gussie's affections, he had reason to believe, would never be deeply engaged; her disposition was both restless and shallow, but this was a matter of no great moment to him. She would be admirably suited to take her place in society as the wife of a man who was one of its leaders, and he did not doubt his ability to keep her in hand if she were to do him the honour of becoming his wife.

The only thing necessary, therefore, to the settling of his future was the speaking of some half dozen words by him, but it was odd how little satisfaction this comfortable reflection appeared to give to him. On the contrary, his mother, when he returned to Mount Street, considered that he looked unwontedly unapproachable, and, attributing his mood to the disagreeable business in regard to Miss Hadley that had been occupying him for the past two days, thought it was as well that he was not escorting her to Hillcourt. She promised herself to settle Miss Hadley and her aunt in some suitable situation quickly; if she did not, she told herself, with a sardonic lift of the brows that made her look momentarily very like her son, it might be some time before Robert decided that he would favour Hillcourt with his presence.

CHAPTER SIX

Miss Hadley, arriving at Mr. Ranleigh's country seat in Sussex on the following day, had, for her part, an exhilarating feeling that she was living in a dream, from which she was not at all anxious to awaken. From the moment when, stepping into Mr. Ranleigh's elegant travelling-chaise, she had leaned her head against its blue-velvet squabs to the moment when, as the chaise rounded a turn in the road that led from the lodge-gates to the house, she saw the rose-pink brick walls of Hillcourt for the first time, she had felt that she had been pitchforked into the very lap of luxury. Lady Frederick, riding before her in her own carriage, impressively flanked by outriders, might, she reflected, have been a fairy godmother, so magical had been the transformation she had wrought from dirt and discomfort of the Running Boar to her present situation.

Her sense of living in a fairy tale did not diminish when, upon entering the house, she was conducted up an imposing staircase to the west wing, where, in a bedchamber furnished in the first style of elegance, she found a comfortable fire sending the light of its flames flickering over the rose silk curtains that shut out the November dusk outside.

She was not aware that Hillcourt—built during the Restoration by a peer who had been obliged to see it pass into the hands of an immensely wealthy Northumberland family—was held in rather low esteem by the Ranleighs, who considered it one of the less interesting of their seats. It had come into the family on the marriage of Mr. Ranleigh's father to the heiress into whose possession it had passed—a damsel who had obligingly died without issue within two years, leaving Lord Frederick free to offer for his first love, Louisa Wymberly, who had unfortunately not possessed the fortune considered necessary for the wife of the fourth son of the Duke of Belfour. Hillcourt, the Ranleighs were used to say, was elegant and convenient, but it had no history; but Cecily, relaxing in an armchair with hot tea and macaroons before her, while an abigail deftly unpacked her few belongings, was in no mood to pine for Tudor glories. She thought the room she was in the most beautiful she had ever seen in her life, and the entire house of a magnificence that was almost breathtaking.

A knock shortly sounded on the door, and, thinking it was her aunt come to compare notes with her on the journey, she called, 'Come in.' To her surprise, a slender boy of about fourteen, with a thin, mischievous countenance, walked into the room.

'Hello!' he said cheerfully. 'Are you Miss Hadley? I'm Neagle—that is, you may call me Charlie if you like. Everyone else does. Don't they, Alice?'

The abigail, who had finished the unpacking, gave him a giggle and then, recollecting herself, a disapproving look.

'Now, my lord,' she said, 'You'd best run along. I'll warrant her la'ship and Mr. Tibble don't know you're here!'

'You're right. They don't,' Lord Neagle agreed, coming across the room and selecting a macaroon from the dish before Cecily. 'Nor are they likely to miss me, I might say, because Mrs. Wixom is having hysterics in the Small Saloon. I knew she would,' he went on, disinterestedly biting into the macaroon. 'As a matter of fact, I tried to lay a wager on it with Tibble, but he wouldn't take it.'

Cecily, regarding the young gentleman with mingled astonishment and amusement, delved into her memory for a reference Lady Frederick had made to the effect that her young grandson, Lord Neagle, and his tutor were at present staying at Hillcourt, during the Dowager Lady Neagle's absence in Jamaica for reasons of health. Cecily had understood that young Lord Neagle had not been sent to Eton as yet, also for reasons of health—but, surveying the boy before her, she was inclined to concur with Lady Frederick's opinion that there was nothing wrong with his lordship's health, but something amiss with his mother's judgment.

'Ever since she lost Neagle—an accident on the hunting field, which had nothing at all to do with the state of his health —she has been quacking herself and fussing over the boy, Lady Frederick had said. 'I see that I shall have to interfere in the matter myself, for he needs to be sent to school; Tibble has no control over him whatsoever. If it were not for Robert's coming down now and then and taking him in hand, he would be quite insupportable! For the worst of it is that he is so engaging, you know, that one cannot be severe with him!'

Cecily, as she looked at Lord Neagle, could well believe this statement to be true. Within the space of five minutes he had routed Alice from the room, devoured half the macaroons on the plate before him, and given her an account of the scene that had just taken place in the Small Saloon, where Mrs. Wixom, put in possession of an urgent message that had arrived for her that morning, to the effect that her niece had come down with influenza and three of the children with the chicken pox, had instantly succumbed to a fit of hysterics.

She would soon, Lord Neagle gave it as his opinion, be on her way to Derbyshire, which would be good riddance, as there was nothing he liked less than being asked regularly how he did, in a tone of voice implying that she rather expected him to announce his imminent demise.

He then asked Cecily directly if she were indeed his cousin, and, if so, why a 'suitable position' must be found for her.

'I should think you had rather marry someone instead,' he remarked. 'You're not at all bad-looking, you know.'

'Oh, I should!' she admitted candidly. 'But in the meantime I am dreadfully poor, you know, so I must find some way to support myself.'

'That's what Tibblè says,' Lord Neagle said, nodding wisely. 'He's my tutor—a curst rum touch, but he *does* manage to get on to most of what happens around here. It's my belief he gossips with the servants. Of course it's devilish hard to get anything out of him, but I have my methods, you see.'

Cecily laughed. 'I should rather think you had!' she said.

He grinned engagingly. 'Well, you know, it's deuced dull down here when Robert's not around,' he said. 'How is Robert, by the way? I haven't clapped eyes on him this month. I rather *thought* he might have come down with Grandmama.'

Cecily said that she believed Mr. Ranleigh was very well, and, conscious of an unaccountable desire to continue the conversation on this subject, unscrupulously encouraged Lord Neagle to go on talking of his uncle.

It was, she found, a topic on which he was most willing to expatiate. In a short space of time she gathered that Mr. Ranleigh was quite by way of being the idol of his nephew, who considered him not only a prime gun, a nonesuch among whips, and a pattern of all those manly accomplishments which such milksops as Mr. Tibble were wont to frown on, but also a friend in need to a boy surrounded by the cautions of a pack of females.

With this opinion Cecily was quite willing to concur. Though she had told Mr. Ranleigh truthfully, on the occasion of his first visit to the Running Boar, that she was relieved to find that his interest in her was not of the kind that might have been expected of a gentleman who had issued an invitation to supper to an actress whom he had never met, she was not on that account immune to the attractions he presented. Moreover, having been reared in the seclusion of a country household, she had had ample time, before she had ever met him, to idealise the distant cousin whose exploits she had had no difficulty in becoming familiar with even in rural Hampshire.

And now that he had stepped into her life to rescue her so unexpectedly from her difficulties—quite in the best style of the heroes of romances—it was scarcely to be wondered at that she should agree even with the most extravagant of young Lord Neagle's encomiums.

He ended his panegyrics, however, on a gloomier note.

'The thing is, though,' he informed her, 'that I shall probably see a good deal less of him soon than I do even now. My mother is bound to come home from Jamaica before long and carry me off to Neagle House, and even if she don't, I expect Robert will be marrying Miss Comerford soon.'

Cecily felt a sudden rather empty sensation in the pit of her stomach. 'Oh?' she said, endeavouring to assume an appearance of impersonal interest. 'Who is Miss Comerford?'

His lordship shrugged. 'Well, they call her *L'Étoile*—that's French for *The Star*, you know,' he said. 'Tall girl, loads of black hair, green eyes—Lord Comerford's eldest daughter. All the Bloods are mad over her, but Tibble says it's Robert who is first oars with her.'

Cecily remarked hollowly that she understood statuesque young ladies were the high kick of fashion just now, and inquired whether Mr. Ranleigh too was mad about *L'Étoile*.

'Oh, I shouldn't think so,' his lordship said frankly. 'But he's expected to marry, you know, so I daresay he will offer for her. I think it's a great nuisance myself; females always spoil things.'

He then asked if Cecily rode, and, being informed that she had done so since she had learned to walk, fell into a conversation with her on the subject of hunting that lasted until a scratching on the door heralded Miss Dowie's appearance.

Miss Dowie, attired in a black bombazine gown of ancient cut, received with some suspicion an introduction to Lord Neagle, and promptly gave it as her opinion that well-bred young gentlemen did not visit young ladies in the latter's bed-chambers.

'Oh, well!' his lordship said, undaunted. 'I'm her cousin—ain't I?'

'I doubt very much that your grandmother would care to hear you claim the relationship,' Miss Dowie said tartly.

His lordship looked intrigued. 'Wouldn't she?' he demanded. 'Why? Ain't you respectable? You look deuced respectable to me!'

Miss Dowie regarded him austerely. 'I daresay,' she snapped, 'if the truth were known, we are a great deal more respectable than a good few of your relations, my lord. We are *not*, however, affluent.'

'Well, that makes no difference to *me*,' Lord Neagle said equably, 'and I shouldn't think it would to Grandmama, either —though,' he added thoughtfully, 'Tibble *did* drop a hint that I needn't go about on the high gab about your being here, because you weren't going into company.'

Perceiving that he was scenting a mystery, Cecily promptly said, 'We are in mourning, you see,' and got up, saying she must not keep her aunt waiting.

The two ladies then went downstairs together, where they were shortly afterward served a dinner of two full courses, including, in addition to a number of side-dishes, semelles of carp removed with a few larded sweetbreads and a raised pie, a dressed lobster, a broiled fowl with mushrooms, and several jellies and creams. Cecily, dazzled by the array of silver dishes, the elegant footmen, and the imposing dimensions of the room, was glad that the company consisted only of Lady Frederick, Mrs. Wixom, and Mr. Tibble, a rather wispy-looking young man whose pale blue eyes wore a permanently disapproving expression, and that the conversation dealt almost exclusively with Mrs. Wixom's projected journey into Derbyshire.

After dinner the four ladies repaired to the Ivory Saloon. This was a double-cube room done in ivory and dull gold, the doorways and ceiling coves being decorated with gilded wood of such gossamer delicacy that Cecily could not refrain from an expression of delight on entering it.

She had little opportunity to examine it further, however, for Lady Frederick, seating herself on a sofa, indicated that she was to place herself beside her and at once began the conversation on a somewhat intimidating note.

'If I am to recommend you to my friends as a governess, child,' she said, 'it may be as well for you to tell me of your accomplishments. You play the harp or the pianoforte tolerably well, I collect?'

Cecily said doubtfully, 'N-no, ma'am. Not very well, that is.

You see I had no instruments at home, though Mrs. Ackling *did* sometimes allow me to practise upon hers.'

Lady Frederick shrugged. 'Well, I daresay you will contrive,' she said. 'You paint in water colours, of course?'

'No, ma'am.'

Her ladyship's brows rose. 'Not?' she said. 'Nor sketch?'

Cecily shook her head, casting an anguished glance of appeal at Miss Dowie.

'Well, upon my word!' her ladyship said, her colour rising slightly. 'I must say I do not know what you can have been thinking of, my dear, to lead me on to believe you were qualified to become a governess! If I had had the slightest notion of your ignorance . . .'

But she got no further, for at that moment Miss Dowie entered the lists.

'Ignorance!' she repeated. 'I'll have you know, ma'am, that I consider my niece to have received as thorough an education as any young woman of her age in England—which is not surprising, since I instructed her myself. She has a considerable knowledge of ancient and modern history, is conversant with the most improving works of our English authors and those of antiquity . . .'

But this time it was her turn to be interrupted. 'A bluestocking!' Lady Frederick exclaimed, in accents of horror. 'But my dear Miss Dowie, such information is *quite* useless for the purposes for which your niece is to be employed. She will be expected to teach the accomplishments—music, sketching, a little French . . .'

'My niece's mind, let me assure you, has not been cluttered with such insipidities, ma'am,' Miss Dowie said grandly. 'It is my opinion that the shocking state of morality today is due solely to the faulty system on which our young females have been educated, and I should have considered myself derelict in my duty if I had not endeavoured to form Cecily's mind on quite other principles.'

Cecily's perceiving that her aunt was launched on one of her favourite subjects, desperately put a question to Mrs. Wixom on the state of the roads she expected to find on her journey, but to no avail. That docile lady merely gave her a nervous stare, quite unwilling to put herself forward to interrupt her patroness's conversation, and the result was that for the ensuing quarter hour a battle-royal was waged over Cecily's hapless head.

As neither of the two ladies was in the least inclined to give ground, hostilities were abated only on the entrance of Mr. Tibble into the room after his enjoyment of a single abstemious glass of brandy in the dining-room. Lady Frederick, perceiving the inadvisability of continuing the subject before him, allowed it to drop, but not before she had promised roundly to write to her son that very evening to request his advice on what she was to do about recommending to her friends as governess a young woman who obviously had not the least qualification for the post.

CHAPTER SEVEN

She was as good as her word, and the letter that she penned duly arrived in Mount Street, just as Mr. Ranleigh was sitting down to breakfast on a chill grey morning. He had time, however, to do no more than break the seal and unfold the single sheet of which the letter consisted before the butler entered to announce the arrival of Lord Portandrew, and the next moment his lordship himself burst impetuously into the room.

'So I've caught you in!' he said, in a wrathful tone that set Mr. Ranleigh's brows instantly on the rise. 'Well, I'm deuced glad of that, or I should have had to go chasing all over the town for you!' He waited until the butler had retreated and closed the door behind him, and then demanded, 'I want to know—and don't try to fob me off, Robert!—exactly what you've done with that girl!'

Mr. Ranleigh carved a slice of ham in a leisurely manner. 'Girl? What girl?' he inquired. 'Care for breakfast, Tony?'

His lordship glanced, revolted, at his cousin's well-filled plate. 'No, I do not care for breakfast!' he said. 'And don't try to flummery me, Robert! You know very well what girl I mean. Miss Daingerfield-Nelson!'

'What about Miss Daingerfield-Nelson?' Mr. Ranleigh asked, still quite unmoved. 'Really, Tony, you might have more tact than to come barging in at this hour posing conundrums. I spent last evening at the Daffy Club, and I don't seem to be quite at my best this morning.'

'Well, I spent it at the theatre,' Lord Portandrew declared, 'and I'll have you know—only you probably know it already—that Miss Daingerfield-Nelson wasn't there!'

'Really? A trifle down pin, perhaps?' Mr. Ranleigh suggested. 'Not feeling quite the thing?'

'She wasn't there,' his lordship said, in a tone which implied that he was keeping his temper only by a heroic exercise of patience, 'because she has disappeared! And what's more, I have a strong suspicion that *you* know where she has gone!'

Mr. Ranleigh's brows again went up. 'What has led you to this rather startling conclusion?' he asked, imperturbably continuing his repast. 'Can it be—let me guess—that you have been consulting the admirable Jillson?'

'Yes, I have!' his lordship said. 'Well, what else was I to do? I go out of town for a few days and, dash it, the girl disappears—nobody knows where she's gone to—vanished into thin air. But that ain't the point,' he continued severely. 'The point is that fellow Jillson says *you* called to see her twice last week at her lodgings, and that on Friday she went off in a travelling-chaise that sounds to me curst like it might have been yours. Now what I want to know is just what kind of rig you're trying to run, Robert!'

'Did he also tell you, I wonder,' Mr. Ranleigh asked, calmly buttering a slice of bread, 'that on the second occasion I called on Miss—er—Daingerfield-Nelson I brought my mother to see her as well? Really, Tony, even you cannot be such a gudgeon as to believe that I should have done that if I had intended to run off with the girl!'

'Yes, but . . .' His lordship looked nonplussed. 'He *did* tell me that,' he confessed, 'and I'll tell *you* that neither of us knew what to make of it. Deuce take it, even Aunt Louisa ain't broad-minded enough to help you make your way with the girl, though I daresay she knows well enough what games you are up to in the petticoat line!'

'Yes, I believe you are right,' Mr. Ranleigh agreed, with a faint smile. 'Mama seems to have an uncanny knack of knowing everything that is going on in town, even when she is buried in Sussex. In the present case, though, there is nothing for her to know. As I told you, I am not interested in Miss Daingerfield-Nelson. She is a very innocent and inexperienced young girl whom Mama has now removed from an excessively uncomfortable situation and placed in one more suitable to her years and education.' He paused, regarding his cousin, whose face was rapidly taking on a beet-red hue, with a solicitous eye. 'Feeling a trifle out of curl, Tony? You don't look at all well,' he remarked.

'Don't look well!' his lordship exploded. 'No, I should think I didn't! Look here, Robert, if you think I'm such a flat that I'll swallow *that* story, you're dicked in the nob! Aunt Louisa wouldn't concern herself over a girl like that, and even if she would—it would have to have been you who put her up to it, and if you think I'll believe *you've* turned philanthropist . . .'

'I haven't,' Mr. Ranleigh assured him. 'And I'm not asking you to believe anything except that the girl is now out of your reach—as well as out of Brackenridge's, Lovett's, and the rest of that set's. If I were you, I should forget her.'

'I'm hanged if I will!' his lordship vowed, his ordinarily good-humoured face still alarmingly wrathful. 'Oh I know what it is: you've crept into her confidence and lured her out of town—though how you brought Aunt Louisa into it I'm dashed if I can think! And what do you intend to do with her when you've tired of your game, you—you Bluebeard! That girl ain't one of your birds of paradise that you can send to the right-about with a king's ransom in diamonds around her neck and no hard feelings on either side! Deuce take it, she's hardly out of the schoolroom!'

'Just so,' Mr. Ranleigh said coolly. 'Which makes me wonder—since you realise that—what your own plans were concerning her. You did not contemplate marrying her, I believe?' Lord Portandrew opened his mouth, shut it again, and contented himself with glaring at his cousin. 'Exactly,' Mr. Ranleigh said. 'And now, if you don't mind—the subject is beginning to bore me. You won't object if I go on reading my letters?'

His lordship did object, but nothing he said seemed to affect Mr. Ranleigh to the extent of distracting his attention from his correspondence. He was, in fact, perusing Lady Frederick's epistle with a frown of irritation, seeing his plans for driving to Epsom that day—where a meeting between a promising young pugilist and a famous veteran of the Ring was to take place—going glimmering in the face of his mother's imperatives. For Lady Frederick had stated in no uncertain terms that she expected him to come down to Hillcourt at once and resolve the question of what was to be done with his protégée now that finding employment for her as a governess was clearly out of the question.

Lord Portandrew, coming out of an indignant harangue to note his cousin's expression of displeased abstraction, momentarily forgot his injuries and inquired with curiosity, 'Bad news? Ain't that my aunt's hand? Can't mistake it—as stiff-backed as if she used a ramrod instead of a pen! Nothing wrong at Hillcourt, I hope?'

'No—nothing of any consequence. But it is a curst nuisance: I expect I shall have to go down there for a few days.' Mr. Ranleigh glanced up, saw a suspicious look cross his lordship's face, and added carelessly, 'It appears that Mrs. Wixom has been obliged to go off suddenly to succour her niece's family, and Mama is at a stand without her. She is not as young as she once was, you know,' he said shamelessly, 'and these things upset her more than they were used to.'

It was fortunate that Lady Frederick did not hear this allusion to her failing powers fall from her son's lips, for she was in poor enough charity with him as it was, when he arrived at Hillcourt later that day. He found her in the Small Saloon, writing letters, and was greeted with an even brusquer coolness than that with which her fondness for him was customarily expressed.

'So you are come!' she said. 'And high time, I must say!'

Mr. Ranleigh laughed, kissing the cheek that was austerely offered to him, and then sitting down in an armchair opposite his mother and stretching his long legs, clad in buckskins and top-boots, comfortably out before him,

'Nonsense!' he said. 'I set out the moment I had your letter, and driving my own curricle, in this weather, so that I should arrive before you had had the opportunity to grow out of reason cross. But I see my best efforts have been in vain.'

'I am *not* cross!' Lady Frederick corrected him starchily. 'I *am*, however, highly perturbed. Tell me at once, if you have the faintest idea—*what* am I to do with that tiresome girl?'

'*Is* she tiresome, ma'am?' Mr. Ranleigh asked. 'I am sorry to hear that; I should not have imagined . . .'

'No, no, of course not!' Lady Frederick made a gesture of compunction. 'I ought not to have used such a term. Miss Dowie, indeed, is one of the most opinionated females I have ever met, so that I am compelled—yes, compelled!—to quarrel with her half a dozen times a day; but the child has been nothing if not obliging. Still, you *must* see what a position you have put me into by cozening me into bringing her down here, Robert! I do not know what I am to do with her, for naturally I cannot send her back to the theatre and that horrid Jillson.'

Mr. Ranleigh, looking at his mother's face, realised, without a great deal of surprise, that what was disturbing her was not the vexation of having an unwanted guest on her hands, but rather a genuine concern for Miss Hadley's future. Lady Frederick's sharp tongue, he knew, concealed a generous heart, and it would have been odd if Miss Hadley, with her engaging ways, had not been able to arouse the same sympathy in it that various categories of philanthropic objects, from mistreated sweeps to unwed mothers, had previously done.

He was wise enough not to put his perceptions into words, however, but merely inquired calmly, 'Where is the girl now?'

'In the billiards-room, with Charlie. He is teaching her the game; the two of them, I should tell you, deal extremely together. She is quite as daring as he in the saddle, it seems, and they have been roaming all over the countryside together—to Damer's dismay. He vows they would be in less danger of breaking their necks if they were hunting with the hardest goers in Leicestershire. What Maria would say if she were to hear of it, I do *not* know!'

Mr. Ranleigh shrugged. 'Well, there is no need to coddle the boy up to Maria's notions,' he said. 'If it is her scheme to confine him to the pace of an elderly groom mounted on a slug . . .'

'Yes, I know!' Lady Frederick agreed, thawing somewhat toward her son in agreement with his criticism of his elder sister. 'Really, I can't think how I ever came to have such an odiously *sober* daughter as Maria, and I am sure it is even worse for Charlie to have her as a mother.' She then recollected herself and said more severely, 'But *that* has nothing to say to the problem. What *are* we to do with that child, Robert? She is *quite* unfit, it seems, to be a governess, for her aunt has stuffed her mind with Latin and history, to the entire neglect of any feminine accomplishments . . .'

'What accomplishments?' Mr. Ranleigh asked impatiently. 'The ability to strum a little upon the pianoforte and to produce abominable water colours? Good God, Mama, if the girl is intelligent enough to learn Latin, she can certainly be crammed with enough of that nonsense in a month or two to permit her to pass herself off with sufficient credit to instruct schoolgirls!'

Lady Frederick stared at him, throwing back her head with an expression of surprise and reluctant approval upon her face. 'Sometimes, Robert, you quite astonish me!' she said. 'That is an excellent plan—I wonder that it did not occur to *me*! I shall send to Binkie at once. Nothing will delight her more than to return to Hillcourt for a time—and though she may be superannuated, she is still perfectly competent, I am sure.'

With her customary impetuosity, she immediately returned to her writing-table to compose an urgent message to Miss Tabitha Binkley, the lady who had instructed her own daughters many years ago and who now lived in retirement in Bognor Regis; and Mr. Ranleigh, seeing that he was *de trop*, strolled off down the hall to the billiards-room.

Here he was at once pounced upon by his young nephew.

'Robert!' Lord Neagle exclaimed, in jubilant tones. 'How long have you been here? You might have told a fellow! *I* didn't know you were coming!'

'Didn't know it myself until this morning,' Mr. Ranleigh

said, allowing his gaze to wander idly from his nephew to Miss Hadley, who was standing at the other side of the room, a billiards cue in her hand and a look of rather shy inquiry on her face. 'Well, Miss Hadley,' he said, 'I am glad to see you have made friends with Charlie.' He glanced down again at his nephew who had not ceased to pour out importunate questions. 'Take a damper, Charlie!' he commanded. 'I don't know myself how long I'm staying. A day or two, I expect—until I can arrange Miss Hadley's affairs to your grandmother's satisfaction.'

'Is that all?' his lordship said indignantly. 'Come all the way down here and then go straight back to London again!' He looked out the window at a few flakes of snow blowing by in the wintry dusk and declared, 'I hope it comes on to snow for a week! Then you won't be able to leave. And I call it dashed unhandsome of you, too, to come for Cecily when you wouldn't for me!'

'Ah,' Mr. Ranleigh said, with a faint smile which Cecily, watching him, could only characterise as perfectly indifferent, 'but Miss Hadley is a responsibility, you see, Charlie, and you are not.'

Miss Hadley, who had spent some few of her waking hours since she had come to Hillcourt in picturing the circumstances of her next meeting with Mr. Ranleigh, in all of which shy dreams she had been distinguished by that gentleman's interested attentions to her, began to experience a sense of strong ill-usage. If, she thought indignantly, Mr. Ranleigh considered her only as a burdensome charge, why had he taken her up in the first place? Obviously his only interest at the present moment was in his nephew, for, though it was clear that it was her dilemma that had drawn him down to Hillcourt, he did not so much as mention that subject to her, but only went on chatting with Lord Neagle about hunting and other such mundane matters.

It did not make her feel any more kindly toward him to learn from Miss Dowie, when she went upstairs to dress for dinner shortly afterward, that he had already settled on a plan for her future. She was, her aunt informed her, to be instructed in the female accomplishments by the lady who had been charged with the education of his sisters, after which her original scheme of becoming a governess might be carried out. Cecily, finding her difficulties thus summarily disposed of, characterised his behaviour roundly as highhanded, only to find, to her surprise, that her aunt quite failed to agree with her.

'Decision,' Miss Dowie said approvingly. 'I like that. No dithering or pondering or beating about the bush. Walked into the house and in ten minutes, Lady Frederick tells me, had the matter in hand.'

'But he did not say a word to *me* about it!' Cecily said, quite unmollified. A recalcitrant expression appeared upon her face, and she said, 'Perhaps I do not choose to be instructed by Miss Binkley!'

'That has nothing to say to the matter!' Miss Dowie said tartly. 'You will do as you are told and apply yourself diligently —*and* express your gratitude properly to Mr. Ranleigh for the considerable trouble and expense you are putting him to. I confess I scarcely expected, when I first met him, to find him a man of sense and proper feeling, but he is acting in this matter just as he ought, and so I have told him. Give the devil his due!' she added, nodding briskly as she went off to her own room to prepare for dinner.

Cecily was left to stare dissatisfiedly at her reflection in the mirror—a quite absurdly youthful one, she considered, for her years—and to wish that, only for this one evening, she might be able to wear any of the fashionable gowns which she had displayed in the theatre, and which would make it quite clear to anyone that she was *not* a child to be ordered off to the school-room.

As it was, she was obliged to content herself with dressing her hair modishly high on her head, and she did not even succeed in exhibiting this piece of sophistication in the dining-room, for Miss Dowie, coming back into her bedchamber when it was time to go below, took one look at her coiffure and, declaring it highly improper for a girl who aspired to be a governess, obliged her to arrange her dark locks in the plainest style.

It appeared, indeed, that Miss Dowie, in spite of her commendation of Mr. Ranleigh's conduct, did not entirely trust that gentleman to keep the line, and was anxious for her niece to attract as little of his attention as possible. But her care was found to be quite unnecessary. Mr. Ranleigh addressed scarcely half a dozen words to Cecily at dinner, and if his eyes rested on her in any but the most casual way it was more than Miss Dowie's sharpest inspection could discover.

Since he behaved toward Miss Dowie herself, however, with the greatest civility, she found herself more than ever of the opinion that she had wronged him in her first summing up at the Running Boar.

'I am quite certain now that it was only that excessively ill-advised wager of his cousin's that made him seek you out,' she said, 'for there was nothing in the least particular in his manner toward you this evening. But that is not surprising, for it would be very odd indeed if a man of his stamp were to look twice at a mere child like you.' She went on, with the air of one making a large concession, 'I have been thinking that it might be proper for you to work a pair of slippers to present to him at Christmas . . .'

But she got no farther, for Cecily, rising impetuously to her feet, declared that she had no intention of spending a moment of her time in preparing gifts for a person who looked upon her in the light of a probably undeserving object of charity.

'I am sure Papa would not have liked it in the least for us to be beholden to someone who cares nothing for us except that anyone connected with *his* family should not be an embarrassment to him!' she said, rather incoherently. 'No, and *I* do not like it . . .'

'Your Papa,' Miss Dowie interrupted scathingly, 'was never in his life averse to being beholden to anyone! You are behaving like a ninnyhammer, Cecily! Sit down!'

Cecily, after a rebellious moment, did so, and was then treated to a pungent lecture on the sin of ingratitude, and an ultimatum to behave toward a gentleman who had nothing but her best interests at heart or risk her aunt's serious displeasure.

'Well, I do not care!' Cecily said unrepentantly, as Miss Dowie wound to a close. 'Everyone else in this house toadeats him abominably, exactly as if he were the Emperor of China; but I do not care how rich and fashionable he is, and how *condescending*! I do not wish to be condescended to! And I shall *not* toadeat him, no matter what *you* choose to do!'

Having relieved her feelings by this outburst, she felt a great deal better, and, as she had quite as much spirit as her aunt, determined to put aside the agreeable dreams in which she had been indulging and think no more about them. This was not the easiest thing to do, with Mr. Ranleigh actually under the same roof, where she would be obliged to see him several times each day. But she consoled herself with the reflection that he would remain at Hillcourt only for a day or two, and that by the time she saw him again—if, indeed, she saw him at all—she would have quite got over her foolishness in regard to him.

CHAPTER EIGHT

As it happened, however, the following day brought a pair of events which made a considerable alteration in Mr. Ranleigh's plans.

The first of these was the fulfillment of Lord Neagle's wish in regard to the weather. Long before noon the leaden skies from which a few snowflakes had occasionally fallen during the night had darkened ominously, and his lordship, who had been induced to leave the house for his customary morning ride with Cecily only by his reluctant realisation that his uncle would undoubtedly feel no overwhelming desire for his company at such an early hour, was obliged to agree with Damer that the thickening snowfall made it advisable for them to return to the house.

The second event was the arrival at Hillcourt, at a moment approximately coinciding with this decision, of a curricle-and-four driven by Lord Portandrew. He was looking extremely cold and uncomfortable—in spite of the splendour of an elegant driving-coat sporting no fewer than sixteen shoulder-capes— as he tossed the reins to his groom and walked up the steps to the front door; and the evident surprise of Welbore, the elderly butler, on seeing him appeared to do nothing to dispel the rather defiant anxiety his mien proclaimed.

'I beg your pardon, my lord—was her ladyship expecting you?' Welbore inquired, as he received the driving-coat, his lordship's curly-brimmed beaver, and his York tan driving gloves and passed them into the care of a footman.

'Well, no, she ain't,' his lordship confessed. 'Matter of fact,

I didn't expect to be here myself, but—long drive—deuced uncomfortable weather, you know . . .'

Welbore, who had been acquainted with his lordship since he had been a schoolboy at Eton, reflected tolerantly that this was another of Master Tony's starts, and said soothingly that he believed her ladyship was in the breakfast-parlour with Mr. Ranleigh. But the mention of his cousin's name, far from soothing his lordship, appeared to have exactly the opposite effect.

'Oh—he's here, is he?' he said nervously. 'Wondered about that. Anyone else, Welbore? I mean to say—any guests staying in the house?'

Welbore, who was quite aware that there was some mystery connected with the two ladies her ladyship had brought back with her from London, coughed and said cautiously that there were.

'Oh?' His lordship appeared struck. 'A young lady?'

'A young lady *and* an older lady,' Welbore replied, still discreet. 'Perhaps you would like me to announce you, my lord?'

'No, I . . . Well I'd as lief announce myself!' his lordship said hastily. 'Deuced awkward business, coming in like this . . . Might be as well . . .'

He did not complete this muddled speech, but walked down the hall in the direction of the breakfast-parlour. The door to this apartment was standing open, and as he approached it he appeared to reconnoitre, for the purpose—it seemed to the puzzled Welbore—of seeing who was inside it.

His behaviour was equally puzzling to Lady Frederick, who was sitting facing the door and thus had the advantage of observing her nephew's peculiarly indirect approach.

'Anthony?' she exclaimed in astonishment. 'Is that you? What in the world are you doing here?'

His lordship, even in his confusion at being thus addressed by the lady who—as he had once confessed to his cousin—always had the ability to make him feel himself nine years old again, with his fingers in a jam jar, was able to observe that there was a none-too-pleased expression in his cousin's eyes as he turned in his chair to survey him. His lordship coughed, and plunged into speech.

'Hello, Robert!' he said, in a propitiatory voice. 'Rather thought I'd find you here. Aunt Louisa . . .' He bent over her hand.

'Why shouldn't you find me here?' Mr. Ranleigh asked, not very cordially. 'I told you I was coming—didn't I? But what the devil are *you* doing here? That's what *I* want to know.'

'Yes,' Lady Frederick concurred, 'for *I* haven't invited you, Anthony; I am quite sure of *that*. Are you absolutely certain you've come to the right house, my dear boy? You *know* what a wretched memory you have!'

Lord Portandrew made a disclamatory sound in his throat. 'Don't mean to stay,' he managed to articulate. 'Took a fancy yesterday afternoon to drive down and see Great-aunt Ethelreda —racked up last night at the King's Head at Cuckfield— thought I'd just pop in on you this morning on the way . . .'

He paused, seeing that both his aunt and his cousin were regarding him with patent disbelief.

'Great-aunt Ethelreda!' Lady Frederick exclaimed. 'Why should you wish to visit her? I am sure you haven't been near her since you were out of short-coats!'

'Exactly the point!' His lordship seized on the idea. 'Deuced long time, you see—old lady growing devilish feeble, I've no doubt . . .'

'And she has *no* fortune at all to dispose of, if you *are* run off your legs—which I don't for a moment believe, with *your* income,' Lady Frederick said, fixing severely penetrating eyes upon him. 'Anthony, tell me this instant—are you *foxed*, at this hour of the morning?'

Mr. Ranleigh smiled a trifle sardonically, as his cousin attempted a horrified denial. 'No, he's not foxed,' he said. 'Nor, may I add, has he any intention of visiting Great-aunt Ethelreda. You came to spy—didn't you, Tony? Have you pumped Welbore yet? What did you discover?'

His lordship reddened indignantly. 'Well, I must say, that's a deuced disagreeable way to put it!' he declared. 'I have half a mind to walk straight out of here and go on with my journey—though,' he added, looking doubtfully at the snow now swirling down thickly outside the window, 'it's come on dashed unpleasant out there in the past half hour. Never would have left the King's Head if I'd known . . .'

'Oh sit down, Tony!' Mr. Ranleigh said, with an impatient shrug. 'Now you are here, I suppose you will have to be told—but I hope to God you will have sense enough to keep a discreet tongue in your head!' He explained to Lady Frederick, 'The fact is, ma'am, that Tony has come in search of Miss Daingerfield-Nelson, whom he is persuaded I have brought down from London, for—er—purposes too indelicate to mention before a lady.'

Lord Portandrew's face had by this time become beet-red, but he stood his ground doggedly.

'Well, dash it, it's true—ain't it?' he demanded. 'The girl *is* here—though how you have persuaded Aunt Louisa . . .'

He paused, intimidated by the affronted stare his aunt now turned upon him.

'Am I to understand, Anthony,' she said awfully, 'that you believe that I—*I!*—am lending countenance to an immoral exploit of my son's?'

Lord Portandrew hastily assured her that such an idea had never crossed his mind.

'Good God, no!' he said. 'Merely occurred to me—plausible fellow, Robert—might have taken you in . . .'

He cast a glance of desperate appeal at Mr. Ranleigh, which his cousin callously ignored.

'No, don't look to *me* to bail you out,' he said unsympathetically. 'You got yourself into this, and you would be properly served now if Mama took it in snuff and showed you the door.'

Her ladyship, as a matter of fact, appeared to be experiencing such strong disapprobation of her nephew's conduct that it did not seem unlikely that she would do just that. But at that moment an interruption occurred in the form of young Lord Neagle, who came prancing into the room with Cecily following rather shyly in his wake.

'Oh, I say, they told me you were having breakfast, Robert!' he began, catching sight first of his uncle. Then, seeing Lord Portandrew, he broke off, staring. 'Tony! What are *you* doing here?' he exclaimed in surprise.

But Lord Portandrew had no eyes for him. He was gazing at Cecily with an expression so comically compounded of incredulity, indignation, and admiration on his face that Lord Neagle was moved to inquire of his grandmother, 'What's the *matter* with him? He looks moonstruck.'

'He *is* moonstruck,' Lady Frederick snapped. 'Close your mouth, Anthony, and *do* try to look less like a perfect knock-in-the-cradle!' She said to Cecily, 'My dear, I think you had best go to your room. I am sure you will find it much more agreeable there until I have got rid of this idiotic nephew of mine!'

Cecily, who was looking quite at a loss over the powerful effect her appearance had had upon the unknown young dandy in her hostess's breakfast-parlour, nodded in bewilderment, and was about to withdraw when Lord Portandrew uttered a resounding negative.

'Not until I've got to the bottom of this!' he said violently. 'Dash it, Aunt Louisa, you *can't* expect to fob me off like this! I want to know what Miss Daingerfield-Nelson is doing here!'

The sound of her stage name brought a modicum of enlightenment to Cecily, and caused Mr. Ranleigh to say, with a flicker of amusement, 'You had as well tell him the whole, Mama, or you'll have him babbling the affair all over London. Miss Hadley, may I make Lord Portandrew known to you? He is the graceless cousin whose wager brought me to the Running Boar. Tony, this is Miss Hadley, a young relative of mine who is staying here at present, and will hopefully soon be employed as a governess in some respectable family. You will oblige her —and me as well—if you will quite erase from your mind the fact that you ever saw her gracing the boards as Miss Daingerfield-Nelson.'

He paused, seeing that Lord Portandrew seemed to be incapable of assimilating more information than had already been given him; but Lord Neagle, quicker of apprehension, said, looking at Cecily with new respect, 'Jupiter! An actress! I always thought there was something smoky about your coming here! But why do you want to be a governess if you can be on the stage?'

'She wishes to become a governess,' Lady Frederick said severely, 'because she values the advantages of respectability— which is more, you scamp, than I can say of you!' She threw up her hands in despair. 'Robert, what in the world are we to do now? Even if Anthony can be trusted to keep a quiet tongue in his head about all this, there is Charlie . . .'

'Charlie will say exactly nothing to anyone,' Mr. Ranleigh said. 'Do you understand that, Charlie? Under threat of my *severest* displeasure!'

Lord Neagle, awed, declared that wild horses would not succeed in dragging information from him, but Lord Portandrew was not so easily brought round. Recovering his tongue, he demanded fuller information, looking at his cousin meanwhile with an expression that appeared to warn him that he was dealing with a man who would see through any attempt to deceive him. Cecily, who was beginning to find the situation diverting, in spite of Mr. Ranleigh's obvious, if rather bored, irritation with his cousin, sat down beside Lady Frederick and listened with attention to the brief account that gentleman gave of her situation, now and then interrupting to clarify some point with a remark of her own. This at length had the effect of turning Mr. Ranleigh's exasperation upon her.

'We shall do very well without your help, Miss Hadley,' he said. 'My mother, I believe, has advised you to go to your room. May I suggest that you do so?'

She stood up, flushing, only to find Lord Portandrew at once springing to her defence.

'No, dash it all, Robert!' he said wrathfully. 'You wouldn't speak to her so if she weren't alone in the world! What right have *you* . . . ?'

'Will you *stop* trying to enact a Cheltenham tragedy over

my breakfast-table, Tony?' Mr. Ranleigh begged. 'I am beginning to find your addiction to high drama more than a little tiresome! Miss Hadley's affairs are no concern of yours; in fact, now that you have succeeded in prying out the information you came for, I strongly suggest that you take your leave of us and go on with your journey.'

Lord Portandrew pointed out the window. 'Can't do that,' he said, in simple triumph. 'Look at the weather. Couldn't send a dog out is a snowstorm like that. I shall have to stay.'

A small chuckle escaped Cecily. Mr. Ranleigh said resignedly, 'Oh, my God!' and then announced, to the unrepentant Miss Hadley, 'In that case, you shall have your meals upstairs until my cousin leaves. I have no idea how much reliance can be placed on *your* good sense, but I have a fair idea of the amount Tony possesses, and—whatever he may think—I did *not* send you down here to have you subjected to improper solicitations.'

'I wouldn't!' Lord Portandrew asseverated indignantly. 'Dash it, Robert, you can't believe I'm such a loose-screw as that! I have the greatest respect for Miss Hadley! And if you think you are going to shut her up, like a dashed Turk with his what-do-you-call-it . . .'

'Harem,' Cecily supplied helpfully.

'That's it!' his lordship said. 'Well, if you think that, you're fair and far out! If you don't trust me to keep the line, I'll have *my* meals in my room!'

'To the best of my knowledge, you have no room,' Mr. Ranleigh reminded him, repressively. 'I don't recall anyone's asking you to stay.'

'Yes, but we shall have to, my dear,' Lady Frederick said, surveying the snow tumbling down outside the window. 'I simply could not face Almeria if I were to turn Anthony out in such weather. You *know* what a hubble-bubble creature she is, and if he were to take a chill she would be certain to lay it at my door! I shall ring for Welbore and have your things taken up, Anthony,' she went on severely, 'but I warn you that if you cast so much as a glance at Miss Hadley that might be construed as particular, or disclose to anyone that she is Miss

Daingerfield-Nelson, I shall be obliged to take steps. Very strong steps, in fact!'

What measures his aunt might take that would materially cut up his peace Lord Portandrew knew no more than any other person in the room, but her warning had the desired effect, and he promised fervently to give her no cause for disapproval if he were allowed to remain at Hillcourt. He was then led away by Welbore, and Cecily, having no desire to face Mr. Ranleigh's displeasure over the part she had played in the scene just past, swiftly took her leave as well and went off to change her riding dress.

CHAPTER NINE

Miss Dowie, whom she found in the little sitting-room next her bedchamber that had been set aside for the visitors' use, received with some suspicion the news that the gentleman who had instigated the infamous wager that had brought Mr. Ranleigh to the Running Boar had arrived at Hillcourt. He was presented to her when the household gathered for luncheon some time later, and was favoured with such a curt acknowledgement of his civilities that he was quite abashed, and scarcely dared open his mouth throughout the repast.

His situation—between two formidable elderly ladies and his disapproving cousin—was indeed so lamentable that Cecily felt obliged to take pity upon him. Mr. Ranleigh's agent having arrived at the house just as they were rising from the table, Mr. Ranleigh went off to closet himself with him in the estate-room, and Cecily, aware that Lady Frederick and Miss Dowie would now enjoy a digestive hour in the Small Saloon, suggested to Lord Neagle that the three younger members of the company might retire to the billiards-room.

Her stratagem was unsuccessful. Miss Dowie, overhearing, said severely that she was to come along with her and Lady Frederick to the Small Saloon. She was obliged to obey, and as a consequence was treated to the unusual spectacle of her aunt and Lady Frederick in amicable conversation together, the two ladies joining in an attack on Lord Portandrew's many faults of character and the excessively bad *ton* of his having forced himself, with the aid of the weather, upon their company.

So engrossed did they become in this agreeable occupation

that she was presently able to slip away and join Lord Neagle and Lord Portandrew in the billiard-room, where, in the course of a friendly game, she soon dropped into the same unceremonious terms with the latter gentleman as those on which she stood with young Lord Neagle. As a matter of fact, when Mr. Ranleigh strolled into the room an hour later, all three of its inmates were laughing immoderately together over the success of one of Cecily's highly unorthodox shots—a circumstance that set that gentleman's brows on the rise. He looked into Cecily's triumphant face and Lord Portandrew's blissfully merry one and said lazily, 'I am glad to see that you are amusing yourselves, children. Miss Hadley, if I am not mistaken, your aunt wishes to see you upstairs.'

Cecily put up her chin. 'I can scarcely believe that you are my aunt's messenger, sir,' she said, with an outspokenness that would have won her that lady's severest censure, 'but I daresay you wish me to leave, so I shall go.'

She then bestowed a dazzling smile upon Lord Portandrew and walked out of the room, having the satisfaction of hearing the beginning of his lordship's expostulation as she departed: 'No, really, Robert! This is the outside of enough! You can't shut Miss Hadley into her room merely because I'm in the house!'

'If she had her deserts, it would be on bread and water,' Mr. Ranleigh said, subduing the amused twitch of the lips that Cecily's defiance had aroused. 'I should be on my guard if I were you, Tony. That abominable brat means to display her independence by flirting with you, unless I very much miss my guess.'

'Flirt with me! Miss Hadley! She's the most innocent creature I've ever clapped eyes on!' Lord Portandrew said indignantly. 'Ask Charlie. Not a word she said to me she wouldn't have said to him as well!'

Mr. Ranleigh, surveying his nephew, said he rather believed he was not a proper judge, and was then tactless enough to inquire whether that young gentleman expected life to be a perpetual holiday simply because his uncle and his cousin had come down from London. Lord Neagle, recalled to a sense of duty, reluctantly left the room, and Mr. Ranleigh then favoured Lord Portandrew with a short but pungent lecture on the conditions of behaviour under which he would not be dismissed from Hillcourt to rack up at the nearest inn—conditions so stringent, as far as Miss Hadley was concerned, as to wring a protest from his lordship.

'I'm dashed if I can see why you are acting this way!' he said. 'If she goes for a governess, she'll have to meet men now and then—won't she? I mean to say, governesses don't dine with the family, but they must run across a fellow or two when they're out walking with the brats. And there are always curates underfoot in the kind of devilish dull sort of place my aunt will look out for . . .'

Mr. Ranleigh, interrupting, observed rather pointedly that Miss Hadley might meet as many men as she liked, with his good will, provided that the object of their attentions to her was matrimony.

'No, dash it—not a curate!' Lord Portandrew said feelingly. 'A girl like that buried in some scrubby country parsonage! I tell you, Robert, she was like to have set the whole town by the ears: never saw a girl so much admired! It ain't so much *what* she looks like, you know; it's the way she has of—of smiling at you as if you was the only person in the world she cared to see . . .'

Mr. Ranleigh, who had himself observed this enchanting effect of Miss Hadley's smile, did not appear pleased to have it called to his attention, but merely remarked that the projecting of it to a theatre full of people must inevitably cause some confusion, to which his cousin seemed to have fallen victim. This his lordship took as an aspersion upon Miss Hadley, and an interchange resulted from which Lord Portandrew, speedily worsted, retired in a miff.

He had recovered his good humour by the dinner hour, however, when he appeared in all the splendour of a corbeau-coloured coat of superfine, much padded at the shoulders and nipped in at the waist, and a neckcloth arranged in the intricacies of the Mathematical style. To his satisfaction, he found that his cousin had repented of his resolution to banish Miss Hadley to her room during his stay in the house, for she was already in the Ivory Saloon with Miss Dowie and Lady Frederick when he entered. He went over to sit beside her, and she inquired at once, with a demure glance, whether he had observed that it was snowing still.

'I should think I have!' he said enthusiastically. 'Devilish disagreeable weather. Shouldn't think I'd be able to go a mile without coming to grief.'

Lady Frederick, overhearing, said dampingly that it was a great pity, since she had depended on his leaving in the morning.

'And I expect it will delay Miss Binkley's arrival as well,' she said, 'since she cannot be expected to travel in such weather. However, at least Robert will not be able to leave, either—which is my *one* consolation in this entire affair.'

Mr. Ranleigh, entering the room on this remark, immediately observed that she was quite right, and said that he had no intention of leaving Hillcourt as long as his cousin remained there.

It began to appear shortly thereafter, however, that even his presence in the house would not be sufficient to dampen the romantic flame in Lord Portandrew's breast. His lordship, never famed for successful subterfuge, had made it plain to everyone in the household by the close of the evening that he was smitten to the point of idiocy with Miss Hadley, and even Cecily herself had begun to grow somewhat uneasy over the matter by the time she carried her candle up to her bedchamber. She refused, however, to confess this to her aunt, who came to her room while she was undressing to lecture her on her conduct.

'I don't know what you are talking of!' she said mendaciously, when Miss Dowie accused her of leading his lordship on. 'I behaved toward him exactly as I did toward Charlie.'

'It might be more to the point if you were to behave toward him as you do toward Mr. Ranleigh,' Miss Dowie said. 'Your conduct toward *him* is enough to make him think you the most ungrateful chit alive—while you *lavish* smiles upon Lord Port-andrew!'

Cecily was about to begin a heated rejoinder, but reconsidered, and after a moment fair-mindedly acknowledged that perhaps she *had* been at fault.

'But I did it only to set Mr. Ranleigh's back up,' she said, in self-defence. 'He is so odiously condescending—as if I were twelve years old and no man in his senses would waste a glance on me!'

Miss Dowie looked at her forebodingly. 'Cecily,' she said, 'are you developing a *tendre* for that man?'

Cecily blushed, but said airily, 'For Lord Portandrew? Good heavens, no!'

'You know very well I do not mean Lord Portandrew,' Miss Dowie said. 'I mean Mr. Ranleigh, miss!'

A deeper colour appeared in Cecily's face. 'Of course not!' she denied quickly. 'I have told you before that I think him quite abominably toplofty—and even Lady Frederick says that he is shockingly highhanded . . .'

'Fiddle!' Miss Dowie snapped. 'He is shockingly attractive —as you very well know. But let me tell you that if you allow yourself to develop a partiality for him you will be the greatest widgeon in England! I have it from Lady Frederick that he is on the point of offering for a young lady who is at all points a highly suitable bride for him—Miss Augusta Comerford. He and Lady Frederick are to spend Christmas in her company at her uncle's seat in Somerset, and Lady Frederick has no doubt that, on the head of it, an announcement will be forthcoming.'

'I am very glad to hear it!' Cecily said, endeavouring to pay no heed to the disturbingly hollow feeling that this piece of intelligence evoked in her. 'Charlie has already described Miss Comerford to me, and, indeed, I believe I have seen her myself, in the box with Mr. Ranleigh the evening he came to the theatre. She is very handsome, but seems a dreadful flirt. I daresay they will be very well matched.'

'Well matched or not, it is no affair of yours,' Miss Dowie

retorted, 'and so I will thank you to remember!' She added, on a fidgeting note, 'I wish that the roads would improve, so that Miss Binkley might arrive. Once *she* is here, your time must be fully occupied, and then I daresay Lord Portandrew will go away, and Mr. Ranleigh as well.'

CHAPTER TEN

But Miss Binkley, a prudent maiden lady on the shady side of sixty, was quite unwilling to entrust herself to roads that progressed, during the following week, from snow-covered thoroughfares to treacherous quagmires as a quick thaw set in. As a result, Cecily was free to enjoy the company not only of Lord Portandrew, but also of Mr. Ranleigh, whose determination to allow his cousin no opportunity for private conversation with her caused him to assume the unlikely role of chaperon when neither Miss Dowie nor Lady Frederick was able to do so.

These occasions consisted chiefly of outdoor excursions. Cecily, country-bred, had no notion of allowing the dismal condition of roads and lanes from deterring her from her favourite diversion, and was to be found hacking a high-couraged chestnut about the countryside each morning that she could prevail on someone to agree with her that the weather was not too bad for such expeditions. Lord Neagle, who had been used to accompany her, would have discontinued his attendance on her to seek his uncle's company if obliged to make a choice between them; but he was not. Lord Portandrew *would* accompany Miss Hadley, and Mr. Ranleigh *would* be of the party if his cousin was. So Lord Neagle made one of Cecily's entourage as well.

She would have been less than human if she had not derived a certain satisfaction from this arrangement. It was certainly agreeable to find herself escorted daily by no fewer than three gentlemen, and if only she could have believed that she owed the pleasure of Mr. Ranleigh's company to inclination, rather than to duty, her cup of enjoyment would have been quite full.

As it was, it frequently had a rather acrid taste. Mr. Ranleigh did not scruple to let her see his cool displeasure at being obliged to guard her from his cousin's ardour, nor was he averse to putting this displeasure into words. Indeed, the frankness of his speech on several occasions drove Lord Portandrew, who had all his life looked up to his Top-of-the-Trees cousin with something like awe, to forget his deference in the heat of his remonstrance, and once even to go so far as to offer to call him out.

'Don't be a gudgeon!' Mr. Ranleigh merely advised him briefly. They had turned their horses homeward after an excursion that had left the gentlemen's top-boots splashed with mud and Cecily's shabby riding habit in an even more disreputable state than it had been in when she had left the house; and Lord Neagle, tiring of the sedate pace at which they were progressing, had already cantered on ahead to the stables. 'In the first place,' Mr. Ranleigh continued, 'it is the height of impropriety for you to say such a thing before Miss Hadley, and in the second, you are such a devilish poor shot that it is folly for you to think of calling anyone out.'

'We'll see that!' his lordship said wrathfully. 'Dash it, Robert, I know I'm no match for you with pistols, but if there's any justice in this world . . .'

'There isn't,' Mr. Ranleigh assured him. 'You'd be cold meat, Tony, so do come down from the boughs and try to behave as if you had *some* modicum of sense left in your head.'

Cecily said to him, taking up the cudgels in Lord Portandrew's defence, '*He* was not the one who began it, you know; *you* were. So I think *you* must be the one to offer apologies—though even if you do not, I warn you that I shan't let him go out with you. Papa fought a duel once, and was brought home on a hurdle, as he well deserved to be, for it was all quite irregular and they were *both* foxed, and a more disagreeable month than Aunt and I spent nursing him you cannot imagine! I made up my mind then that I should not allow anyone *ever* to fight a duel over me.'

'My good child,' Mr. Ranleigh said wearily, 'I wish you will disabuse yourself of the notion that I have the slightest intention of letting Tony's blood. If you would have the propriety not to encourage his remarkably absurd predilection for you, there would be no need for heroics on your part—or on his, either.'

'No, dash it, Robert!' Lord Portandrew interrupted. 'You won't say such things of her in *my* presence!'

Unfortunately for the remainder of the speech which his lordship intended to make, his vehemence at this point led him to clap his heels into his horse's sides, and that spirited animal at once bolted off down the lane, leaving Cecily dissolved in helpless laughter behind him.

Mr. Ranleigh, controlling a telltale twitch of his own lips, said to her, 'Yes, it's very well for you to laugh, you incorrigible brat—but you are causing the devil of an amount of trouble, you know! Do you realise how shockingly you imposed on me the first time we met, with that schoolroom demureness of yours?'

'Oh, I didn't! That is, I didn't mean . . .' Cecily suddenly ceased laughing and looked at him with some anxiety. 'You don't *really* believe I set out to deceive you?' she asked. 'Pray do not, because it is not at all true! It's only that—I *do* try to behave with propriety, but Aunt says all the Hadleys are sadly unsteady, and I *am* a Hadley—well, I can't help that!' she ended, smiling at him again, a little shyly and ruefully.

'No, you cannot,' Mr. Ranleigh agreed, with slight acerbity. 'But you *can* refrain from encouraging my cousin to make a cake of himself over you. He will not marry you, you know, and I can't believe you are birdwitted enough to wish to lead him on to offer you a *carte blanche*.'

The smile died out suddenly from Cecily's eyes. She turned pale, and jerked out, in a voice of anger quite different from her youthful indignation of a few moments before, 'You would not say such things to me if I were not—if I were Miss Comerford!'

She put her horse into a gallop on the instant; before he could reply she was flying—heedless of mud and snow—toward the house. A startled frown creased Mr. Ranleigh's brow; he uttered a vexed exclamation and followed her.

He was not vouchsafed an opportunity to make his apologies to her, however, if that were his intention, for she reached the house before he did and, consigning her mount to a groom, ran indoors at once. She went immediately to her bedchamber and did not reappear until it was time for luncheon, when she came downstairs in Miss Dowie's company, looking pale and a little subdued. Miss Dowie said that she had the headache, and recommended that she drink a glass of camphorated spirits of lavender and lie down upon her bed. Whether she followed this excellent advice or not Mr. Ranleigh had no way of knowing, for she disappeared into the west wing of the house at the end of the brief repast and was seen no more that afternoon.

Lord Portandrew, meanwhile, having received unmistakable hints from his aunt and his cousin that the state of the roads need no longer prevent his departure, found himself in a quandary. A period of solitary reflection in the library, and the consumption of an amount of his cousin's excellent brandy that might be considered reasonable in a man screwing his courage to the sticking-point, sent him, at about four o'clock, in search of Miss Dowie, whom he found in her small sitting-room. What passed there between them was to remain unknown, but it had the effect of sending Miss Dowie, after a considerable period of time, into Cecily's bedchamber with a very odd expression on her face.

She found her niece seated by the window with the handkerchief she had taken up to hem dropped upon her lap, and said to her at once, 'My dear, I have come on a very delicate errand. It is not at all what I like, but his lordship is quite determined, and indeed I scarcely know what to do in the matter. He contends that neither Lady Frederick nor Mr. Ranleigh has the authority to control your actions, and that if he has *my* permission to pay his addresses to you it is everything that is needful. *My* feeling is that if you do not wish to receive them there is no need for me to embarrass him by drawing Lady Frederick into the matter. On the other hand, if you wish to give him an affirmative answer, I should not consider it at all proper to allow him to address you without her knowledge. You know, my dear, it is a very serious matter to marry a man whose entire family is set against you . . .'

Cecily, who had been listening with eyes growing wide with surprise, at this point could contain herself no longer.

'Marry?' she exclaimed. 'Lord Portandrew? Is *that* what you are talking of, Aunt?'

Miss Dowie sat down. 'Well, of course!' she said testily. 'What else have I been saying these five minutes past? He has asked my permission to pay his addresses to you, exactly as I have told you . . .'

'But is he serious?' Cecily interrupted, her head in a whirl, but uppermost in her thoughts the rather bitter triumph of knowing that Mr. Ranleigh had been mistaken when he had informed her that his cousin would not offer her marriage. 'He truly wishes to *marry* me?'

Miss Dowie adjusted her spectacles upon her nose. 'You are not ordinarily slow of comprehension, Cecily,' she said severely. 'Have I not told you that, as plainly as it is in my power to do? However,' she went on, relenting, 'I daresay it may come as something of a surprise to you, and it is possible, I am aware, to be somewhat bewildered by the headache. How *is* your headache?'

'My headache?' Cecily passed one hand mechanically over her brow. 'Oh, it has quite left me, Aunt! But—but Lord Portandrew . . .'

'A very amiable young man,' Miss Dowie conceded, 'although not, I fear, possessed of the highest powers of intellect. However, his manners are excellent and his birth unexceptionable, and he assures me that his affairs stand in such a case that he has no need to look for fortune in choosing a wife. There is also the advantage of the title: as little store as I set on such matters personally, I expect you would find it agreeable to be a Countess.'

Cecily, who did not appear to be attending to her, but had pressed her hands to her temples as if she were endeavouring to quiet the whirling thoughts within them, said at this point, in a stifled voice, 'But I do not love him, Aunt! Indeed, I never thought—I never expected . . .'

Miss Dowie looked affronted. 'Love!' she said roundly. 'Romantic fancies! Pray, what has that to say to the matter? A rational regard on both sides is what must be looked for in such affairs. Of course, if you have taken Lord Portandrew in dislike...'

'But I have not!' Cecily said. 'I mean, I do not *dislike* him—but—but I am sure I could never feel for him the regard which —I should like to feel for the man I marry ...' She sprang up, and began to pace the room. 'Oh dear, Aunt, indeed I *do* see that this might be the end of all our difficulties!' she said miserably. 'I expect I am perfectly birdwitted even to think of refusing such an offer, for I should be Lady Portandrew, and never have to return to that odious Jillson, or go for a governess, or do anything disagreeable so that we may not find ourselves without a roof over our heads...'

Miss Dowie, who, for all her lack of sentimentality, was not wanting in feeling, saw the distress in her niece's eyes and said brusquely, 'Now, my dear, there is no need for you to put yourself into a taking! It would be in the highest degree repugnant to me to think of your entering into marriage only for an establishment. I assure you that I have always believed it to be a much lesser evil to be obliged to earn one's own bread.'

Cecily came across the room and dropped impetuously on her knees beside her aunt's chair.

'Dear Aunt,' she said gratefully, 'it is exactly like you to say that, when I am sure anyone else in your place would be telling me that I *must* accept this offer or be cast off by them forever! And I *do* feel a perfect monster not to wish to do so, for I quite see how splendid it would be for both of us.'

Miss Dowie nodded, shrugging her shoulders with the air of one casting away some agreeable dream, and gave Cecily's hand a bracing pat.

'Fiddle!' she said. 'If you don't wish to marry the man, you don't. I need not scruple to tell you, at any rate, that I had hoped for something better for you—for though he may be an Earl, and wealthy into the bargain, he does *not* appear to me to be a man of sense. Now *don't* go off into any high flights!' she concluded, regarding with disapproval the tears welling up in Cecily's eyes. She rose and shook out the voluminous folds of her old-fashioned gown. 'I shall give him his answer,' she said briskly. 'No need for this to go any further.'

Cecily jumped up. 'Oh, no—if you please, Aunt, I had much rather tell him myself,' she said.

Her feelings might oblige her to reject Lord Portandrew's offer, but she was aware that Miss Dowie's outspoken tongue might make the manner of that refusal doubly unpalatable to him, and she was unwilling to wound him further than was necessary.

Miss Dowie was not at once prepared to accede to this idea, but she eventually allowed her scruples to be overcome and Cecily went off to the sitting-room. Here she found his lordship nervously pacing up and down. His face lighted when he saw her, but she dashed his hopes by saying quickly, 'Oh, my lord, my aunt has told me what an honour you have done me, but indeed it will not do! I am quite sure that we should not suit, and—and that you would be far better advised to offer for some young lady whose circumstances are more similar to your own.'

His lordship's face fell. 'No, dash it!' he objected, looking revolted by this prospect. 'Never met a girl before I saw you I'd care to offer for—well, perhaps one or two,' he added hastily, recalling certain events having to do with what his long-suffering mama customarily referred to as 'Anthony's fatal propensity to fancy himself in love with the *most* ineligible young females.' 'But that don't signify: I never knew *true* love before I met *you*, Miss Hadley. And as for your circumstances, I don't care a rush about them, so *that* has nothing to say to the matter.' He looked at her with a slight appearance of hope dawning on his face. 'Perhaps I've been too quick for you,' he said. 'The thing is, I haven't had time to fix my interest with you, what with Robert and my aunt taking the deuced gothic position they have. You wouldn't like to take time to think it over?'

'No, I am afraid not,' Cecily said gently. 'You see, I am *quite* certain of my own mind.'

'Yes, I can see that,' his lordship said, in the dismals again.

'Thought you was—but it never does any harm to try one's luck.' He reflected for a moment. 'I shall have to leave here tomorrow, you know,' he said gloomily. 'No telling when I shall see you again.'

'I think that will be all for the best,' Cecily said encouragingly. 'I am sure you will soon forget me under those circumstances.'

'Will I? No, dash it, I won't!' his lordship said feelingly. 'I expect I shall wear the willow for the deuce of a time.'

Obviously he was not in the mood to be comforted by such philosophic reflections as Cecily was able to call to mind from her aunt's many improving lectures on the subject of young persons who fancied their lives blighted by unrequited affection; and when she was at last able to induce him to leave her she felt that she could congratulate herself upon only one point— that at least he would be spared the mortification of having the fact of his rejection known to anyone but himself.

CHAPTER ELEVEN

But here she was reckoning without Lord Portandrew. It was quite out of his character to keep such an event to himself, and the result was that the first words she heard addressed to her by Lady Frederick, when she came downstairs with her aunt at the dinner hour, were: 'Well, my dear, so you have had the good sense to refuse my nephew! I was most gratified to hear it—quite as much as I was mortified by his having had the bad taste to pursue you with his attentions under my roof.'

Cecily blushed and, at a loss for words, looked to her aunt. That lady, appearing to take Lady Frederick's words as an affront, informed her at once in a starchy tone that, except for her lack of fortune, she considered Cecily in no way an unsuitable match for Lord Portandrew.

'Not,' she conceded, 'that I should have allowed him to address himself to her if she had not assured me that she had no intention of accepting his offer, for I do not consider—in view of the obligation under which we stand to you—that she is free to act as she chooses in a matter that touches your family so nearly.'

This speech, which implied a certain criticism of Lady Frederick's attitude in taking it for granted that it was out of the question for Cecily to think of becoming Lady Portandrew, led to a spirited dialogue between the two elder ladies, which was interrupted only by the appearance of Mr. Ranleigh, who, taking the situation in at a glance, turned the conversation into more unexciting conversational channels. His maner, as he did so, seemed quite as usual, and he did not allude to his cousin's offer, but Cecily guessed that it could not be unknown to him. She rather wished that he *would* speak of it, if only to give her the satisfaction of seeing that he was aware how unfounded his assertion had been that Lord Portandrew had no thought of offering her marriage; but, as he continued to engage her aunt and Lady Frederick in civil chitchat, the lowering reflection was gradually forced upon her that the whole affair was one of indifference to him.

In this conclusion, however, she was not correct, for the news that his cousin had thrown caution to the winds and made an offer for Cecily's hand had had an odd and highly disagreeable effect on Mr. Ranleigh. He was, in fact, startled to find that the absurd child in whose concerns he had so negligently involved himself had the power to move him out of his boredom into positive anger—anger with Tony for having placed a girl who might be considered as being, at the moment, under his protection in the awkward position of being obliged to reject his addresses, and anger with Cecily herself for having led his cousin on to make those addresses.

Lady Frederick, in discussing the matter with him, had been much inclined to praise Cecily for her good sense in rejecting a match which—however repugnant it must have been to his lordship's family—would certainly have been to the highest degree advantageous to herself. But with this encomium her son was far from agreeing.

'Good sense!' he repeated impatiently. 'The two of them together have not exhibited as much of that commodity as one might reasonably expect from Charlie! Tony cannot marry that chit; he knows that as well as you and I do. The moment Aunt Almeria got wind of such a scheme she would be down on him with every argument and entreaty known to female igenuity, and he is no more capable of withstanding her than he is of flying to the moon. There would be a scandal, and the engagement would be broken off at once. That, let me assure you, ma'am, would effectively put an end to any hopes you may have of establishing the girl respectable, for her career in the theatre could not possibly escape notice under such circumstances!'

Lady Frederick, though obliged to acknowledge the justice of these observations, was still, however, inclined to credit Cecily with having behaved very properly in the circumstances.

'For it was quite to be expected, you know,' she remarked, 'that a girl in her situation would be so dazzled by the idea of marrying an Earl—even such a nodcock as Anthony—that she would spend not a moment's thought on the unsuitability of the match.'

Mr. Ranleigh gave a short laugh. 'The unsuitability of the match!' he said. 'Do you believe for a moment, ma'am, that *that* was what decided her against accepting Tony? If you have been in her company this many days without learning that she has no more worldly wisdom than an infant, you must suddenly have become strangely lacking in perception. Depend upon it, she has acted from impulse and nothing more—an impulse I can scarcely wonder at, for poor Tony is far from being a romantic figure in the eyes of a schoolroom miss.'

Lady Frederick, who could not remember the time when her son had been sufficiently exercised by the conduct of any young lady to be moved by it out of his usual satirical calm, gave him a sharp glance. It had occurred to her once or twice during the days just past that his irritation over his cousin's pursuit of Cecily was somewhat excessive, but she had not previously imagined that it might be due to any interest of his own in that direction. She still did not believe that this was likely—it was more than probable that his exasperation arose from his dislike of the sort of scandal into which his befriending of the girl had threatened to plunge them—but she kept a watchful eye on him during dinner.

Nothing, however, could have been more indifferent than Mr. Ranleigh's manner toward Miss Hadley. His conversation was addressed almost exclusively to Miss Dowie and to Mr. Tibble, the latter of whom, in happy ignorance of the emotions under which the remainder of the company were labouring, was flattered to receive so much of his attention and fervently agreed with every word that fell from his lips. Lord Portandrew, who sat throughout the meal in depressed silence, was vouchsafed no more than the curtest of civilities from his cousin. As for Cecily herself, she appeared quite subdued, scarcely lifting her eyes from her plate throughout the meal.

Lady Frederick would have had her doubts concerning her son set even more to rest had she been privileged to be present during the conversation that took place between him and Miss Hadley just before that young lady retired to her bedchamber. Cecily had pleaded a recurrence of her headache to escape the prospect of an evening spent under the surveillance of the all too many persons who knew what had occurred that day, and had just set her foot on the lowest step of the staircase, when Mr. Ranleigh strolled into the hall from the library.

'Going up so early, Miss Hadley?' he inquired, with a rather sardonic inflexion that at once set her hackles on the rise.

'Yes,' she said shortly. 'I have the headache.'

He did not appear to receive this news with sympathy; as a matter of fact, he did not appear even to believe it.

'You are wise,' he said coolly. 'May I suggest, however, that if you had displayed this delicacy a little earlier you might have spared both yourself and my cousin an excessively disagreeable interview?'

Her colour heightened. She said warmly, 'It was not my fault; I never imagined . . .'

'Then you cannot have attended very carefully to the several warnings I dropped on the subject,' Mr. Ranleigh said bluntly. She tried to speak again, but he went on ruthlessly. 'I realise, of course, that you are very young, but you appear to have been brought up with *some* notions of propriety, and if you are not to fall into a far worse scrape than this in the very near future, I should recommend that you adhere to them.'

Cecily said, her eyes positively flashing now, 'I have fallen into no "scrape", as you put it, Mr. Ranleigh! I have received an offer of marriage—which *you* predicted I should not be honoured with—and I have refused it. That is no more than hundreds of other perfectly respectable young women might say —and I am sure you would not think of casting aspersions upon *them*!'

'Should I not? But I rather believe I should, Miss Hadley, if they were in your position. If you intend to conduct yourself on these principles, you had as well go back to the theatre, for it is quite as simple a matter for a giddy chit to be taken in by a callow youth who makes up, with a promise of marriage that he will never keep, to the pretty governess hired to instruct his sisters as it is for her to be ruined in *that* profession!'

She stared at him, startled. 'Oh!' she said, after a moment, moved out of her anger by a sudden sense of mortification. 'Do you mean—Lord Portandrew would not *really* have married me, even if I had accepted his offer?'

'No, my girl, he would not. I do not say he might not *wish* to, as the young fools you will meet as a governess may do as well—for a time. But if *you* are persuadable, you would do well to remember that so are they, and that there will always be weeping mamas and adamant fathers to do the persuading.'

Cecily felt her sense of importance over having received her first offer rapidly diminishing. Under Mr. Ranleigh's cool summing up of the situation, she was made to perceive herself as she no doubt appeared in *his* eyes—a silly chit who had been playing with fire, and who had embroiled a peaceful household in a tiresome brouhaha. The colour flamed up into her face; she said hotly, 'I think you are the most disagreeable person I have ever met—and I don't wish to be obliged to you—and I shall leave this house tomorrow!'

'You will do nothing of the sort,' Mr. Ranleigh said calmly. 'Tomorrow Miss Binkley will be here, and you will then devote your energies to learning as rapidly as possible all those abominable female "accomplishments" that you will be expected to impart to your future charges.'

She gave him a smouldering look, which had the unexpected effect of making him laugh.

'Don't look at me as if you were contemplating murder, you absurd brat!' he said. 'You will thank me for this some day'—a statement which, however, as he turned away from her to go back into the library, seemed to him to ring with a somewhat hollow optimism.

Would she thank him for helping her to a life of respectable drudgery? It was a bleak prospect—certainly one unworthy of a creature as vital and glowing as this one. He frowned over the selection of a book from the shelves, took one down, and riffled through its pages.

'Damn Tony!' was the rather unusual reflection engendered by this inspection.

He replaced the book on the shelf and left the library forthwith to return to the Ivory Saloon. It was not often that Mr. Ranleigh was driven to seek company to save himself from the necessity of encountering his own thoughts; but it was certain that that was what he was doing at this moment.

CHAPTER TWELVE

On the following morning Cecily, coming down to breakfast, found both Lord Portandrew and Mr. Ranleigh on the point of departing for London. When they had gone, the house rapidly appeared to sink into a quiet gloom, which could scarcely be said to have been enlivened by the arrival, at an hour somewhat past noon, of Miss Tabitha Binkley.

Miss Binkley, a tall, silent female in a hair-brown pelisse and bonnet, lost no time in coming down to business with her new pupil. Not an hour after her arrival, Cecily was summoned to the schoolroom on the third floor where she had formerly held sway, and found herself set down at once with a sketch-book before her, being inaugurated into the mysteries of depicting in water colours the trees, shrubbery, and similar innocuous objects Miss Binkley considered suitable subjects for a young lady's brush.

From this she escaped only to one of the back drawing-rooms below, where a pianoforte awaited her attention, and where she spent an arduous pair of hours in practising five-finger exercises and stumbling perseveringly through a Haydn sonata.

This regimen was repeated on the following morning, much to Lord Neagle's disgust. His lordship had looked forward to enjoying an early ride with Cecily, and expressed himself in terms of strong disapprobation when he learned that henceforth she would be too much occupied with her studies to have the leisure for such diversions.

Cecily herself was privately only too ready to agree with his sentiments. The prospect of an unremitting schedule of schoolroom drudgery was certainly bleak when one had been enjoying the pleasures of life at a country seat of the first elegance, complete with the attentions of a peer and the company of the Nonpareil; but she had some of her aunt's good sense, in spite of her inexperience, and was prepared to realise that *that* interlude had been in the nature of a blissful dream.

The dream became even more remote when Lady Frederick and Lord Neagle shortly afterward departed from Hillcourt on holiday visits—the first to spend the Christmas season at the Somerset estate of Lady Comerford's brother, Lord Langworthy, whose wife was a connexion of hers, and the second to go to the Lincolnshire home of his aunt, Lady Fursebrook. Cecily, aware that Mr. Ranleigh and Miss Augusta Comerford were both to be of the Somerset party, found that she was rapidly descending into a case of the dismals as the month of December drew on, for the contrast between her own days and the pleasures being enjoyed by the beautiful Miss Comerford was a severe trial to her. No doubt, she thought bitterly, *that* young lady was now being assiduously courted by Mr. Ranleigh, who would probably consider this a suitable occasion for making her an offer in form.

Sometimes it seemed to Cecily that she would have done a great deal better to have accepted Lord Portandrew's offer and married him in the teeth of his family's opposition, if only to prove to his odious cousin that she *could* enter his world and Miss Comerford's as an equal—for that, it seemed to her, was all she was longing to do. If she were Lady Portandrew it was quite certain that Mr. Ranleigh could not lecture her as if she had been a tiresome child!

So she spent an agreeable hour picturing herself, clad in an elegant satin-and-gauze gown, seated in her own box at the opera and receiving the compliments of a great many gentlemen of the *ton*, while Mr. Ranleigh stood by in an attitude of dark and brooding jealousy, looking somewhat as one might imagine Lord Byron to do. However, the fact that Mr. Ranleigh had not the slightest tinge of romantic melancholy in his nature presently caused this agreeable tableau to fade, and she was left to face the unalterable fact that in order to give him the opportunity to develop these sentiments she would be obliged first to marry Lord Portandrew—something which she did not at all desire to do.

Neither Lady Frederick nor Lord Neagle returned to Hill-court until almost a fortnight after the New Year, by which time Cecily had made such excellent progress in her studies that Miss Binkley reported to her patroness that she believed she might soon be capable of undertaking the education at least of young ladies of tender years.

'Good!' Lady Frederick said approvingly. She had sent for Miss Binkley to her dressing-room, where she was undergoing the ministrations of her dresser in preparation for dinner. The whole household was in a bustle, for Mr. Ranleigh had escorted his mother back to Hillcourt from Somerset, and Lord Neagle, too, had arrived only an hour before under the charge of Mr. Tibble. 'In that case,' Lady Frederick went on, 'I have found just the situation for her. Lady Langworthy was most kind in inquiring whether anyone in the neighbourhood might require the services of a governess, and learned of a Lady Bonshawe who is in need of someone to undertake the education of her two little girls, aged, I believe, eight and eleven. I made it my business to call upon Lady Bonshawe—*not*, I may say, a woman of the slightest distinction, for her father was in trade, and her husband as well, before he was knighted—but a very comfort-able, good-hearted creature.'

Miss Binkley, who would not have dreamed of disputing any of her patroness's pronouncements, at once agreed that such a situation must suit Miss Hadley exactly; but Miss Dowie, when the same information was imparted to her, said she wondered that Lady Frederick should snatch at the first situation that offered, for she believed Lady Bonshawe might well be one of those noisy, vulgar creatures whose household would not be at all the sort of place for Cecily.

Lady Frederick eyed her quellingly. 'My dear Miss Dowie,' she said, 'I am *not*, as you phrase it, snatching at the first thing that offers. In fact, I have already rejected two other situations for which I might have recommended your niece—both in households of considerable rank and fashion.'

Miss Dowie bristled. 'Then perhaps, ma'am, you do not believe that my niece belongs in such *elevated* surroundings?' she inquired.

'To put it to you roundly—no, I do not!' said Lady Frederick. Then, observing that Miss Dowie was preparing to fire a broadside of her own, she went on with some acerbity, 'Don't be a ninnyhammer, woman! Have you not sense enough to see what must be the outcome of it if Cecily is placed in a household where there are gentlemen of fashion who may recognise her as a young woman they have seen upon the London stage? Even if she were not recognised, with her charm she would be fair game for any young man of rakish tendencies who was familiar in the household.'

Miss Dowie, holding her fire to consider this statement, was obliged to acknowledge its merit.

'Exactly!' Lady Frederick said. 'The Bonshawes, on the other hand, are worthy people of no fashion whatever, and have as well, I believe, that mania for respectability that one so often finds among people who are desirous of forgetting their origins. And, as their family consists only of the two little girls whose education Cecily will be called upon to superintend, I believe I may assure you that their house will *not* be frequented by young men of fashion. Lady Bonshawe and Sir William live quite retired, as a matter of fact, on his very respectable estate not far from Bath. I have not met him, but have been assured that he is some years older than his wife, and addicted to nothing more dangerous than whist.'

Miss Dowie, considering this information, was moved to the unusual concession of granting that Lady Frederick's remarks showed a good deal of sense. Her ladyship shrugged.

'Naturally!' she said. 'I have grown very fond of Cecily, and have expended a great deal of thought over the matter of her future. She must marry some day, of course, but she is very young still, and until the proper young man has been found for her I believe she will do very well with Lady Bonshawe. In the meantime,' she added, 'I have a matter to propose to *you*, Miss Dowie. I am aware that you have had it in mind, when Cecily should be settled, to seek some employment as well. What should you say to remaining here? That foolish creature, Maria Wixom, has been persuaded to stay on in Derbyshire indefinitely and devote herself to her niece's family, and so it happens that I am left in need of a companion.'

If she had expected to astonish Miss Dowie with this statement, she was disappointed. Miss Dowie sat primly in her chair, with her hands folded calmly in her lap, and gave the matter her consideration. After some moments, she nodded briskly.

'Very well,' she said. 'No doubt you will regret it, but so, I daresay, shall I. On the other hand, mistaken as I consider your opinions frequently to be, I find your conversation quite stimulating.'

Lady Frederick gave an appreciative crack of laughter. 'And I yours,' she said. 'There is nothing so boring as living with someone who merely echoes one's own opinions, and quakes like a blancmange at the very hint of a set-down. Now *you*, my dear Miss Dowie, are quite incapable, I should think, of quaking.'

'Oh, yes!' Miss Dowie said simply. 'You see, I have lived with my brother, and, compared to the disagreements I have had with *him*, ours have been merely bagatelles.'

'Indeed!' said Lady Frederick—and was spared further comment by the entrance of Lord Neagle into the room.

Dinner that evening was a lively meal, with the two elder ladies both in excellent spirits and Mr. Ranleigh his usual urbane self. Only Cecily seemed subdued. She had been acquainted by her aunt with the plans that had been made for her, and for that lady herself, but she had displayed a surprising lack of interest in them, seeming more concerned with endeavouring to discover whether Lady Frederick had had any news involving her son to impart to Miss Dowie.

Miss Dowie, however, had shown herself impervious to hints, and Cecily had eventually been obliged to ask her directly if

Mr. Ranleigh had returned to Hillcourt betrothed to Miss Comerford.

'And what business is it of yours if he has?' Miss Dowie inquired dampingly.

Cecily's heart went down. 'Oh!' she said, rather faintly. 'Do you mean—he has?'

'I know nothing whatever of the matter,' Miss Dowie said. 'Lady Frederick did not confide in me, nor did I feel it proper to make any inquiries on the subject.'

She looked so unencouraging that Cecily did not pursue the matter further, but she scanned Mr. Ranleigh's countenance rather anxiously when she saw him a little later, as the household gathered for dinner that evening. It told her nothing at all, however, and, as the conversation during the meal did not touch on Miss Comerford, she was left as much in the dark at its conclusion as she had been at its outset.

Nor was she more fortunate when the gentlemen joined the ladies in the Ivory Saloon after dinner. Lady Frederick, her energies not at all diminished by her journey, was all for making up a table for whist before retiring, and Mr. Ranleigh, Mr. Tibble, and Miss Dowie accordingly sat down with her, while Cecily was encouraged by her patroness to demonstrate her new proficiency on the pianoforte that stood in the room.

She was obliged to comply, though with considerable misgiving over the quality of the performance she was about to give. At the conclusion of her efforts she received a kind commendation from Lady Frederick, who was quite unmusical, but, encountering Mr. Ranleigh's quizzical glance, she excused herself in some dudgeon from any further exhibition of her skill—or lack of it—and went immediately to her room.

She was too young for her problems to interfere greatly with her slumbers, but she awoke early in the morning and, finding that sleep had deserted her, rose and dressed, intending to go for a walk before breakfast. The sun had just risen on a fine midwinter morning when she came down the stairs, expecting to find no one stirring but the servants. As she reached the last step, however, she was surprised to hear a quick, firm tread in the hall, and a moment later Mr. Ranleigh himself came into view. He wore top-boots and a long, many-caped driving-coat, and was apparently on the point of leaving the house.

He checked on seeing her, surveying her cloaked figure in slight surprise.

'Miss Hadley? Where are you off to?'

She was annoyed to feel that her colour was heightening at this sudden encounter with the person who had been occupying her thoughts so disturbingly, and replied rather more coolly than was necessary, 'For a walk.'

'Alone? At this hour?'

'Yes, alone!' Her colour rose still further at the disapproval implied in his tone, and she went on rashly, 'I am not a governess *yet*, Mr. Ranleigh! I suppose I may do as I please for a few days more, and I please to go for a walk, and I *shall* go!'

Somewhat to her surprise, he did not take umbrage at this speech, but smiled—a most disturbing smile, as a number of ladies of his acquaintance could attest, for it at once erased the coolly ironic expression his face habitually wore and made one realise what a warm and humorous light could appear in those glinting grey eyes.

'Spoken like a true Hadley!' he remarked. 'I expect you were not acquainted with my grandmother, but my own rather imperfect memories of her all seem to have to do with the fact that the merest hint of opposition was enough to bring out the Tartar in her.'

Cecily laughed, her brow clearing. 'Yes—isn't it abominable!' she said penitently. 'I should not have said it, I am quite aware! It makes me sound dreadfully ungrateful.'

He shrugged. 'Oh, as for gratitude . . . !' he said. 'You may be wishing you had never clapped eyes on either me or my mother, once you are immured at the Bonshawes'. Taking charge of a pair of brats who have not the slightest claim upon you except for the wages that are paid you is scarcely a matter for congratulation, it would appear to me.'

As these were exactly her own sentiments, she could not dispute them with any degree of conviction, but she did manage to summon up enough civility to say, 'Yes, but it *was* very kind of you and Lady Frederick to give me such an excellent opportunity, and Aunt is forever saying that I do not show my appreciation properly.' She blushed furiously all at once and went on, 'In fact, I daresay she is right and you think me quite ragmannered—but now that I am going away and may never see you again, I should like you to know that I—that I shall never forget...'

She paused, seeing a suddenly arrested look in his eyes that confused her. For a moment she took the full light of a very penetrating gaze: then the cooler, more familiar look returned and he said lightly, 'Oh, I don't believe we need be quite so final as that. I have no doubt you have not seen the last of my mother. She has grown very fond of you, you know.'

'Oh, yes!' Cecily said, with unsuitable mournfulness. 'But that is different. I expect she will not be living *here* after—when you are married.'

As for the look he had surprised in those great candid eyes—a look that should certainly not have astonished him, for young girls were notoriously liable to romantic fancies—*that*, if anything, should only have put him more on his guard. But the odd fact was that it had taken him *off* his guard, for he had not until that moment imagined that his protégée had come to regard him with anything but a rather smouldering dislike.

Gathering his reins and nodding to Sivil to let go the leaders' heads, he found a sudden question as to why he had not, after all, offered for Gussie Comerford flickering through his mind. Certainly it could have nothing to do with that abominable child! His interest in her was simply a desire to see her respectably established, out of the reach of that rascal, Jillson: only the night before, as a matter of fact, he had approved his mother's plan of taking her again under her own roof in a year or two, when the notoriety attaching to her appearance on the London stage should have been forgotten, so that she might find a suitable husband for her.

Yet it was strange that the thought of her being given in marriage to some red-faced country squire or earnest young man with an eye to a minor post in the diplomatic service seemed so unsatisfactory to him now. Mr. Ranleigh, turning out of the lodge-gates on to the road, found himself thinking somewhat sardonically that it might be as well that he had remained only one night at Hillcourt on this occasion. It would have been too much indeed if little Miss Hadley, having driven Lord Portandrew into a most unbecoming state of confusion on the occasion of *his* last visit to Hillcourt, should have succeeded this time in doing the same for his cousin.

'When I am *what*?'

'Married—to Miss Comerford,' Cecily said perseveringly. 'Should I not speak of that, either? Charlie—I mean, Lord Neagle said . . .'

'I see that I shall have to have a word with Charlie,' Mr. Ranleigh said. 'No, you should *not* speak of it, Miss Hadley; in fact, if you will heed a word of advice from me, you will wait until you read an announcement in the *Gazette* before you run to conclusions on any of your acquaintances' matrimonial plans.'

She looked a little daunted, but was unable to prevent the improved state of her spirits from appearing as she said defensively, 'Well, I did not know. And I expect *I* am not to blame if you lead people on to think you are going to offer for them and then do not!' A thought occurred to her and she said seriously, 'It must have been *very* depressing for poor Miss Comerford.'

He flung back his head and laughed. 'When last I saw Miss Comerford, she was enjoying a dashing flirtation with a handsome captain in the Guards,' he assured her, and then, collecting himself, went on with a severer air, 'Good God, how came we to be talking of such matters? If you feel that you genuinely wish to express your gratitude to me, you will oblige me by curbing your wish to discuss my affairs with anyone—including myself!'

Again the smile in his eyes belied the sternness of his words. Cecily, hesitating on the stairs, said rather shyly, 'Well, I shan't do so again, if you do not like it.'

'See that you don't,' he recommended. Unexpectedly, he took one of her hands in his, lifted it to his lips, and imprinted a light kiss upon it. 'Good-bye! I am going into Leicestershire and shan't see you before you leave, so you must take my good wishes now,' he said. 'You will let us know—will you not?—if you find the tyranny of those two brats more than you can endure.'

He was gone, leaving Cecily staring rather dazedly at the hand he had kissed. Of course, she was obliged to tell herself, he had meant nothing by it; he had merely intended to be kind and civil. But it was a great deal, at any rate, to know that he had not offered for Miss Comerford!

Had she but realised it, Mr. Ranleigh, getting into the curricle awaiting him before the front door, was not feeling at all kind and civil; he was asking himself, in rueful wrath, what the devil he had meant by behaving toward that chit as if she were not merely an engaging child for whom he had enlisted his mother's good offices. Certainly it was no excuse that she had looked so absurdly young and vulnerable, standing there on the stairs in her shabby cloak, that it had suddenly seemed a wickedly cruel thing to send her into the world alone to earn her bread.

CHAPTER THIRTEEN

Not quite a fortnight after Mr. Ranleigh's departure from Hill-court, on a dark winter morning near the end of January, Cecily too set out from it on her journey into Somerset.

Lady Frederick, who quite agreed with Miss Dowie's notions that it would not do for her to travel alone, had also not been amenable to the idea of her making the journey on the stage, and as a result she enjoyed the luxury of Lady Frederick's own travelling-chaise and the company of one of her ladyship's abigails. Lady Frederick, who had taken Lady Bonshawe's measure most accurately during her brief meeting with her, had shrewdly calculated that nothing would be more likely to ensure that lady's kindest behaviour toward the new governess than the latter's arriving in an elegant private chaise, accompanied by an abigail.

Lady Frederick was quite correct. Lady Bonshawe was so impressed by these unmistakable tokens that Lady Frederick considered Miss Hadley rather in the light of a relation than as a dependant that she made a hasty rearrangement of her domestic plans, which resulted in Cecily's being shown up to a pleasant guest-bedchamber instead of to the bleak little room on the third storey that had been intended for her.

She was also honoured with an invitation to dine with the family that evening—'for we shall not be seeing company, you know,' Lady Bonshawe said, in defence of her own condescension. 'Not that I expect you mightn't sit down with us even if we was, for—lord!—I daresay the Arberrys and the Casewits would like nothing better than to meet a young lady who is connected with the Ranleighs and has been staying at Hillcourt! I am sure I shall be only too glad to hear all about it from you myself!'

Cecily had been forewarned by Lady Frederick what she was to expect of her new employer, but she found Lady Bonshawe's fluctuations between patronising condescension and respectful curiosity too much for her lively sense of humour, and surprised that good lady on at least two occasions by what appeared to her to be a quite inappropriate ripple of laughter, immediately repressed.

'But, there! You are not much more than a slip of a girl yourself,' Lady Bonshawe said good-naturedly. 'And I am glad to see that you are not one of the prim sort, for that would never do for my Millie and Clemmie. As lively as grigs they are, the pair of them. But here they are now!' she added, as a pair of schoolgirls, both of them fair and plump like their mama, peeped into the room. 'Amelia! Clementina! Come in, my dears! This is Miss Hadley, your new governess.'

Cecily, who had been brooding with some foreboding during her journey over her shortcomings in the field of the female accomplishments, was relieved to see that neither Amelia nor Clementina appeared to be of a studious nature. A visit to the schoolroom, where the two young ladies were commanded by their mama to display their skill on the pianoforte that had been installed there for their use, did even more to erase the doubts of her competence to instruct them that had been assailing Cecily. Her pupils were evidently a pair of romps, and the most arduous of their governess's duties would be that of attempting to imbue in them some notion of the proper conduct expected of well-bred young ladies, rather than that of burdening their heads with any more esoteric knowledge.

When Cecily was left alone in her bedchamber to change her dress for dinner she took stock of her situation, and acknowledged that it might have been a great deal worse. Inglesant itself, which had been purchased by Sir William Bonshawe some few years before, was a handsome Tudor manor, and it had received every modern improvement at its new owner's hands.

Her own bedchamber was furnished elegantly, though without a great deal of taste, in green damask and mahogany, and the rest of the house had been done in the same expensive fashion. She had not the least doubt that she would live there exceedingly comfortably; it also appeared to her that she need anticipate few difficulties in dealing with Lady Bonshawe. Amelia and Clementina were not ideal pupils, perhaps, but, though they appeared to have been indulged by their mama, they were not spoiled beyond reason.

All in all, she told herself, resolutely putting from her mind the remembrance of a tall, broad-shouldered gentleman whom she had last seen at the foot of the staircase at Hillcourt, she had much for which to be grateful. And what, after all, had so elegant a figure as Mr. Ranleigh to do with a governess in the establishment of what he would unhesitatingly have characterised as a mushroom squire? She might, in fact, never see him again, and it assuredly behooved her to think no more about him, but to devote her energies instead to satisfying her new employers.

She was privileged to meet Sir William Bonshawe at dinner that evening, and was favoured by him during the meal with several items of conversation, most of which dealt with the prices he had paid for the dinner service from which they ate, the ornate epergne that graced the table, and the crystal chandelier that glittered above it.

'Everything in the first style,' he said complacently. 'No expense spared, and no trumpery, either, for I meant to make Inglesant—and so I told 'em!—the equal of any gentleman's seat in the county. Well! What d'ye think of it, Miss Hadley? Have I succeeded, or haven't I?'

Cecily said civilly that she was quite sure he had, and was rewarded by an approving nod of her employer's bald head.

'Ay! I thought you must say so! And Lady Bonshawe tells me *you'd* be the first to know, because of your being connected with all the nobs. Hillcourt, eh? I looked it up in the guidebooks but it ain't as old as Inglesant. Still I daresay it's a fine place in its way. Well kept up, I expect?'

Cecily said demurely that it was.

'Well, I don't doubt it,' Sir William handsomely allowed, 'for they say Ranleigh is nearly as rich as Golden Ball. But no handle to his name, Lady Bonshawe says! Hanged if I see why he'd settle for an "Honourable" when he has that much brass! And a Duke for a cousin! Now if *I* stood in his shoes . . .'

The picture was too much for Miss Hadley; she choked, hastily drank a sip of water, and thought with unholy anticipation of the probable look on Mr. Ranleigh's face when she told him of this conversation. She then reminded herself that it was not at all likely that she would ever have the opportunity of doing so—a damping thought which made it possible for her to attend to the remainder of Sir William's remarks without the slightest desire to give way again to laughter.

On the following morning she took up her duties in the schoolroom. However, in the midst of a persevering attempt to instruct her pupils in the use of the globes, a message arrived summoning her downstairs: one of Lady Bonshawe's neighbours, Mrs. Casewit, was below, and Lady Bonshawe was desirous of introducing the new governess to her. Cecily was obliged to sit for a quarter of an hour answering the inquiries of the two ladies about her noble connexions—for it appeared that Mrs. Casewit, a native of Sussex and well-acquainted with the exalted position occupied by the Ranleighs, was willing to display her curiosity concerning them even more undisguisedly than was Lady Bonshawe.

'A very pretty, well-behaved young woman, I am sure,' she pronounced Miss Hadley to be in a quite audible voice as Cecily was leaving the room. 'But, I declare, Amelia, she is wearing a positively plain gown! Ay, they are very great people, the Ranleighs, I don't doubt, but I'd take shame to myself to see *my* connexions looking no more elegant than that!'

Fortunately for Cecily, Mrs. Casewit's stout figure, encased in a purple-bloom silk gown and surmounted by a dazzling hat with a huge poke-front lined with Sardinian-blue silk, had already engaged her risibilities, and she was therefore able to smile at the bluntness of the lady's remarks instead of taking offence at them. In point of fact, it had been Lady Frederick's wish to equip her young protégée for her post with an entire new wardrobe; but, as neither Miss Dowie nor Cecily could be prevailed on to accept so lavish a gift, she had been obliged to confine her generosity to adding to Cecily's own modest wardrobe two new gowns—a long-sleeved walking-dress of French cambric and a pretty jaconet muslin.

Cecily had occasion to wear both of these frequently as the days progressed, for her duties, she found, were not confined to the schoolroom. Lady Bonshawe might have complied with her spouse's wish to live in the country, but she was herself city-bred, and liked nothing better than to drive in to Bath for an agreeable hour or two of shopping in Milsom Street. On such occasions she frequently yielded to the importunities of Amelia and Clementina to be allowed to accompany her, and Cecily too then made one of the party, for Lady Bonshawe, once set down in a silk warehouse amid the distractions of satins and gauzes, could not be expected to concern herself with looking after her lively offspring.

Cecily was not at all averse to these interruptions in a daily routine which, while it could not be said to be dull, with such damsels as Amelia and Clementina in her charge, was scarcely an agreeable one to her. It never occurred to her that she might meet anyone on these excursions who would recognise her as Miss Daingerfield-Nelson, for, even were someone who had seen her on the London stage to come across her in Bath, they would scarcely connect that dashing young lady with the demurely attired governess shepherding two schoolgirls through the Milsom Street shops.

But her feeling of security in this respect was quite shattered one afternoon in late February when, as the carriage proceeded along George Street, she suddenly perceived Mr. Jillson in the throng passing on the flagway. She uttered a startled exclamation and shrank back against the squabs.

'What is it, my dear?' Lady Bonshawe asked, with her ready curiosity.

'Nothing at all!' Cecily said hastily. 'That is—I thought for a moment that I had seen someone I knew, but it is no such thing.'

Lady Bonshawe gave her hearty laugh. 'Well, it is someone you don't much care to see, I'll be bound,' she said, 'for you have turned quite as pale as a sheet, my dear.'

Cecily, who was wondering anxiously whether Mr. Jillson had seen her through the window of the chaise, tried to smile and return a negligent answer, but she was conscious that she succeeded ill in this endeavour.

The sight of Mr. Jillson had, in fact, given her the severest cause for apprehension. She had been long enough in Lady Bonshawe's household to realise that propriety was the goddess before whom that worthy dame worshipped, for it was the highest ambition of both her and Sir William to advance themselves in the world which Sir William's wealth had enabled them to enter. Therefore, if Mr. Jillson were to betray her to them, it was quite impossible that they would wish to continue to employ her. Even the aura cast about her by her highborn connexions would not then be sufficient, she feared, to cause them to accept the gossip that must arise when it became known that they were employing as governess a young woman who had appeared upon the London stage. She would be sent back to Hillcourt without ceremony, and, what was worse, Lady Frederick must be exposed to the censure of Lady Bonshawe and Mrs. Casewit and their set, which would certainly spread beyond it and perhaps eventually reach even those more elevated circles in which Lady Frederick and Mr. Ranleigh themselves moved.

When the chaise stopped in Milsom Street and she was obliged to step down from it, she cast a glance of trepidation along the street, but to her relief Mr. Jillson was nowhere in sight. She hurried Amelia and Clementina into the shop—much to the discontent of Clementina, who had spied a street-crier selling hot spiced gingerbread—and was able to breathe more easily once the door had closed behind them.

It was not to be supposed, however, that one of Lady Bonshawe's shopping expeditions would be confined to her entering a single warehouse, and, once she had settled upon the purchase of a spotted ermine muff, she led the way down the street in search of a set of silver filigree head ornaments. Again Cecily's eyes anxiously scanned the passing pedestrians, and again she found herself safely inside a jeweller's shop without having had a sight of Mr. Jillson.

A half hour had now passed since she had seen him in George Street, and she was beginning to feel that she might relax when Lady Bonshawe, recollecting that she had brought along a book to change at Duffield's Library, requested her to undertake that errand for her while she decided among the several sets of ornaments that had been brought out for her approval. Cecily was obliged to comply, and set out alone from the shop.

She had not gone ten paces from it, however, when she saw, to her dismay, that Mr. Jillson was crossing the street toward her, nimbly dodging between the wheels of a gentleman's tilbury and those of a lumbering wagon. She averted her eyes and hurried on, hoping that he had not as yet seen her and that she would be able to make her escape before he had done so; but her hope was in vain. In the space of thirty seconds he was beside her, raising his hat and falling into step with her as she continued to hurry along the flagway.

'Miss Hadley!' he said. 'I thought I could not be mistaken! What an agreeable surprise!'

For a moment she thought of refusing to recognise him, but it would not do: she knew him well enough to be sure that she could not be rid of him by any means so simple as a quelling stare and icy silence.

She tried a direct attack instead. Halting on the flagway, she said to him determinedly, 'What do you want of me, Mr. Jillson?'

He looked at her reproachfully. 'Why, my dear, what an unhandsome greeting to an old friend!' he said. 'One might almost imagine you were not pleased to see me.'

'Well, I am not pleased,' Cecily said downrightly. 'I wish to have no more to do with you, Mr. Jillson—and if it is that money you lent us, you know very well that Aunt left all that was still owing of it for you at the Running Boar before we set out from London.'

'But, my dear young lady, of course she did! And even if she had not—can you think I should have been guilty of such a solecism as to approach you with a dun in mind?'

She looked him up and down, noting that his raiment, though decidedly fashionable, displayed a telltale shabbiness.

'Well, you certainly look as if you might be in need of money,' she said frankly, 'so I should not be at all surprised if you had.'

'A merely temporary embarrassment,' he assured her, waving the observation away with an airy hand. 'Owing to an unfortunate concatenation of circumstances, my spouse and I find ourselves at the present moment between engagements, but we shall be returning next week to London, where the managers of the Surrey Theatre have assured me that a prominent place awaits us in their company, so that we shall soon be living as high as coach-horses. Which I have reason to think, my dear, *you* are not doing at the present moment, any more than I am. If my eyes have not deceived me, you are wasting your considerable talents in the capacity of governess to those two female imps in whose company I saw you a half hour back.'

'So you *did* see me!' Cecily said accusingly. 'And have been hanging about ever since, I daresay, hoping for the chance to speak to me!'

'Exactly,' said Mr. Jillson, unabashed. 'Not,' he added, 'that I was unprepared, if need be, to approach you in the company of the estimable, if somewhat overdressed, female who appears to be your present employer . . .'

'You wouldn't!' Cecily interrupted, indignantly.

Mr. Jillson regarded her with an expression of some interest. 'Ah!' he said. 'So the good lady is *not* informed of your career as Miss Daingerfield-Nelson? I rather fancied that she might not be.'

Cecily, her eyes flashing, gave him back look for look. 'No, she is not!' she said. 'And if you are thinking of telling her, you are the shabbiest creature alive! What is more,' she added, 'if you believe I shall go back to the theatre if she dismisses me, you are *quite* mistaken. I—I am by no means as friendless as you think me, Mr. Jillson!'

'No?' he said, interested. 'And who *are* these obliging friends of yours, Miss Hadley? Do they still include in their number, for instance, the famous Mr. Ranleigh? That appears to me highly doubtful, I must confess, considering your present situation . . .'

He paused, observing that Cecily's brows had drawn together in a distinctly menacing frown.

'That is none of your affair,' she said, beginning to walk on down the street.

'Well, well, at any rate, it need not concern us now,' he agreed. 'The point of the matter is that I am prepared to offer you a handsome future—infinitely more appealing than the grubby drudgery into which you have at present fallen—if you will agree to throw in your lot with me once more.'

Cecily halted again. 'Well, I shan't!' she said bluntly. 'You are wasting your time, Mr. Jillson. I am *quite* content where I am!'

'My dear,' he said, frankly surveying her, 'if you could but see your face when you say that, you would not make such a ridiculous statement! Content to bury yourself here in Bath—or is it in the country, which is even worse?—looking after another woman's brats, when you might be the reigning toast of London? I do not believe it.'

Cecily, about to make a heated denial that she found anything in the least repellent in the notion of spending the remainder of her days as a governess, checked, conscious that she would be quite unable to make such a statement at all convincing. After a pause, she said instead, 'Well, it does not signify whether you believe it or not, because, whatever happens, I am *not* going back to the theatre.'

'Another rash statement,' Mr. Jillson said, shaking his head. 'I see that it is matrimony you have in mind, dear child—but let me point out to you that to achieve that happy end is not a simple matter for a penniless young lady. On the other hand, were you to gain the plaudits and the fortune which I am offering you, you might look to establishing yourself eventually in the first style. Why, my dear, there are any of half a dozen you might have if you played your cards properly—Brackenridge, Lovett, young Portandrew . . . They were all cast into flat despair when you disappeared; in fact, they made devilish nuisances of themselves, trying to find out where you were gone to!'

'I do not care about that!' she said obstinately. 'And I beg you will stop following me, for I do not at all wish to talk to you any longer, and I must get back to Lady—to my employer.'

He shook his head again, with a more melancholy air. 'If you wish, my dear,' he said. 'But you are making a great mistake, you know.' He viewed her unyielding profile and sighed. 'Very well,' he said. 'I shall importune you no further. But if you should change your mind, pray remember that a message conveyed to the Running Boar will reach me promptly, and that news of my whereabouts can always be obtained there.'

He then raised his hat politely and walked off, leaving her free to pursue her errand alone.

The encounter had been an unnerving one, but by the time she rejoined Lady Bonshawe and her charges she had succeeded in shaking off the greater part of her agitation, and was able to present a tolerably cheerful countenance to her employer. She was excessively relieved, however, to find that she saw no more of Mr. Jillson that afternoon, and she returned to Inglesant with far less than her usual regret at leaving the bustle of Bath for the quiet of the country once more.

CHAPTER FOURTEEN

But her relief at having escaped having her career as Miss Daingerfield-Nelson called to Lady Bonshawe's attention was short-lived. Not a fortnight later, on an afternoon early in March, Lady Bonshawe arrived home from a drive with her friend, Mrs. Casewit, in a flutter of pleasurable agitation.

'Only think, my dear, whom I have met today!' she exclaimed, unbosoming herself, for want of a better confidante, to Cecily, whom she found supervising Clementina's practice upon the pianoforte. 'Do leave the girls for a moment and come into my dressing-room, for I must tell someone about it or I shall burst!'

Cecily, surveying the bronze-green carriage dress into which her ladyship had squeezed her ample form, was of the opinion that such a fate was not improbable, whether she succeeded in unburdening herself of her news or not. But she was too happy to escape from Amelia and Clementina to waste more than a moment on considering the appropriateness of Lady Bonshawe's words, and followed her thankfully down the stairs to her dressing-room.

Here Lady Bonshawe discarded her high-crowned Pamela bonnet without ceremony and, plumping herself down in an easy chair, immediately inquired of Cecily if she had ever heard of Sir Harry Brackenridge.

'But I daresay you have not,' she went on, too unobservant to note the start which the name had drawn from Cecily, 'living retired in the country as you have done. I assure you, though, that he is quite as well-known as Mr. Ranleigh—a very Pink of the Ton. Well! Would you believe it?—it turns out that he is a nephew to Lady Kerwin and has come down on a visit to her, and Maria Casewit is to get up a party for next Saturday, which he means to come to, and, depend upon it, will come to Inglesant as well if I can but prevail on Sir William to allow me to send out cards for a dinner party. For he is all condescension, my dear, not in the least what one would expect, for he moves in the very *highest* circles, and, while Lady Kerwin *did* call when Sir William and I came into the neighbourhood, we are not at all intimate with her, and I have always considered her odiously toplofty.'

Cecily, sitting in stunned silence before this conversational avalanche, paid very little heed to it; she had, in fact, heard nothing after Lady Bonshawe's announcement that Sir Harry Brackenridge had come into the neighbourhood. She would not recognise Sir Harry if she walked straight into him at high noon, but it was certain that he would recognise *her*, for his name had been signed to one of the invitations to supper that she had received during her brief theatrical career. What was more, Mr. Jillson had mentioned him, not a fortnight since, as being one of the gentlemen who had made strenuous efforts to discover her whereabouts, and it was to be gathered, therefore, that his interest in her was more than a casual one.

A horrid suspicion that her meeting with Mr. Jillson might have had something to do with Sir Harry's sudden appearance on the scene in Somerset crossed her mind, and the suspicion, far from being allayed, rose to more ominous heights as Lady Bonshawe rambled on, 'To be sure, no one could have expected that he would not set himself on as high a form as Lady Kerwin does, so that I thought, when we met him, that he would certainly give us the go-by with no more than a bow, but not at all! He drew up his curricle, just as Maria promised me he would—for he had been introduced to her yesterday at the Allens' and was the *soul* of amiability, so that she had quite decided to ask him for Saturday if she were to see him again. And he accepted without the least hesitation! It quite provokes me with Sir William, that he will not exert himself to go about as Mr. Casewit does, for Maria is always stealing a march on me in this way. But I am determined that he shall give me the chance to ask Sir Harry here to dine, and so I shall tell him as soon as ever he comes in!'

Cecily could only hope that Sir William would find it expedient to veto this plan or that, if he did not, she herself would be permitted to dine upstairs in the schoolroom with Amelia and Clementina; but neither of these wishes was destined to be granted. Sir William, when approached on the matter, was quite as eager as his lady to entertain so notable a social figure as Sir Harry Brackenridge, and Lady Bonshawe, in making up her table for the projected dinner, informed Cecily that she would expect her to be one of the company.

'For of course Sir Harry must be well acquainted with Mr. Ranleigh,' she said, 'since they move, I understand, in the very same circles, so that I am sure nothing could be more proper than for me to introduce a connexion of his to him. And you need not put yourself into a taking over what you will wear, for I shall have Trimmer take in my sea-green Italian crape for you, for Sir William does not at all care for it and, indeed, the colour is very trying to my complexion.'

No argument that Cecily dared advance succeeded in prevailing against her determination. Cecily saw that she intended to make her presence a proof to Sir Harry of her own intimate acquaintance with the Ranleighs, and understood that she would be made to figure rather as a protégée of the Bonshawes than as anything so common as a mere governess. What Brackenridge's response to all this would be, she could not venture the remotest guess. That he must recognise her, she could not doubt; but whether he would betray her or not was something that must be left wholly to the future to reveal.

Tuesday, the day set for the dinner party, arrived all too quickly. No fortuitous illness had smitten her to allow her to absent herself from Lady Bonshawe's table, nor had the happy news arrived at Inglesant that Sir Harry had broken his collarbone in a fall from his horse, or some other such fortunate minor accident. Quite desperate, Cecily ventured to approach Lady Bonshawe at five o'clock with her last forlorn hope, the plea that she felt a dreadful headache coming on.

But Lady Bonshawe, usually the soul of sympathy, merely stared at her in a flustered way.

'A headache!' she said. 'Well, I am very sorry, my dear, but it cannot signify, for I can't and won't have my table put out at this hour, not if it was ever so! If you will go and lie down upon your bed for a time, I have no doubt it will soon pass off —though, indeed, I shall be sorry if you feel you must do so, for I have been depending upon you to keep Millie and Clemmie from getting into everyone's way.'

In the face of these remarks, Cecily could do nothing but return to her young charges, her problem quite unsolved.

She dressed herself a little later in Lady Bonshawe's sea-green Italian crape with emotions very similar to those of one going to the gallows. Her only hope, it appeared, now lay in Brackenridge's having the good breeding not to betray his surprise at having a young lady whom he had known as an actress named Miss Daingerfield-Nelson introduced to him as Miss Hadley, a governess. If that were the case, she might manage somehow to take him aside during the evening and throw herself upon his generosity. It was a scene which she had the greatest difficulty in imagining herself playing, but at least it would not be so trying as another scene that kept recurring hideously to her mind, in which Sir Harry, already apprised by Mr. Jillson of her deception, exposed her ruthlessly to the company at the moment of their introduction.

That moment soon arrived. She was in the Green Saloon with Sir William and Lady Bonshawe and the early arrivals among their guests when Sir Harry Brackenridge was announced, and her eyes at once flew to the door. She saw a tall man with cold blue eyes and hair of an odd brassy-yellow colour come into the room, his exquisite fitting coat, intricately tied neckcloth, and air of distinction at once casting every other gentleman in the room into the shade. Cecily gazed at him in despair: nothing in his attitude, as he bowed with what seemed to her rather mocking civility over Lady Bonshawe's hand, appeared to indicate the sort of good nature to which one might readily appeal. She swallowed convulsively as she saw his eyes, languidly surveying the assembled company, come to rest upon her own face for a moment, and when she was finally brought forward to be introduced to him she felt as if she must sink through the floor.

'And this is my young friend, Miss Hadley, who is so kind as to lend me her help in looking after my two darling girls,' Lady Bonshawe said, her face beaming with the broad, triumphant smile that had creased it ever since she had beheld Brackenridge step into her saloon. 'I daresay you have never met her, but she is a connexion of the Ranleighs, and was recommended most highly to me by Lady Frederick Ranleigh.'

Cecily, who had been anxiously watching Brackenridge's face for any sign that he had recognised her, saw the merest flicker of surprise enter his eyes as Lady Bonshawe uttered these last words. But it was gone on the instant, and he said to her with the utmost composure, 'Delighted, Miss Hadley! The Ranleighs, you said, Lady Bonshawe? Then I take it that Miss Hadley may be well acquainted with a gentleman with whom I was in company myself not two days before I came into Somerset—Mr. Robert Ranleigh?'

'Oh, indeed she is!' Lady Bonshawe said volubly. 'In point of fact, she had been staying at Hillcourt just before she came to us here—such an elegant house, I am sure! I quite long to see it!'

The arrival of new guests claimed her attention at that moment, and, as Brackenridge was seized on by Mrs. Casewit, Cecily was free to move away and to congratulate herself breathlessly on having at least got through that first dreadful moment without discovery.

But by the time the company went in to dinner her self-congratulation had already given way to renewed anxiety. Certainly Brackenridge had not betrayed that he was conscious of having seen her before, but there had been an almost mockingly amused expression on his face as he had looked at her that gave her the uneasy feeling that she might be about to be made the unwilling participant in a game of cat-and-mouse.

In fact, the more she turned the matter over in her mind the clearer it became to her that he must have been aware before he entered the house that evening that he would meet Miss Daingerfield-Nelson there as Miss Hadley. Jillson! she thought furiously. It would have been a simple enough matter for him to find out Lady Bonshawe's identity in Bath, for she was well-known there, and, once he had realised that his desire to profit by placing Cecily upon the stage under his own aegis could not be fulfilled, he had undoubtedly followed what had appeared to him the next best course by passing his information on to Brackenridge—no doubt at a handsome price, she reflected bitterly.

It was disturbing to her to think that Brackenridge would go to such lengths to pursue her. She was not vain, which gave her the clarity of vision to realise that it might not be infatuation alone that was his motive. Remembrance of the wager that had first brought Mr. Ranleigh to the Running Boar crossed her mind. A rivalry between the two men there well might be: even she was aware that Sir Harry's exploits were almost as famous in the Corinthian set as were those of the Nonpareil himself, nor could she forget the ambiguous flicker of light that had leapt into his eyes when Lady Bonshawe had mentioned her connexion with the Ranleighs.

He was beginning to put the pieces of the puzzle together, she felt; and she felt, too, that if he saw in the situation the opportunity to discomfit Robert Ranleigh he would be willing to use her quite ruthlessly to attain that end.

Fortunately, she was placed at such a distance from him at table that he could neither converse with her nor observe her while the meal lasted. It was a very elaborate one, for Lady Bonshawe had urged her cook to frenzied heights, and as a result the company was treated to two full courses, consisting of half a dozen removes and more than a score of side-dishes. There was a tureen of turtle, removed with fillets of turbot, which in turn were removed with a haunch of venison served with chevreuil sauce; and the second course offered a green goose with French beans and broiled mushrooms, tenderones of veal and truffles, a Gâteau Mellifleur, and a quantity of jellies and creams.

As far as Cecily was concerned, however, she might have dined on cold porridge with equal pleasure, and she was grateful for the cook's efforts only to the extent that the dishes she had prepared were absorbing the attention of the two gentlemen between whom she sat, leaving her free from the necessity of carrying on any extensive conversation with them. This freedom enabled her to gather, from the scraps of talk she overheard from Brackenridge's vicinity, that he was in excellent spirits, and was succeeding in captivating Lady Bonshawe to such an extent that it was probable he might have the entrée at Inglesant whenever he chose during the remainder of his stay in Somerset.

She had a brief respite from his company when the ladies rose from the table to return to the Green Saloon, but not even Sir William's excellent brandy was sufficient to hold the gentlemen long in the dining-room. All too soon Cecily saw Brackenridge's tall figure enter the saloon. He went at once, with graceful address, to Lady Bonshawe, and Cecily took advantage of his preoccupation with her to rise from a seat which she felt placed her in undesirable prominence and retire to one of the pillared alcoves in the corners of the room.

She had reason to regret her choice of retreat, however, when, some quarter hour later, she saw Brackenridge leave Lady Bonshawe and, by amiable degrees, with a word here and a bow there, stroll over to her side of the room. A few moments afterward he was standing beside her, leaning against one of the alcove's fluted pillars and surveying her with a composed smile on his lips.

'So, Miss Hadley,' he said, with a slight, satirical emphasis on the name, 'you are a connexion of Robert Ranleigh's, it seems. How odd that he has never mentioned it to me!'

She scarcely knew where to look, but pride came to her rescue as she saw how well he was enjoying her discomfiture, and she put up her chin defiantly.

'I do not think it at all odd,' she said. 'I daresay he does not recite a catalogue of his connexions to all his friends—if you *are* indeed his friend, sir.'

'How acute of you to gather that I am not!' Brackenridge murmured, thwarting the efforts of a stout matron in a pomona-green turban to catch his eye. 'And you, Miss Hadley?' he went on. 'Are *you* entirely satisfied with the quality of Robert's friendship? I must own that I find myself somewhat surprised in your case, for he has the reputation of being excessively generous to those who may feel themselves entitled to the reward of his—er—gratitude.'

Cecily coloured vividly. 'You have quite mistaken the situation, sir!' she said, with as much ice in her voice as she could summon. 'I have no such claim upon Mr. Ranleigh.'

His brows went up. 'No?' he said softly. 'Dear me, you modern young females . . . ! No doubt I am sadly old-fashioned to think otherwise.'

She was growing more indignant by the moment at his having the audacity to speak to her so, but with the eyes of half the room upon her she was obliged to control herself. She said stiffly, 'I should like you to know, sir, that I consider that Mr. Ranleigh and his mother have *both* been excessively kind to me. And if I may suggest it to you—you had much better go and talk to someone else, for I am only the governess here, and it is not at all suitable for you to single me out in this way.'

'But I do not wish to talk to anyone else,' Brackenridge said, with his teasing smile. 'I wish to talk to you, *Miss Daingerfield-Nelson*. As a matter of fact, I came here this evening particularly for that purpose.'

She had started visibly at the sound of the name, and could not prevent herself from giving him an imploring glance.

'Oh, that is better! Much better!' he said approvingly. 'I infinitely prefer that melting look to your termagant one, my dear!'

Her lips curled angrily. 'You are the most detestable man I have ever met!' she said. 'Are you going to give me away?'

Brackenridge, raising his quizzing-glass to his eye, became

absorbed in the details of a portrait across the room. 'That, my dear,' he said, 'depends entirely upon you.'

'Upon *me*? How can I prevent you . . . ?'

He allowed the quizzing-glass to fall and looked down at her again. 'Oh, quite easily!' he said. 'You have only to ask it of me with the proper complaisance.'

Cecily's eyes flashed. 'Well, I shan't! I shan't ask anything of you—ever!'

'What a singularly rash statement to make!' Brackenridge said, smiling once more. 'Are you fond of wagers, Miss Hadley? I should like to lay one with you that you will very soon find you are *quite* mistaken.'

Cecily said grittily, maintaining an appearance of decorous calm only with the greatest of efforts, 'If you do not go away at once, sir, I shall get up from this chair and walk away from *you*.'

'Oh, no, you will not,' Brackenridge assured her silkily. 'That is, of course, unless you have a fancy to hear me entertaining this worthy company with an exact description of the circumstances under which Robert Ranleigh first became acquainted with you.'

'Oh!' she gasped. 'You would not! You could not be so odious!'

'That,' he agreed, 'is entirely possible. Let us say, at any rate, that I am open to persuasion. However, this scarcely seems the proper place to allow you to put forth your best efforts in that regard. Shall I look forward to a more private conversation with you tomorrow?'

'But I can't! You must know I can't!'

'Nonsense!' he said encouragingly. 'I am sure, if you consider the alternative . . .'

'Oh, very well!' she said, casting a despairing glance at him. 'I—I shall come down early tomorrow morning and—go for a walk in the shrubbery—alone.'

'Excellent! Shall we say eight o'clock?'

She nodded miserably, and had the inestimable relief of seeing him bow and walk off, just in time to prevent their being joined by Sir William, who evidently considered it his duty as host to see to it that Brackenridge spent his time with more exalted personages than a governess. He bore Sir Harry off, and Cecily was left to calm her agitated feelings as best she might.

Brackenridge did not approach her again during the evening, which was of some assistance to her in this endeavour. But she could not think without the greatest foreboding about the assignation that she had appointed with him for the following morning, for unless she could succeed in persuading him then not to reveal to the Bonshawes the facts of her career as 'Miss Daingerfield-Nelson', her employment at Inglesant, she was convinced, must come to an end.

She went to bed that night in flat despair, and could only hope that the morrow might bring new counsel to enable her to extricate herself from her dilemma.

CHAPTER FIFTEEN

But the morrow—a cloudy March morning, threatening rain—
offered no new ideas to her troubled mind. She arose early
and, dressing quickly and throwing a cloak around her shoulders, stole downstairs and out to the shrubbery. It was shortly
before the appointed hour of eight and the household was hardly
stirring yet, after the festivities of the previous evening. She
paced up and down anxiously for several minutes in the bare
shrubbery, so immersed in her own reflections that she quite
failed to hear the tall gentleman in the coat of dandy russet and
the exquisitely fitting buckskins strolling up behind her until
he was almost upon her. Then she gave a little jump of surprise
and whirled around.

'Sir Harry!' she exclaimed. 'Oh! You startled me!'

'But you were expecting me, surely?' Brackenridge said,
smiling at her in the tantalising way she had already come to
detest. He reached out and calmly possessed himself of both
her hands. 'Come, my dear, don't let us play games with each
other,' he said. 'We have both of us come here this morning
with a very definite purpose in mind. Yours, I imagine, is to
persuade me not to reveal to the worthy, but exceedingly un-
interesting, Sir William and his wife the details of your past
career . . .'

'Yes, yes!' she interrupted him eagerly. 'That is it, exactly!
And you will not do so, will you? Surely you were only teasing
me last night! You can have nothing to gain . . .'

'On the contrary,' he said, still maintaining his hold on her
cold, ungloved hands and pausing to raise first one and then the

other to his lips, 'I have everything to gain, my dear. In other words, your compliance.'

'My—my compliance?' Cecily stammered, endeavouring to wrest her hands from the hold which he kept on them and observing with increasing alarm the intent smile on his face as he prevented her from doing so. 'I don't understand . . .'

'But you understand perfectly,' Brackenridge contradicted her with the utmost tranquillity. 'I should like to take you back to London with me. Failing that—if you still wish to persist in your peculiar determination to remain in this dull, but undoubtedly respectable, position in life—I intend to make it the principal end of my existence to persuade you to be at least as kind to me as you have been to Robert.'

'But I—I haven't been k-kind to *him* at all!' Cecily said desperately. 'Indeed, you have quite mistaken the matter, sir!'

'Have I?' Sir Harry surveyed her through suddenly narrowed eyes. 'Almost, my pet, you persuade me to believe you! But in that case I am doubly determined not to fail as he has done.'

'But he didn't fail!' Cecily said urgently. 'I mean—he—he didn't *want* to . . . Oh, you don't understand! He doesn't even *like* me! The only reason he asked his mother to invite me to Hillcourt was that I am *truly* connected with his family.' She dashed into a breathless explanation: 'You see, my grandfather and his grandmother . . .'

Brackenridge, releasing her hands, held up one of his own in protest. 'Spare me the details!' he said. 'I am quite w lling to accept your word that you are connected with the Ranleighs. But, my dear girl, what has that to say to *our* affair? You surely cannot believe that the fact that you are related to Robert makes it any the less piquant for me?'

She looked him full in the face, the earnest flush dying out of her cheeks and an expression of warm contempt suddenly appearing on her countenance.

'I see,' she said. 'I *was* right, then. You are doing this merely to spite Mr. Ranleigh.'

He met her accusing gaze, his own quite unmoved. 'What an excessively crude way to put it!' he remarked composedly.

'I assure you, I was quite smitten with your charms before Robert had ever appeared upon the scene. You know, my dear, you really are something quite out of the common way. That rogue Jillson is entirely correct in thinking that you might make your fortune upon the stage, if only you could be brought to drop your foolish prejudice against it.'

'Well, I shan't drop it,' Cecily said bluntly. 'But I had a good deal rather do so than do what *you* would like me to do.'

Brackenridge laughed, not entirely pleasantly. 'That is plain enough!' he said. 'But it is the privilege of your sex to change your mind, and we must see if I cannot persuade you to do so. I might tell you that I am thought not to be an ungenerous fellow; in fact, knowing that I should meet you when I came into Somerset, I had the forethought to bring with me this small token of my regard.' He reached into his pocket and took from it a jeweller's box, which he opened to reveal a pair of diamond ear-drops. 'For you, my dear,' he said.

Cecily looked at the elegant jewels, and then gazed up into his face in astonishment.

'For *me*?' she said. 'I think you must be mad, sir! I could not possibly accept such a gift from you!'

'Oh, I think you will find it quite a simple matter to do so,' he observed. 'You have merely to hold out one of your hands . . .'

Cecily placed both her hands behind her and backed away a pace or two. 'No! I shall do nothing of the kind!'

'But I think you will,' Brackenridge said, and, reaching out, drew one of the hidden hands into view and opened its tightly clenched fingers. 'You need breaking to bridle, my dear,' he said, 'but I believe you will find the process not entirely disagreeable, with my hands on the reins.' He placed the box in her hand and closed the fingers over it. 'No,' he said softly, looking into her face, which had flushed with anger and determination, 'I should advise you *not* to throw it down upon the ground. Only think what a hue and cry there would be when it was discovered, and explanations can be so difficult—can they not?—when one is dealing with people as hopelessly conventional as Sir William and his lady.'

He released her hand and Cecily, forced to concede the truth of what he had said, continued to hold the box in it, regarding him with a smouldering gaze.

'I think you are quite abominable!' she said hotly. 'And I shan't wear these—I couldn't!'

'Not here, certainly,' he agreed. 'But, you see, my dear, I do not think that you will remain at Inglesant forever.' He reached out to flick her cheek with a careless finger. 'I shall leave you now,' he said. 'Shall we say tomorrow at the same hour? I shall be seeing you later in the day as well, for I am getting up a little expedition to Wells on which I believe I shall be able to persuade Lady Bonshawe to permit you to go. But that will be meeting in the company of others, and private meetings offer so many more possibilities. Don't you agree?'

He did not wait for an answer, but, slipping one arm about her waist, dropped a kiss upon her averted face as she struggled to free herself and strolled away as he had come, through the shrubbery. Cecily remained standing motionless behind him, seething with fury. This soon gave way, however, to a cold realisation of the almost hopeless position in which he had placed her. If she did not accede to his wishes, he had it in his power to have her dismissed from Inglesant—and what she was to do then she did not know.

But, in any case, she could not remain away from the house any longer. She hurried inside and up to her bedchamber, which she was obliged to leave almost at once, however, on hearing unmistakable intimations that Amelia and Clementina had arisen and required her supervision. She breakfasted with them in the schoolroom, her mind all the while racked with her problem to such an extent that her two young charges misbehaved themselves disgracefully, and were in the act of conducting a battle by flinging lumps of sugar from the bowl on the table at each other when their preceptress finally roused herself sufficiently to part them.

The intrusion of one of the housemaids with a letter that had arrived for her in the post diverted her mind from her problems for a few minutes. It was from her aunt, but, fond as she was of that lady, a letter from her describing a daily routine enlivened by nothing more exciting than young Lord Neagle's latest misdeeds, and containing no reference whatever to Mr. Ranleigh, was quite unable to retain her attention for a longer period of time than was required for her to glance quickly through it.

If it had offered her an excuse for absenting herself for a few weeks from her duties at Inglesant, it might have been otherwise; but both Miss Dowie and Lady Frederick apparently believed that she was content where she was, and neither sent a message that could in any way be construed as an invitation to her to return to Hillcourt.

She set the letter aside disconsolately, only to be seized at once by an idea so breathtakingly brilliant in its simplicity that she could only wonder at her own genius in conceiving it. She could not flee to Hillcourt, ignominiously confessing that she was unable to cope with the situation at Inglesant and throwing herself once again on Lady Frederick's charity: pride forbade that, and the fear that Lady Frederick might simply wash her hands of her and refuse to put herself to any further inconvenience in attempting to obtain another position for her. But her uncle's house lay only a matter of some thirty miles distant, in Hampshire, and she might contrive to make some excuse to go there for a time and thus throw a rub in the way of Sir Harry's schemes. The small matter that no invitation had been offered her did not concern her; Sir Timothy, she felt, could not refuse to receive her when she had stated her dilemma to him, and she had every confidence that, were Brackenridge to go to the length of pursuing her into Hampshire, Sir Timothy would know how to deal with him.

She thought it more probable, however, that Brackenridge, finding her gone—to attend her uncle's deathbed, she improvised further, with a superb disregard for Sir Timothy's notoriously robust health—would have the propriety not to intrude upon her there, and, as he scarcely seemed the man to enjoy kicking his heels in the rural quiet of his aunt's home, she hoped that he would soon return to London.

The more she turned the idea over in her mind, the more satisfactory it appeared to her. She was on tenterhooks to see Lady Bonshawe and obtain her permission to start off for Hampshire, but she was obliged to wait for her interview with her almost until noon, when, on her request, she was admitted to Lady Bonshawe's bedchamber.

She found her sitting up in bed, sipping chocolate, wearing a lace-bedecked wrapper and a cap with lilac ribbons tied under her chin, and at once launched into a hurried and quite mendacious account of the events that required her to go at once into Hampshire.

Lady Bonshawe was astonished. 'Your uncle?' she exclaimed. 'But, my dear, I'm sure Lady Frederick gave me to understand that you weren't on terms with him?'

'No—yes—that is—you see, it is my aunt, rather, that he has quarrelled with,' Cecily explained, somewhat incoherently, 'and that is why he wishes to see *me*. People do—do change their minds about their relations sometimes when they are on their deathbeds, ma'am.'

'To be sure they do,' Lady Bonshawe said feelingly, 'and none can know it better than me, for my aunt Kirkmichael left everything she had in the world to her sister Kate, though she had promised me faithfully that I was to have her garnet set and her pearl brooch. But must you go at once, my dear?'

'Oh, yes!' Cecily said fervently. 'That is—I do not think I ought to delay, for the letter was quite *gloomy* about the outcome of his illness.'

'An apoplexy, you said?' Lady Bonshawe clicked her tongue commiseratingly. 'Well, well, it's a wonder it did not carry him off at once, but what a fortunate thing for you that it did not! For if he should have made his will against you, this will give him the chance to alter it, and, though I should be sorry to lose you, for I am sure Millie and Clemmie have taken to you amazingly, of course I should not wish to stand in your way if it is a matter of inheriting your uncle's estate.'

She was beginning, Cecily saw, to enter into the spirit of the event with her usual good-humoured extravagance, to the extent that, by the end of a quarter hour, her imagination had magnified Sir Timothy's much encumbered estate into a respectable fortune, and bestowed upon Cecily a future husband—possibly titled—and a country house of some magnificence, where she herself and Sir William would frequently be invited to stay in company with such exalted guests as Lady Frederick and Mr. Ranleigh.

It was not surprising that, in this mood, she should consider it her duty to send Miss Hadley into Hampshire in her own chaise, rather than subject her to the rigours of travelling on the stage. Cecily made some attempt to dissuade her, for she was beginning to feel rather anxiously that the deception she had been obliged to practise upon her to induce her to let her go to her uncle was getting quite out of hand, but to no avail.

'Lord, my dear, what would Lady Frederick say if she was to hear I had sent you jauntering about the countryside on the common stage!' said Lady Bonshawe. 'And it is not as though the horses could not easily make the journey within the day, and then Henson may rack up at Romsey and be back here on Friday, which will not discommode me in the least, for we are to go in the Casewits' carriage on the expedition Sir Harry Brackenridge has got up to go to Wells tomorrow.'

The mention of Sir Harry's name, with all the disagreeable memories it brought up of their conversation earlier that day, silenced Cecily's objections. She thanked Lady Bonshawe and assured her that she would be ready to start on her journey in the morning, and then returned to her young charges to forestall any further discussion of Sir Timothy's fictitious illness.

No doubt, she told herself remorsefully, she was an unprincipled wretch to deceive the poor lady so grossly; but when she remembered the alternative, and imagined herself obliged either to face Brackenridge in the shrubbery on the following morning or to await his disclosure to Lady Bonshawe of her London career, she could not regret the course that she had taken.

CHAPTER SIXTEEN

So intent had Cecily been on escaping from her meeting with Brackenridge that it was not until she was several miles distant from Inglesant on the following morning that she was able to withdraw her mind from picturing that gentleman's probable wrath when he found she did not intend to appear at their appointed rendezvous and cast it forward to the reception she might receive from her uncle.

She had never visited Sir Timothy's home, her previous meetings with him having been confined to the occasions of the rare visits he had made to her father's house. These had always been brief, and had been discontinued altogether of late years, so that her memories of him were imperfect, consisting chiefly of a picture of a powerfully built but undersized gentleman in an old-fashioned, full-skirted, snuff-coloured coat and knee-breeches, with a red face and an alarmingly loud voice. He had never betrayed the slightest interest in her, but she had Lady Frederick's word for it that he had expressed his willingness to provide her with a home if she should wish it, and it therefore seemed unlikely that he would be averse to allowing her to remain with him now for the space of a few weeks.

She found herself growing increasingly apprehensive, however, as mile after mile of rolling green Somerset countryside fell behind her, and rehearsed in her mind with some trepidation the speech of explanation with which she would greet her uncle.

But, as it happened, it was not Sir Timothy to whom she was obliged to make this speech, but the redoubtable Mrs. Cassaday.

Arriving late in the afternoon at Dowie House, a 'black-and-white' half-timbered Elizabethan manor approached by an ancient stone bridge over a dry moat, she found herself facing a buxom middle-aged dame with her carroty curls imperfectly confined under a cap, who demanded to be told what her business was.

'I am Sir Timothy's niece, Miss Hadley,' Cecily said, summoning up her dignity under the grinning gaze of the young fellow in greasy corduroys who, though he had opened the door for her, had the look more of an ostler than a footman or a porter. 'If you will tell him, please, that I am here . . .'

'Sir Timothy's gone to Romsey,' Mrs Cassaday said uncompromisingly. 'You'll have to let *me* know what it is you want.'

Cecily's heart sank, but she said, with as much sang-froid as she could muster, 'Well, you see—I've come to visit him. I daresay you will not know about it . . .'

'No more I do, nor he don't, neither, I'll be bound, for he wouldn't have gone off without telling me if he'd been expecting you,' Mrs. Cassaday said, her gaze going over Cecily suspiciously. 'And I'll tell you something else—*I* don't know if you're Miss Hadley or Adam's off ox! Nor you needn't be thinking I'll take you in here, when that old nip-farthing as like as not will be in a rare tweak if he comes home and finds I've done it without him telling me to!'

She was interrupted by a look from Miss Hadley that made her realise with some uneasiness that what she had taken for a mere dab of a girl had suddenly become a young lady with an air of decided resolution and a directness of gaze that it was singularly difficult to encounter with impertinence.

'What is your name?' the young lady asked quietly.

Mrs. Cassaday, in spite of herself, found herself dropping a grudging curtsey.

'Mrs. Cassaday, miss.'

'Very well, Mrs. Cassaday. I have had a long journey, and I should like to be taken upstairs to a bedchamber immediately. You may send someone out to the chaise to fetch in my portmanteau, and when my uncle arrives you will, of course, inform me at once.'

This speech, though delivered, unknown to Mrs. Cassaday, with a good deal of inward trepidation, had the desired effect. The youth in the greasy corduroys was sent outside to fetch in her portmanteau, and she herself was led up the great carved oak staircase to a bedchamber, which, though it had a dusty, unused look, yet held out the comfort of a huge four-post bed.

'You'll be wanting dinner, too, I daresay,' Mrs. Cassaday said, tossing her curls with some asperity as she showed her inside. 'Well, I hope you ain't too niffy-naffy to have it with me, for that, I can tell you, is what Sir Timothy does!'

She gazed at Cecily, as she spoke, with a bold, meaningful air, and Cecily, her eyes widening, suddenly realised the full significance of the dark hints she had heard her aunt cast out on the subject of Mrs. Cassaday's character. She examined that martially waiting dame with unmaidenly curiosity, wondering rather perplexedly how much she was expected to indicate that she understood from this announcement.

'No,' she said at last, cautiously, 'I do not *think* I am niffy-naffy, and I am certainly very hungry. Do you dine soon, or do you wait upon my uncle's return?'

Mrs. Cassaday, appearing only slightly mollified by her failure to make any objection to her company, snorted.

'Wait on *him*!' she said scornfully. '*He's* as like as not to stop out all night! *Not*,' she added darkly, 'that he won't fly into one of his takings if he *does* come home and finds his dinner ain't on the table on the stroke of five. You'd best see to it that *you* don't keep him waiting, either, or it's a cold welcome you'll get from him!'

And she thereupon flounced out of the room, leaving Cecily alone to assess her rather dismal situation.

She had not much time in which to indulge in reflection, however, if she wished to refresh her appearance after her journey so that she might appear downstairs before her uncle's early dinner hour had arrived. As a matter of fact, she was still putting the finishing touches on her toilette when she heard a door slam violently somewhere below and the sound of a loud masculine voice. She drew a thin shawl over her shoulders against the chill of the old house, gave a last pat to the skirt of her jaconet muslin frock, and, gathering her courage, went downstairs, where she found Sir Timothy already in the dining-room, engaged in refreshing himself from the contents of a large tankard and in conversation with Mrs. Cassaday. She recognised him at once, for he appeared to be wearing the same snuff-coloured coat in which she had last seen him years ago, and, except that the bald head had grown balder and the vinous colour of the face more pronounced, he himself had altered little over the period.

She was aware that the same could not be said in her case, and, indeed, from the blank stare with which he greeted her entrance, she gathered that he did not recognise her at all.

He recovered from his astonishment immediately, however, and, to her intense relief, greeted her with a satisfied chuckle.

'What!' he said to Mrs. Cassaday. 'Do ye mean to tell me *that's* Grisell's little wench! Well, she's not got the look of her, and that's the mercy of God, for poor Grisell was muffin-faced, whatever ye may say to her good! Come here, lass!' He set the tankard down and extended both his hands toward her. 'Ha' ye a kiss for your old uncle?'

Cecily advanced and found herself seized upon and soundly kissed.

'Ay, that's a good lass!' Sir Timothy exclaimed, holding her off at arm's length and examining her with the eye of a man looking over the points of a new filly. 'A trifle short of bone, but a sweet goer, I've no doubt!' he decided. 'Come to visit me, ha' ye? Well, I won't say ye ain't gi'e me a surprise, but ye're welcome, my dear, as long as ye ain't thinking of staying too long. Not that ye've the look of a strong trencherwoman, so the expense of keeping ye mightn't put me out too much if ye'll be saving on candles.'

Cecily, somewhat dazed by this handsome acknowledgement, allowed herself to be led to one of the high-backed oak chairs set around a huge table, over one end of which a none-too-clean cloth had carelessly been cast. Her uncle having sat down beside her, and Mrs. Cassaday opposite, the business of the meal was commenced with the appearance of the youth of the greasy corduroys, which he had now exchanged for an ancient suit of black-and-silver livery, bearing a roast shoulder of mutton and a boiled tongue with turnips. Sir Timothy, once he had doled out frugal portions of these dishes upon Cecily's plate and inquired if she would drink porter or tea, apparently considered that he had fulfilled his obligations as host and applied himself exclusively to his dinner, replying only in grunts to the flow of complaints launched at him by Mrs. Cassaday on the subject of the delinquencies of various members of the household.

When a curd pudding was brought in, Cecily made her own attempt to contribute to the conversation by commenting politely on the antiquity of the house, but Sir Timothy, his mouth full of pudding, only waved her to silence. This was somewhat discouraging, but his mood appeared to mellow a little later, when, having completed his repast, he pushed back his plate, called loudly for Jem to bring him another tankard of porter, and calmly invited Mrs. Cassaday to leave the room.

'I must talk to my niece now, old girl,' he said to her simply. 'You be off, and see that them gals in the kitchen don't gorge themselves into an apoplexy on what's left of that mutton, or we'll all go home by beggar's bush.'

His use of the word 'apoplexy' sent a faint blush into Cecily's cheeks, which she was relieved to see that Sir Timothy did not appear to notice. He was, however, regarding her shrewdly, and, when Mrs. Cassaday had gone out, said to her, 'Out with it now, my dear! Why did ye come here? The last I heard of ye, from that Blood that came to see me about ye in London, ye'd gone on the stage. Ain't married him and run off from him already, ha' ye?'

'Mr. Ranleigh? Oh, no!' Cecily said, blushing now in good earnest. 'He didn't want to—I mean, he was so very kind—and Lady Frederick Ranleigh, his mother, as well—as to put me in the way of obtaining a position as governess in a—a very respectable family . . .'

'A governess, eh?' Sir Timothy did not appear best pleased by this intelligence, but, having considered it, acknowledged, 'Why, it's board and wages till ye find some young fellow who's willing to leg-shackle himself with ye, at any rate. But why ha' ye come to me, then? Got yourself in some sort of hobble, I'll be bound, or ye'd not ha' done so. Not with Mab Dowie dinning it in your ears night and day that ye'd be better off to go to the devil than to me.'

Cecily, finding herself obliged at last to make some explanation for her visit, plunged desperately into words.

'Why, you see, sir, I found that I—that is, there was a gentleman arrived to pay a visit in the neighbourhood who . . . In short, he made me the object of such particular attentions that I . . .'

Sir Timothy banged his tankard down upon the table in some irritation. 'Zounds, can ye not gi'e me a plain tale?' he demanded. 'Some rogue has been trying to get at ye—is that it? And what of this *respectable family* that ye're working for? Can they not put a stop to such goings-on under their own roof?'

'Truly, sir, the fact is that they know nothing of the matter,' Cecily said, 'and I dare not tell them, for if I do so the gentleman will certainly inform them that he has seen me performing in the theatre, and then I shall lose my employment. But I thought if I were to come to you for a few weeks he might grow discouraged and leave Somerset . . .'

'Don't want to offer you marriage—is that it?' Sir Timothy said, wrath kindling upon his face. 'A-ah, let him come nosing down here after ye and I'll gi'e him a lesson he won't forget in a month! Damned puppy!' He nodded decisively. 'Ye've done the right thing—what's your name?—Cecily?' he informed her. 'Damn him, let him come if he likes! I'll send him to the right-about!'

Cecily was much relieved to see her uncle take the matter in this spirit, but her relief turned to dismay when Sir Timothy, after gazing at her ruminatively for several moments, said, with a wise leer, 'Ay, but the thing of it is, my dear, ye ought to have a husband, for ye're a well-looking gal, and are bound to ha' the dogs after ye when they zee ye're put out to work with no one to look after ye. And I'm thinking I know just the man for ye—Ned Goodgame it is, for he'd like nothing better than to join his land to mine, and I'd a deal rather zee it go to him than to some dandy I've never laid eyes on. Marry him, my dear, and ye may ha' everything I own when I go, with my blessing.'

But Cecily interrupted him here, between amusement and alarm. 'Uncle, how can you say so?' she protested. 'The gentleman has never set eyes on me, nor I on him. Surely you cannot propose a marriage between us.'

'Can't I? Why can't I?' Sir Timothy demanded. Cecily, whose experience with her father had made her quite cognisant of the signs that a gentleman was, to phrase it politely, a trifle above par, began to perceive that the liberal potations in which Sir Timothy had been indulging were beginning to have their effect upon him. There was a mulish look in his eyes, and his temper, never, it seemed, an equal one, appeared to be showing alarming signs of slipping its leash entirely. 'Ye're a well-looking lass, ain't ye?—and Dowie blood in ye, as well, that's been here in the county since kingdom come. And *he's* as right a lad as ye'd zee in a day's journey—a regular good 'un to go, will ride like a streak across the trappiest country, takes his fences in flying style . . .' He set down his tankard and halloo'd for Jem to come in and fill it again. 'I'll send Jem with a message to ha' him to dinner with us tomorrow,' he said. 'Ay, and he's a warm man, too, for there's a tidy property and old Micah, his father, broke his neck on Michaelmas last, so Ned came into his inheritance only three months after he came of age. Ye needn't be thinking it's an old man I'd be saddling ye with, my dear; nay, it's a lively young un, and a fit match for ye . . .'

Cecily endeavoured in vain to stem the progress of these optimistic plans. Sir Timothy, growing more and more enamoured of his own device for ensuring the passing of his lands into the hands of a young man who apparently had won his approval by the twin virtues of being a bruising rider to hounds and possessing an unassuming nature, would hear none of her objections. He ended by growing so irritated with her that he said he could see Mab Dowie had had the raising of her, and that for his own part he had no use for a wench who would whistle a fine young fellow like Ned Goodgame down the wind for no more than a set of Bath-miss airs.

'Damme, if I thought ye'd ha' made such a piece of work over it, I'd never ha' opened my door to ye!' he declared. 'But ye'll zee him tomorrow or my name's not Tim Dowie, and then, if he likes to offer for ye, ye'd best think twice before ye gi'e him your answer, for *I* won't gi'e house-room to a stubborn jade—not if she was a dozen times my niece!'

Cecily, managing at last to escape from this tirade, went up-stairs to her bedchamber between tears and laughter, for, even in the anxiety into which Sir Timothy's sudden penchant for matchmaking had cast her, she could not but find something comical in this new complication. She thought she might place some reliance, too, on young Mr. Goodgame's not pressing his suit quite so rapidly as Sir Timothy desired, even if he were to fall in with the idea of marrying her, for he seemed, by Sir Timothy's description, to be a bashful young man, who was shy even of those damsels in the neighbourhood with whom he had been acquainted all his life.

It was therefore quite possible, she thought, that she might succeed in remaining for a few weeks under her uncle's roof without finding her situation made too uncomfortable by Mr. Goodgame's importunities. At any rate, she believed that she might prefer them to Sir Harry Brackenridge's, and she was almost certain that she would find them a great deal easier to deal with.

CHAPTER SEVENTEEN

The idea had never entered Cecily's head that her flight to her uncle would become known at Hillcourt; but she had reckoned without Lady Bonshawe. That worthy dame, though she could by no means have been called an acute observer, had not failed to notice the manner in which Miss Hadley had been singled out by Brackenridge on the evening of the dinner party at Inglesant, and when Sir Harry, on the expedition to Wells that took place on the day of Cecily's departure, showed a pressing curiosity over all the details of that departure and the reasons that lay behind it, certain agreeable ideas began to stir in her brain.

What a thing it would be, she confided to Sir William, if Miss Hadley and Sir Harry, meeting under her roof, were to make a match of it! Certainly he had displayed the most gratifying interest in the girl, and, since she was so well-connected and Sir Harry's own circumstances were such that he need not look for a fortune in a wife, it would not be so strange a match, after all, as might at first appear.

She would write to Lady Frederick at once, she decided, and apprise her of the good fortune that might be in store for her protégée assuring her at the same time that she herself would do everything in her power to forward so delightful a scheme.

The letter, concluding with proper expressions of sympathy for the unfortunate illness which had called Miss Hadley to her uncle's bedside, arrived at Hillcourt on a windy March morning, four-and-twenty hours before Mr. Ranleigh was to drive down from London to spend a few days there over business matters with his agent. Lady Frederick read it with a puzzled crease between her brows, and then walked upstairs in search of Miss Dowie, whom she found in her sitting-room, her spectacles upon her nose and a weighty-appearing tome in her hands.

'This is very odd,' Lady Frederick said, sitting down beside her. 'Here is a letter from Lady Bonshawe, saying that Cecily has been sent for to Hampshire to your brother, Sir Timothy, who is on his deathbed with an apoplexy. Do you know anything of this?'

Miss Dowie's spectacles dropped from her nose. 'On his deathbed? Timothy!' she said incredulously. 'Nonsense! He drinks far too much, but he is as healthy as a horse; he is good for another twenty years, at least. And even if he *were* ill, he would never send for Cecily. He could not, for he has not the least notion that she is at Inglesant.'

She took the letter which Lady Frederick held out to her and perused it, uttering a contemptuous—'Humph!'—as she returned it to its owner.

'The woman's a fool,' she said decidedly. 'Who is this fellow, Brackenridge?'

'Sir Harry?' Lady Frederick made a grimace of distaste. 'Oh, a man of the town—a dandy in the forefront of fashion—a rather dangerous creature, I suspect. It seems to me in the highest degree unlikely that he can have lost his head over Cecily to the extent of wishing to marry her. That he has made her the object of his gallantry I can well believe—but that is another matter altogether.' She frowned slightly. 'I cannot recall exactly, but it seems to me he was involved in that ridiculous wager that was responsible for Robert's becoming acquainted with the child. If that is so, it is too vexatious! One cannot in the least rely upon his good will, and if he recognised her when he met her in Lady Bonshawe's house . . .' She consulted the letter again. 'But if he did, he cannot have mentioned it to the Bonshawes,' she said, looking increasingly puzzled, 'for I am sure that, in that case, Lady Bonshawe would never risk her reputation for respectability by promoting a match between him and Cecily.'

Miss Dowie, who seemed more perturbed by the possibility

of Cecily's being at the present moment under her uncle's roof than by any speculations concerning Sir Harry Brackenridge, said baldly that, in her opinion, it had been a mistake to send Cecily to the Bonshawes in the first place.

'They do not appear to be at all the sort of people to look after her properly,' she said. 'If that woman really has allowed her to go gallivanting off to Hampshire, she must be a perfect looby. Who wrote the letter to the child that Lady Bonshawe says she received I do not know, but that it was not Timothy I will take my oath!'

'Naturally he did not write it himself if he is expiring from an apoplexy!' Lady Frederick said impatiently. 'But I *must* believe that it came from his household. Only think of the dreadful possibilities if it did not! She may even have been induced to go off to a rendezvous with Sir Harry, giving her uncle's illness as a pretext . . .'

Miss Dowie sat up straight in her chair. 'Do you mean to tell me, my lady,' she inquired ominously, 'that you believe *my* niece would be guilty of such impropriety?'

Lady Frederick shrugged distractedly. 'She is very young, you know. And Sir Harry is attractive and experienced—a rake, if you must have the truth. She would not be the first young female . . .'

'My niece, ma'am, is *not* "a young female"! She is a lady—as much a lady as you are, and with notions of propriety that are, I have no doubt, a good deal stricter than those on which *you* were reared!' Miss Dowie got up from her chair and stood confronting Lady Frederick with rigid determination. 'There has been quite enough of this,' she said. 'I shall set off for Dowie House at once, and see for myself if the child is there. If she is not . . .'

'If she is not, you will have not the least notion where to look for her,' Lady Frederick said witheringly. 'No, really—we had a great deal better wait until Robert arrives tomorrow. I assure you that I am as upset over the matter as you are, but I am sensible enough to recognise that it is scarcely a matter that we can undertake ourselves. If Brackenridge *is* involved in the affair, you will have no idea how to deal with him, or even how to go about finding him.'

Miss Dowie, considering, was obliged to acknowledge the truth of this, but she did so grudgingly, unwilling to give up her plan of going instantly in search of her niece. A little further reflection, however, and Lady Frederick's promise to send her into Hampshire in her own travelling-chaise as soon as Robert arrived, if he had no better plan to propose, reconciled her to the short delay involved in carrying out Lady Frederick's wishes. Obviously she would gain little time by setting out on the earliest stagecoach, and, if she did not find Cecily at Dowie House, she realised that she would be brought quite to a stand-still.

She therefore determined to await Mr. Ranleigh's arrival with what patience she could muster, but, as neither her anxiety nor Lady Frederick's abated overnight, frayed nerves caused hostilities to break out between them afresh on the following morning, and it was a pair of highly militant females whom Mr. Ranleigh, arriving at Hillcourt in good time for dinner, found awaiting him in the Small Saloon.

He strolled in, still wearing the top-boots, buckskins, and riding-coat in which he had driven from London, and regarded the two of them with a look of considerable amusement on his face.

'What have I done to merit *this*?' he inquired, crossing the room to his mother's chair and, after bowing over her hand, bestowing a civil greeting upon Miss Dowie. 'Do you know, I rather flattered myself, on the way down, that you would be glad to see me?'

'I *am* glad to see you,' Lady Frederick said bitterly. 'We have been waiting for you, as a matter of fact, since yesterday morning.' She held a sheet of elegant hot-pressed notepaper out to him and commanded briefly: 'Read this!'

Mr. Ranleigh's brows rose, but he took Lady Bonshawe's letter and perused it. As he did so, the two ladies saw the smile disappear from his face, and, in their relief at having been able to shift the burden of their anxiety on to masculine shoulders, burst simultaneously into speech, demanding to know his opinion of the matter.

His only immediate response was a rather grim frown. He was reading the letter again, more carefully this time, it seemed. When he had done, he looked over at Miss Dowie.

'You knew nothing about this, ma'am?' he asked curtly.

'No, indeed I did not!' she replied. 'Nor do I credit a word of it, Mr. Ranleigh. As I have told Lady Frederick, my brother could have had no notion that Cecily was at Inglesant, and even if he were on his deathbed he would not have sent for her.'

'I am dreadfully afraid, Robert,' Lady Frederick put in, 'that it has something to do with that horrid creature, Brackenridge. Was it not he who laid the wager with Anthony over Cecily that brought about your acquaintance with her?'

'It was,' Mr. Ranleigh said. Miss Dowie was surprised to see that a slight flush had crept into his lean face and an implacable expression into his grey eyes; she was not a timid woman, but it occurred to her that she would not care to face those eyes if she were the person who had incurred their owner's displeasure. 'It is quite possible,' he went on deliberately, 'that he is involved in this affair in some way.' He turned to Miss Dowie. 'In what part of Hampshire is your brother's house, ma'am?' he asked. 'I believe I had best pay a call on him.'

'Oh, will you go yourself, sir? That would be very good of you!' Miss Dowie exclaimed. 'It is near Romsey—but of course I shall go with you, and shall be able to direct you.'

Lady Frederick, who had been watching her son's face rather anxiously, interrupted at this point to ask him, 'But what will you do, Robert, if you find that the girl is *not* with Sir Timothy? Surely, if she *has* been so imprudent as to run off with Brackenridge, it is not your responsibility . . .'

'On the contrary, ma'am, it is very much my responsibility,' Mr. Ranleigh said levelly. 'Miss Hadley is under my protection.'

'But you would not feel obliged to call Brackenridge out!' Lady Frederick exclaimed, her alarm rising even higher at these words. 'No, really, Robert . . . !'

Miss Dowie, her own cheeks beginning to fly martial colours, said tartly, 'I must beg you to refrain from casting aspersions upon my niece's character, my lady! Cecily would never demean herself so as to run off with a man! You may depend upon it, if she is found to be with Brackenridge, he has abducted her—and in that case, though I have always held the practice of duelling in the greatest abhorrence, I hope that Mr. Ranleigh *may* shoot him!'

'But *he* may shoot Robert, you idiotish woman!' Lady Frederick cried. 'And I will not have it! Do you understand that, Robert? If that odious man has indeed succeeded in ruining the child, you will bring her here to me, and *I* shall see to it that any scandal is scotched—which it most assuredly will *not* be, you must see, if you are foolish enough to call Brackenridge out!'

Mr. Ranleigh, perceiving that the two ladies were quite ready, in their agitation, to run to the most extreme lengths of conjecture, at this point deemed it prudent to pour cold water upon their imaginations by remarking that he had no doubt they should find Miss Hadley safe with her uncle, and thereupon announced that he was going upstairs to change his dress for dinner.

He then walked out of the room, but in the hall was at once pounced upon by young Lord Neagle, who greeted him with great cordiality and inquired hopefully if he would have time on the morrow to take him out in his curricle and let him handle the reins, so that he might learn how to point the leaders and turn a corner in style as he himself did.

'No, not tomorrow,' Mr. Ranleigh replied, proceeding up the stairs with his nephew hot on his heels. 'I find that I shall have to go into Hampshire tomorrow.'

'Hampshire! But you've only just got here! Are you bamming me?' Lord Neagle inquired suspiciously. 'Grandmama said you were coming down to see Dyson about estate business.'

He followed Mr. Ranleigh into his bedchamber, where Dawe, his valet, was engaged in laying out his clothes for the evening.

'I say, exactly *what* is going on here?' Lord Neagle persisted.

'Hampshire? Has it something to do with Cecily? Grandmama had a letter from Lady Bonshawe yesterday, and, while she wouldn't tell *me* what it was about, I could see she and Miss Dowie were both . . .'

He broke off, under the weight of a resigned stare from his uncle, and glanced impatiently at Dawe, who, having proceeded to brush an imaginary speck of dust from an exquisitely cut coat of blue superfine, unhurriedly bowed himself out of the room.

When he had gone, Lord Neagle sat down on the bed and said, undaunted, 'It *is* about Cecily—ain't it? The two old ladies have been in high fidgets ever since yesterday morning. Has she run off from that governess place? I rather thought she might, you know. A dashed dull business *I* should think it was for her, after being in the theatre.'

Mr. Ranleigh looked down at him, a faint smile appearing on his hitherto frowningly preoccupied face.

'If your grandmother overhears you referring to her as "the old lady" at any time, I should advise *you* to run off, my lad,' he said, 'for you won't be able to weather the storm!'

His lordship grinned. 'Know what you mean,' he said sagely. 'But you haven't answered me.'

'I didn't intend to.'

'Oh! I see. She *is* in some sort of hobble, then. I rather thought she might be. Good sort of girl—I don't mind telling you I'm deuced fond of her—but things seem to happen to her. Like Tony, for instance. Made her an offer—didn't he?'

'That,' said Mr. Ranleigh repressively, 'is not, to the best of my knowledge, your affair.'

'No, I expect not. Still, it would have been if she'd accepted him, wouldn't it? I mean to say—member of the family then.' He considered the matter and acknowledged handsomely, 'I shouldn't mind making her an offer myself when I come of age; she's not so *very* much older than I am, you know.' Advised briefly by his uncle not to be a gudgeon, he went on, with unimpaired frankness, 'Well, I know *you* don't like her, but I can't see what you can have against her, except that she does

152

seem to be always getting into some sort of scrape that makes you stir about. What is it this time? She *must* have run off from the Bonshawes if you are going into Hampshire because of her.'

Mr. Ranleigh, into whose eyes a rather odd expression had leapt on the allegation of his dislike of Miss Hadley, refrained from commenting on this matter, and, changing the subject rather pointedly, began to inquire into his nephew's recent activities. The device succeeded, and, an agreeable conversation following, in the course of which Mr. Ranleigh promised to make up for the time that would be lost by his going into Hampshire by remaining a few days longer than he had planned at Hillcourt, the topic of Miss Hadley's present whereabouts was allowed to drop.

CHAPTER EIGHTEEN

Meanwhile, Miss Hadley herself, having spent nearly a week under Sir Timothy's roof, had been driven to the point of wondering rather desperately if she dared return to Inglesant, on the hopeful chance that Brackenridge would by this time have gone back to London.

There were two reasons for her desire to leave her uncle's house. The first was a very large, very fair, square-jawed young man named Ned Goodgame. The second was Mrs. Cassaday.

Mr. Goodgame, whose acquaintance she had made on the day following her arrival, had fallen in, with what Sir Timothy considered commendable promptness, with that gentleman's plans for his future. He had no sooner set eyes upon Cecily than he succumbed, dazzled, to the future that had been laid out for him. Fortunately, he was too bashful to have—as Sir Timothy impatiently phrased it—'got down to business' yet, but he spent every available hour at Dowie House, feasting his eyes upon Cecily in all the blissful misery of calf-love.

As for Mrs. Cassaday, the second prong of the pitchfork urging Cecily away from Dowie House, her behaviour toward her employer's niece was based upon the purest self-interest. She had hopes, Cecily had discovered, of yet bringing Sir Timothy to the altar, and, as the future Lady Dowie, she had every objection to Sir Timothy's plans to leave his entire property to his niece.

As a result, she sought by every means in her power to discourage Cecily from remaining in Hampshire, and, since these means included a studied lack of attention to her comfort and convenience, it was not surprising that Cecily found the circumstances of her daily life at Dowie House excessively disagreeable.

On the day following Mr. Ranleigh's arrival at Hillcourt Mr. Goodgame had, as had become customary over the past several days, ridden over to Dowie House to dine with Sir Timothy and his young guest. He arrived shortly before five and walked into the Great Parlour to find Cecily seated with a book on the settle beside the fireplace, where a miserable blaze flickered beneath the huge oak mantel. It was a fine afternoon in late March, but with a wintry chill still in the air. Mr. Goodgame, blushing fiery red at the sight of Cecily, walked over to the fire as he greeted her and busied himself quite unnecessarily with a show of warming himself at the dying blaze.

'Squire not about?' he inquired.

Cecily put aside her book with regret, for she could not look forward with any pleasure to the prospect of a tête-à-tête with Mr. Goodgame.

'I believe he has not come in as yet,' she said, 'but I expect he will not be late. Won't you sit down?'

'Ay. I'll do that, thank ye.'

Mr. Goodgame cast his eye about the room, as if debating the choice of several high-backed chairs which offered him their dubious comfort, but abruptly, with an air of casting caution to the winds, took a pair of hasty strides toward her and seated himself beside her on the settle.

Once he had placed himself there, however, he seemed to have no idea how to go on. He twisted his great hands together between his knees, stared down at the tips of his imperfectly blacked boots, and heaved a pair of laboured breaths, which seemed to be a prelude to an announcement of some sort.

'It is—it is *quite* cool for March,' Cecily said hastily, in what she hoped was a completely impersonal and discouraging voice. 'Don't *you* find it so, Mr. Goodgame?'

Mr. Goodgame, appearing to be somewhat thrown off his stride by this interruption to his mental processes, considered the matter.

'Ay,' he agreed at last. 'It is.' He added ominously, 'That ain't what I came to talk to you about.'

'No, I—I expect it is not,' Cecily said, casting an anguished glance toward the door in the hope of seeing Sir Timothy appear. 'But it is very—very odd—don't you agree?—that we are having such a late spring, when everyone expected . . .'

She shrank back suddenly, for Mr. Goodgame, wisely refusing to clutter his brain with a search for any further preliminaries, at that moment swooped down and enveloped her in a crushing embrace, remarking thickly, 'Came to ask you to marry me. Hope you don't dislike it. The old gentleman's agreeable.'

'Mr. Goodgame! Please!' Cecily cried, spiritedly fending off his attempts to kiss her by pushing as hard as she could with both hands against his chest. 'I *beg* you will not . . .'

A third voice interrupted her. 'Ay, that's it! To her, lad! She'll ha' ye—never doubt it! They're all alike, ye know—she'll hold ye off at the first, but she'll ha' ye, or my name ain't Tim Dowie!'

Mr. Goodgame, almost as embarrassed as Cecily by this gleeful harangue, loosed his hold upon her as abruptly as if cold water had been poured upon him and sprang to his feet, regarding his host, who stood rubbing his hands together in the doorway, with a discomposed air.

'Sir!' he gasped. 'I never heerd ye come in!'

'Nay,' Sir Timothy said encouragingly, 'never mind me, lad! Ye were doing famously!' He turned suddenly as Cecily, recovering herself somewhat on finding herself released from Mr. Goodgame's grasp, also jumped up from the settle and made as if to walk past him out of the room. 'Here! Where are ye off to?' he inquired, in the liveliest astonishment. 'Ha' ye gi'e him your answer yet? It's time for dinner, ye know, and we must ha' the thing settled now, so we shall be able to dine in peace!'

Cecily, finding her progress arrested by Sir Timothy's determined grasp upon her arm, halted and said, without raising her eyes to his face, in a voice suffocated with embarrassment, 'I must beg you to excuse me, Uncle. Indeed, I do not wish for any dinner today! And as for Mr. Goodgame—I have never encouraged him to believe . . .'

'Why, what miff-maff is this!' Sir Timothy exclaimed, his colour beginning to rise. 'Never encouraged him! *That's* a loud one! Ain't I zeed the two o' ye sitting here together night after night, as thick as inkle-weavers!'

Cecily looked at him imploringly. 'Indeed, Uncle, I have never showed him anything but the civility that was due him as your guest!' she said. 'You must know . . .'

'Showed him anything!' Sir Timothy interrupted her wrathfully. 'Ay, I should hope ye never showed him anything, and the two o' ye not even betrothed! But what has that to say to the matter? Nay, all that's needed is to clap hands together and strike the bargain, for ye'll ha' him in the end, ye silly jade, and well ye know it!'

'No, Uncle, I know nothing of the kind!' Cecily said resolutely. She turned to Mr. Goodgame, who had been following the conversation with the greatest attention. 'Mr. Goodgame,' she appealed to him, 'I am persuaded that *you* will not be so ungentlemanly as to press your suit upon me when I tell you that I do not desire it—that indeed I cannot marry you . . .'

Mr. Goodgame opened his mouth to speak, but was forestalled by Sir Timothy.

'Cannot marry him!' he exclaimed irefully. 'And why can ye not, I should like to know! He's a likely lad, ain't he?— None o' your damned caper-merchants, and top-over-tail in love wi' ye into the bargain . . .'

'Yes, yes, I know, but I *cannot* wish to marry him, Uncle,' Cecily said earnestly. She turned to Mr. Goodgame again. '*Please* speak to my uncle, sir!' she said. 'Tell him that you will not importune me against my wishes . . .'

But at that moment an interruption occurred that made all three occupants of the room turn hastily and face the door. None of them, in the warmth of the discussion, had heard the sound of carriage wheels upon the drive outside or the vigorous plying of the knocker, and it was only Mrs. Cassaday's announcement now, delivered from the doorway, that first acquainted them with the fact that visitors had arrived at the house.

'Begging your pardon, sir,' Mrs. Cassaday said, in a hollow voice which plainly declared that she had already met the enemy and been put to rout, 'but here's Miss Dowie come to see you. *And* Mr. Ranleigh!'

Since Miss Dowie herself entered the room hard on the heels of this announcement, Sir Timothy had time to do no more than blink before he found himself confronting the diminutive figure of his sister, still attired in the pelisse and bonnet in which she had journeyed from Sussex.

'Ha!' she exclaimed, her eyes upon Cecily. 'So you *do* have the child here, Timothy! And attempting to force her into a marriage with this—this clodpole,' she said, turning to regard Mr. Goodgame with no friendly glance, 'if my ears are to be believed! You are, as always, quite disgusting, Brother!'

Mr. Ranleigh, who had come quietly into the room behind Miss Dowie, said civilly to Sir Timothy, who appeared quite thunderstruck by the sudden appearance of his sister within his house, 'I must ask your pardon for this intrusion, sir, but the fact of the matter is that we have been quite concerned for Miss Hadley's safety.'

'But how did you know that I was here?' Cecily cried, the first of the bewildered trio to recover her tongue. 'I didn't tell anyone but Lady Bonshawe and Sir William!'

'Lady Bonshawe,' said Miss Dowie, 'wrote to us, my dear. An excessively stupid letter it was, with Timothy's expiring of an apoplexy all mixed up with Sir Harry Brackenridge's attentions to you. It is no wonder that Lady Frederick and I were quite at a loss to think what could have happened to you.'

Cecily's hands flew to her burning cheeks. 'Oh, dear!' she said. 'I didn't know—I never imagined—I only told her that, you see, because I *had* to get away . . .'

She got no further, for Sir Timothy, shaking off his astonishment, at this point burst into speech, demanding to know what the devil his sister meant by it to set her foot inside his door.

'Didn't I tell ye, the last time ever I zeed ye, that I wouldn't ha' ye in my house again?' he roared. 'Damme, and here ye come a-marching in as bold as brass, looking to tell me my duty, do ye? Well, I won't ha' it, I tell ye! The girl's come to me now, and *I*'ll ha' the settling o' her in life—and a better business I'll make of it than *you* ever did, I'll be bound, that had her first showing herself off on a stage and then sent to live wi' a pack o' boobies that couldn't tell how to look after her so she wouldn't be in the way to be ruined by some damned dandy!'

'Ruined!' Miss Dowie gasped. She turned to Cecily, her cheeks blanching. 'Oh, my poor child! Is it true, then?'

'No, no!' Cecily cried hastily. 'Pray do not distress yourself, Aunt! My uncle only means that I was obliged to come to him because—because a certain gentleman's attentions . . .'

'Brackenridge?' Mr. Ranleigh interrupted curtly.

She glanced up in dismay at his cold, thunderous face. 'Yes, but—but, truly—it is not at all as you think!' she stammered. 'It was only that he said he should inform Lady Bonshawe of my having been on the stage if I would not—if I . . . You see, he has *quite* the wrong impression of why you took me away from London . . .'

She broke off, seeing that her explanations, far from assuaging Mr. Ranleigh's displeasure, seemed merely to be intensifying it. She had no opportunity to mend the matter, however, for Sir Timothy interrupted at this juncture, declaring that he would not have it, to be set upon by a parcel of meddling busyheads just as he was about to sit down to his dinner.

'Ay, and as pretty a rump of beef as ever I zeed dressed and ready in the kitchen,' he said, adding pertinaciously, for his sister's ears, 'but you needn't ha' it in mind that I'll ask *you* to sit down to it, for I shan't!'

'And *you* need not think,' Miss Dowie replied with spirit, 'that I would taste a morsel of food in this house, Brother, while you are master in it! I came here for one purpose only— to remove my niece from the contamination of your presence.'

'Contamination!' Sir Timothy sputtered. 'Zounds, am I *con-taminating* the chit to be offering to wed her to as fine a lad as you'll find in the county, with a neat property besides? But I should ha' known,' he went on bitterly, 'that ye'd turn up to throw a rub in the way, for ye've no sense in your cockloft and never had—coming here blethering about an apoplexy! What apoplexy? Do I look to ye as if I was dying of an apoplexy?' And in his rage he capered about the room in a hornpipe, coming to a halt before his sister and glaring belligerently into her face.

Miss Dowie, unperturbed by the red visage thrust so close to her own, remarked coldly, 'Again, *quite* disgusting, Brother! What Mr. Ranleigh must think of such a performance, I blush to imagine!'

'Ranleigh! What do I care for Ranleigh?' Sir Timothy inquired rudely. '*I* never asked him to thrust his nose into my niece's affairs—and if ye're thinking to marry the wench to him, Sister, ye've less brains than even I gave ye credit for, for it ain't an honest country lass like *her* a Blood o' *his* cut would take a liking to wed, but one o' them painted fine ladies mincing about London with their simpering graces and their airs.'

'I believe,' Mr. Ranleigh observed, stepping forward at this juncture and addressing Sir Timothy with the cool civility that never failed to depress presumption, 'that a discussion of *my* affairs is scarcely to the point, sir. Miss Dowie and I came only to assure ourselves of Miss Hadley's safety and to carry her back with us to Sussex.' He turned to Cecily. 'If you will instruct a servant to pack up the things you have brought with you, I think we need delay no longer,' he said.

Cecily, who was ready to sink at her uncle's bald coupling of her name with Mr. Ranleigh's, and the latter's biting reception of this impertinence, murmured an almost inaudible assent and fled from the room. Her uncle gazed after her in amazement.

'And what might she think to be up to, to go off and flout a good lad like Ned Goodgame, that's ready to offer her honest wedlock?' he demanded. 'Damme, what more could I do for her than put her in the way of such a match?—for she might set up her own carriage and live as fine as any lady in the parish. I tell ye, there's no understanding wenches; they're all alike, one minute meek as a nun's hen, and the next giving ye the devil's own amount of trouble with their curst contrary ways!'

The honest bewilderment on his face set a telltale muscle to quivering at the corner of Mr. Ranleigh's mouth, and caused him to say in a more cordial tone, 'Indeed, I believe you have the right of it, sir. Still, it will not do for you to attempt to force Miss Hadley's inclinations, no matter how contrary to yours and this young man's they run. I am sure that Mr.—Goodgame, is it?—would not himself desire you to do so.'

Mr. Goodgame, finding the eyes of the company upon him, coloured beetroot-red and agreed hastily, 'Ay! I mean no!' He added hoarsely, 'Not that I'd not be glad to wed with her— that is to say, her being willing . . .'

'But she is not willing, you see,' Mr. Ranleigh said remorselessly, 'which must alter the matter—must it not?'

Mr. Goodgame nodded glumly, at which point Sir Timothy, who had been momentarily floored by this desertion of his single ally, rattled in once more to the attack.

'Ay, but if she *ain't* to wed him, what will ye do wi' her then?' he demanded. 'Send her back to those rubbishing folk in Somerset that couldn't keep her out o' the reach of a damned dandy that meant nothing but her ruin? I tell ye to your head, I'd not gi'e a brass varden for her virtue if ye do—ay, and ye needn't think to be sending her to me to house when she's damaged goods, for I'll ha' none o' such a stubborn toad, that won't ha' an honest gentleman when he's willing to wed her.'

'Brother, you are an idiot!' Miss Dowie remarked roundly. 'Do you think for a moment that *my* notions of what is a proper situation for my niece are less nice than yours? I assure you that Cecily will *not* return to the Bonshawes . . .' She broke off, seeing that Cecily, wearing her pelisse and bonnet, had returned to the room and was standing in the doorway. 'Oh, are you back already, my love?' she said approvingly. 'Where is your portmanteau?'

'Mrs. Cassaday has been kind enough to see to putting up my things and having them brought downstairs,' Cecily said faintly, scarcely daring to meet either Mr. Goodgame's or Mr. Ranleigh's eyes.

She went up to Sir Timothy, however, and thanked him earnestly for having given her the shelter of his roof in the time of her need, which caused him to relent toward her somewhat and to remark grudgingly that she was a pretty-behaved gal, after all, if only she would give over her curst airs and·wed as he would wish her to.

'I am truly sorry, sir, but I *cannot*!' she said imploringly.

He shot her a darkling glance from under his bushy brows. 'Ay, this is what comes o' being in company with lords and ladies in Bond Street fribbles,' he said severely, 'for it's plain to me that your head has been turned by them so ye can see neither your duty nor your own interest.'

Nevertheless, he kissed her and, clapping her upon the shoulder as if she had been a favourite filly, enjoined her to be a good girl and never give cause to her uncle to blush for her.

'For I'd rather see ye dead than ruined,' he said frankly, and then, turning to his sister, said to her in a truculent voice, 'Do ye hear that? See that ye keep her out o' the way o' dandies, and if *that* one'—sending a challenging glance at Mr. Ranleigh— 'gi'es ye trouble with her, ye'll ha' no more than ye deserve.'

'Mr. Ranleigh,' said Miss Dowie, 'has been the soul of chivalry in this matter. And let me tell you, Brother, that becomes *you*, of all people, to speak of virtue, when your own life is a daily scandal, to the point where I consider it to the highest degree improper for Cecily to have spent even a few nights under your roof.' She would have gone on, but, seeing that Mr. Ranleigh was regarding with no great appearance of complaisance this introduction of a new subject of contention between herself and her brother, altered her intention and said instead, 'But we shall trespass no more upon your *hospitality*' (the last word uttered with a great deal of sarcastic emphasis). 'Cecily, come, my love. No doubt your things have been brought down by now.'

In truth, Mrs. Cassaday, her efforts spurred by the desire to have both Cecily and Miss Dowie out of the house as quickly as possible, had flung Cecily's few belongings into her portmanteau and already summoned Jem to carry it out to the waiting chaise. A few moments saw it strapped into place; Cecily mounted up beside her aunt, while Mr. Ranleigh took the reins of his own curricle from Sivil. No extended farewells being made, the little cavalcade soon set out on its way, its destination being—as Mr. Ranleigh informed Miss Dowie—a very respectable inn in the neighbourhood, where they might dine and lie overnight before beginning their return journey into Sussex on the following day.

CHAPTER NINETEEN

It was a very silent party that took the road for Hillcourt the next morning. Mr. Ranleigh, in the experienced eyes of Sivil, looked remarkably like a man with a question of such vexing moment on his mind that he—Sivil—must have resigned himself to being absentmindedly overturned in some unfriendly ditch had it not been for his knowledge of his master's proficiency as a whip. He drove through the chill spring morning mizzle with his eyes fixed frowningly upon the road ahead; and even when the mizzle thickened to a disagreeably cold rain he only turned up the collar of his driving-coat and proceeded on as if he were as impervious to the weather as to any desire for human companionship.

In the chaise ahead, Cecily and Miss Dowie were equally taciturn. Miss Dowie, who on the previous evening had been inclined to be very well pleased with herself after her victorious encounter with Sir Timothy, was beginning to perceive that she had solved only the most pressing of the problems concerning her niece's future. Obviously, it was impossible for her to return to Inglesant, where Brackenridge might turn up at any moment to communicate the damaging information in his possession to the Bonshawes. But, on the other hand, what was to prevent him from seeking Cecily out elsewhere, if he really was determined to pursue her? A chance meeting with someone who had seen her in the theatre had seemed a risk that might reasonably be taken; but to gamble on Brackenridge's abandoning his deliberate attempt to win the girl to his wishes was a more dangerous matter altogether.

Had she but known it, Cecily, whose silence she presumed to be due to the same considerations that were occupying her, had actually spared not two thoughts to Sir Harry that morning. *She* was preoccupied with the recollection of the ice in Mr. Ranleigh's voice when Sir Timothy had committed the impertinence of linking her name with his. Not by a word or a glance, when her uncle had scornfully referred to the unlikelihood of his wishing to marry her, had he given a sign that Sir Timothy had misread his intentions regarding her. Of course he did not wish to marry her! He was a proud man, and the bearer of one of the proudest names in England: was it likely that he would wish to ally himself with a nobody, a young woman who was no longer even respectable, since she had performed as an actress upon the stage?

Cecily, finding that there were tears in her eyes, turned her head away so that her aunt should not see them. As usual, however, Miss Dowie missed nothing. She reached out and patted Cecily's hand.

'I am sure I do not blame you for giving way to your feelings, my love,' she said sympathetically. 'The events of this past week have been enough quite to overset your nerves. But you must not despair, for Lady Frederick is not at all averse to exerting herself once more on your behalf. Indeed, I believe she will be so overjoyed when she learns that you have come by no harm from that odious Brackenridge that she will do everything in her power to establish you respectably—for you must know, my dear, that she was in mortal dread that Mr. Ranleigh would feel obliged to call Sir Harry to account if you had.'

Cecily turned astonished eyes upon her. 'But what can you mean, Aunt?' she faltered. 'Mr. Ranleigh call Sir Harry to account . . . ? You cannot mean that he would have felt he must fight a duel with him because of me?'

Miss Dowie shook her head disapprovingly. 'Well, my dear, you know what gentlemen are!' she said. 'There is no telling what maggots they may take into their heads on the subject of honour! And I must confess that there is a certain propriety in Mr. Ranleigh's feeling called upon to do for you what your father or your brother, if you had one, would consider it incumbent upon him to do, had you come by harm at Sir Harry's hands. You are, in a manner of speaking, under his protection.'

This was a new and dismaying idea for Cecily. It was no wonder, she thought dismally, that Mr. Ranleigh had appeared so withdrawn that morning at breakfast. If he had disliked being brought into her affairs in the first place, it must be doubly disagreeable for him to feel now that he had been placed in a position in which it might be necessary for him to hazard his own safety for her protection. It would no doubt have been a great deal better, she told herself miserably, if she had never revealed the connexion between them to him, and had remained upon the stage instead.

They arrived at Hillcourt late in the afternoon. Lady Frederick, who had been fidgeting over a game of Patience in the Small Saloon, swept the cards away at the sound of voices in the hall and herself came anxiously out to greet them. The instant she saw that Cecily was of the party her face brightened.

'So you have brought her back! How clever of you, Robert!' she said. 'My dear Miss Dowie, how very much relieved you must be!'

She was interrupted by Lord Neagle, who came bounding down the stairs to add his own impetuous greetings to hers.

'Oh, I say, you've brought Cecily with you!' he said. '*Did* you run off from that governess place, Cecily? I told Robert I expected you might. Was it very grim there? Did you dislike it very much?'

'Now *do* give over asking questions, Charlie, and let Robert tell me what has happened!' Lady Frederick said reprovingly. 'As a matter of fact, you had much better go upstairs again to Mr. Tibble . . .'

'Well, I shan't!' his lordship said indignantly. 'I am not a child, Grandmama! *I* know there's something smoky going on, and if you think I am going to wait to learn what it is until Tibble has a chance to worm it out of the servants . . .'

Mr. Ranleigh, allowing Welbore to take his dripping beaver and driving-coat, said wearily, 'It is quite all right for him to remain, ma'am. There is nothing to tell except that we found Miss Hadley at her uncle's house, and that he did *not* appear to be suffering from an apoplexy. And now, if you will excuse me, I am going upstairs.'

'Oh, in that case, I'll go too!' Lord Neagle said buoyantly.

He followed his uncle up the stairs, while Lady Frederick led Miss Dowie and Cecily into the Small Saloon. Here, steaming cups of tea having been produced to lend assistance to a cheerful fire in dispelling the chill of the journey, Miss Dowie and Lady Frederick at once fell into animated conversation. The nefarious behaviour of Sir Harry Brackenridge was brought up for review; Sir Timothy's rudeness and Lady Bonshawe's stupidity were animadverted upon; and it appeared to Cecily that, for once, the two ladies were about to enjoy a half hour of unremitting agreement in each other's company when Mr. Goodgame's offer was touched upon.

This at once put a different complexion upon the conversation. Lady Frederick, who had been racking her brains quite as busily as Miss Dowie in search of a solution to the new set of difficulties regarding Cecily's future introduced by Brackenridge's pursuit of her, instantly pounced upon what appeared to her to be a gleam of light in the darkness of her dilemma. She instituted an immediate inquiry into the young man's age, appearance, and situation in life, and, upon Miss Dowie's acknowledging that he was twenty-one, not unprepossessing in spite of his unpolished manners, and the owner of a considerable property, unhesitatingly gave it as her opinion that Cecily was a great goose to have whistled him down the wind.

This at once set Miss Dowie's back up. 'Indeed, ma'am, I do not at all take your meaning,' she said. 'Is my niece to be coerced into marriage at my brother's desire?'

'Coerced? Fiddle!' Lady Frederick said. 'He sounds a very respectable young man to me.'

'A country clodpole!' Miss Dowie said wrathfully.

Lady Frederick shrugged. 'My dear, his lack of polish might be mended by his wife, if she chose to take the pains. You refine too much upon the matter.'

Miss Dowie's blue eyes sparkled with resolution. 'That is very well, ma'am, but if you believe that I shall allow my brother to force a husband for whom she has no liking upon this child . . .'

'Liking! Pho!' said Lady Frederick downrightly. 'You do not appear to understand that neither you nor Cecily is in a position to be picking and choosing, after this unfortunate business with Brackenridge! The rogue will spread the tale all over town; you may be assured of that! It may become quite out of my power to place her in another such position as she was in at the Bonshawes', and yet you will turn up your nose at an opportunity to see her respectably established!'

Cecily, who had been listening to this dialogue in acute discomfort, at this point could remain quiet no longer, and, rising, begged to be excused so that she might go upstairs.

'Ay, and I shall go with you!' Miss Dowie said, getting up in her turn. She added with great sarcasm to Lady Frederick, before she swept out of the room, 'It is a pity that you have never become acquainted with my brother, ma'am, for I am persuaded that the two of you would deal extremely!'

Fortunately for Cecily, who had no desire to continue on the subject of Mr. Goodgame, the dinner hour was approaching, so that Miss Dowie was able to give vent only to a few pungent observations on Lady Frederick's interference in Cecily's affairs before she was obliged to retire to her bedchamber to change her dress. Cecily herself, with a heavy heart, donned the pretty jaconet muslin that Lady Frederick had given her. The more she thought of her own affairs, the more tangled they appeared to her to become, and she could almost have wished that she had never set eyes on either Lady Frederick or her son.

At dinner it appeared to her that Mr. Ranleigh had not at all recovered his customary air of imperturbability. He seemed abstracted, and took no part in the conversation except when he was obliged to do so. Once or twice she was conscious that his eyes were resting upon her, but he addressed not a single syllable to her at any time, and she was obliged to believe that he was still out of charity with her over the inconvenience to which she had put him.

Lady Frederick too, it appeared to her, had only severity in her mien when she gazed at her, so that, all in all, she felt the meal to be an ordeal from which she was glad to be released when Lady Frederick at last arose and led the ladies of the party into the Ivory Saloon.

Here Lady Frederick discovered that there was a disagreeable draught, and requested Cecily to run upstairs and fetch a shawl for her. It was not difficult for Cecily to guess that what she actually desired was the opportunity of speaking a few words in private to Miss Dowie before the gentlemen had left sitting over their wine and joined the ladies, and she therefore took her time over the errand. She did not anticipate that her aunt would be won over to take Lady Frederick's view of Mr. Goodgame's suit, but there was still the possibility that Lady Frederick, displeased by her opposition, might wash her hands of any further attempts to find some suitable occupation for Cecily.

With these thoughts disturbingly in her mind, Cecily came slowly down the stairs again, a handsome shawl of Norwich silk over her arm. The door of the Ivory Saloon was open, and she could hear her aunt's voice, delivering some determined statement; then Lady Frederick's, speaking in agitated accents, came to her ears.

'My dear woman, pray do not be such a goosecap! Do you not see what the result of this may be? From something Robert let fall to me just before dinner, I very much fear that he has taken the quixotic notion into his head that the only way out of the muddle is for him to offer for the girl himself! It is quite nonsensical of him, but you must see that she has been placed in such a position by this affair with Brackenridge that marriage with *someone* is now the only practical way out of her difficulties!'

Cecily, her face gone very pale, stood rooted to the spot, the shawl clasped tightly in her arms. She heard her aunt say, with acerbity, 'Indeed, my lady, as to that, you need have no fear—my niece does not aspire to the honour of being Mr. Ranleigh's wife. You may believe, too, that I should not countenance such a business for a moment. Cecily is in no way your son's responsibility, and, though I am grateful to him for having so much consideration for her, she has no right to expect such a sacrifice of his own inclinations.'

'Exactly!' said Lady Frederick. 'But how am I to convince him of that? Men, my dear, are the most obstinate creatures in the world when it is a question of something they believe touches their honour, and I am sure there will be no moving him if he feels he must really make the child an offer. He will certainly not allow that a mere female can know anything of the matter!'

Cecily, composing herself with a desperate effort, forced a smile to her lips and walked into the saloon.

'Here is your shawl, ma'am,' she said to Lady Frederick, in a voice that quivered in spite of herself. 'I hope you will not mind if I leave you and Aunt alone now; I find I am quite worn out after my journey, and I believe I should like to retire early this evening.'

Both the elder ladies looked at her sharply, but, as she betrayed no consciousness of having overheard what had been said just prior to her entrance, Lady Frederick merely said, 'Yes, my dear, of course you must go up if you are tired. I am sure we shall all feel much better after a good night's rest, for this has been an upsetting affair for all of us.'

Miss Dowie too said good night to her niece, intimating that she would remain downstairs until the hour at which she usually retired. Cecily was thereupon free to run upstairs. One great sob escaped her as she reached the head of the staircase, but she swallowed it down fiercely and went at once to her own bedchamber. Here she sat down beside the window and for some quarter of an hour remained in the deepest thought, after which she rose and made her way swiftly to the part of the house where Lord Neagle's bedchamber lay.

His lordship was already abed and asleep, as the lack of response to her cautious scratching upon the door informed her.

Hearing footsteps approaching down the corridor, she tried the doorknob in desperation and, finding the latch free, whisked herself inside. Lord Neagle's regular breathing announced that he was quite unconscious of her intrusion. She approached the bed.

'Charlie!' she hissed intensely. 'Wake up! It's Cecily! I *must* talk to you!'

He merely stirred and yawned. Discerning his sleeping figure dimly in the moonlight that peeped through the drawn curtains, she reached out and shook him vigorously.

His lordship sat bolt upright on the instant. '*What?*' he exclaimed. 'Who is it?'

'It's Cecily! *Do* be quiet! Do you want Mr. Tibble to hear you?'

'I don't know. Do I?' his lordship inquired sleepily.

'No! I've come to ask you to help me, and *nobody* must know. Do you understand me?'

Lord Neagle gradually appeared to take a firmer grasp of the situation. 'Might tell Robert,' he remarked presently. 'You in some sort of scrape, Cecily? Dashed good fellow to help a person out of a scrape, Robert.'

'*Especially* you are not to tell Mr. Ranleigh!' Cecily insisted fiercely. 'Do you understand me, Charlie? If you are going to tell *him*, I won't say another word.'

'Oh, very well, in that case . . .' his lordship conceded. 'What is it, then? You must be in the deuce of a pucker, to come to me at this time of night.'

'I am!' Cecily said. She was silent for a moment, and then went on in a rush, 'The thing is—I overheard your grandmother talking to Aunt Mab just now. She says Mr. Ranleigh feels himself obliged to make me an offer of marriage because—because I am under his protection and that odious Brackenridge will make it impossible for me to obtain another respectable position, now that he knows I am Miss Daingerfield-Nelson. And—and I find that I do not wish to be respectable, after all, and so I am going back to the theatre!'

Having poured this information rather incoherently into Lord

171

Neagle's ears, she halted and waited anxiously for his response. It was not immediately forthcoming, his lordship, it seemed, finding the matter a rather involved one to cope with on being awakened from a sound slumber.

After some time, however, he remarked sapiently, 'I take you. You don't want to marry Robert. Cork-brained scheme, at any rate. He don't want to marry you. Don't even like you. Told me so the other day.'

'Did—did he?' Cecily faltered, feeling crushed, in spite of her resolution not to allow Mr. Ranleigh to sacrifice himself to his ideas of honourable behaviour. 'When did he say that?'

'Well, he didn't actually *say* it,' Lord Neagle acknowledged. 'We were talking about his being obliged to go into Hampshire after you, and *I* said it was a pity he had you on his hands because he didn't even like you. Well—he didn't say he *did* . . .'

'I don't suppose he does,' Cecily said, in a small voice. 'You see, I have been such a great deal of trouble to him. So I have decided that the best thing for me to do is to go back to the theatre—because Lady Frederick says herself that it will be impossible to establish me respectably now except I am married to someone, and I do not at all wish to be married.'

'Well, no one could blame you for *that*,' his lordship said. 'I mean to say, you'd need to be perfectly birdwitted not to prefer being on the stage. But there'll be a rare dust kicked up when they find out about it, you know.'

'They are not going to find out about it until it is too late,' Cecily said, resolutely. 'Too late for them even to *think* of trying to make me respectable again, that is. And that is why I have come to you, Charlie. *You* must help me to get away from here without anyone's knowing, and lend me some of your clothes, and some money, if you have any—for I am not sure I have enough of my own—and tell me exactly how I am to get to Cuckfield, so that I can take the stage to London.'

Lord Neagle appeared to find nothing at all unreasonable in this request, although he did demand to know, after a moment's cogitation, why she had need of his clothes.

'Because I shall go dressed as a boy,' Cecily said promptly.

'It will not look nearly so odd as if I were to go jauntering about dressed as a young lady, for I shall have to walk to Cuckfield, you know. And then it will throw my aunt and Mr. Ranleigh quite off the scent, for they will not be inquiring after a boy.'

'But will you be able to carry it off?' his lordship asked doubtfully. 'You'll have to do something about your hair, for one thing.'

'Oh, yes,' agreed Cecily, quite unperturbed. 'Isn't it lucky that the front is already cropped? I shall simply snip the back short too and be quite in the latest mode. And as for carrying it off, there is nothing in the least difficult about it, if one remembers to take long strides and speak in a gruff voice—like this.'

And she gave a creditable imitation of his lordship's own boyishly offhand tones.

Lord Neagle nodded. 'Well, I daresay you might do it,' he said judiciously. 'And I must say it's a dashed clever notion, for I don't suppose even Robert would think it was you if he found out about a boy's having been seen on the road to Cuckfield.'

'And you won't tell him, Charlie?' Cecily said anxiously. 'Will you promise me that? Because it will be worse than anything if he finds me before *I* can find Mr. Jillson and go on the stage again.'

His lordship said indignantly, 'What do you take me for? Of course I won't split on you! But they'll be in a deuced pucker, you know. May think you've been murdered, or kidnapped, or something of that sort.'

'No, for I shall leave a note for Aunt and tell her that I have gone away of my own accord,' Cecily said. 'And I shall tell her not to search for me, for I am *quite* able to look after myself now, and—and to arrange my own future for myself.'

His lordship agreed that this was the thing to do, and a candle was then lighted so that a search might be instituted for the proper clothing for her to wear upon her journey, and for such sums of money as might be found to be in his lordship's possession. The gratifying amount of three half-crowns, together with a guinea bestowed upon him two days before by his uncle, was

173

turned over to her in its entirety, and his lordship's wardrobe was next ransacked for jacket, breeches, hat, and shirt, together with footwear more suitable for a youth with a long, muddy walk before him than Cecily herself owned.

'You ought to have a cloak-bag or a portmanteau for your own things, though—oughtn't you?' Lord Neagle inquired, frowning.

'Yes, but that is quite all right, for they haven't taken mine away to the box-room yet,' Cecily informed him. 'I am glad it is small, since I shall have to carry it all the way.'

'*I* think it would be better if I went with you. Couldn't they find something for me to do in the theatre? It would be a good deal more to my taste than staying on here, poring over books with old Tibble.'

'Oh, Charlie, do try not to be such a *clunch*!' Cecily said. 'Of course you cannot go with me! This isn't a lark; indeed, it is a very serious affair, and I am half out of my mind with worrying that I shan't be able to get away without being discovered, or that Mr. Ranleigh will come after me and find me . . .'

'Well, he can't *make* you marry him, even if he does,' Lord Neagle said reasonably.

'I know that! But I d-don't wish him to m-make me an offer when he doesn't c-care about me in the least . . .' She broke off, found her handkerchief, and blew her nose defiantly. 'And if I do not marry *him*, I shall be plagued to marry Mr. Goodgame, and I had rather die!' she said. 'So you see I *must* go back to the theatre, where I can earn my own living and not have to be beholden to *anyone*.'

'Yes, I can see that. Well, I will tell you how you must go about slipping out of the house—for I have done it myself once or twice, you know—and then how you must go to get to Cuckfield.'

When this information had been satisfactorily memorised by Cecily, she said good-bye to Lord Neagle with many expressions of gratitude and left his bedchamber, fortunately meeting no one while returning to her own room, where she quickly packed up a few necessaries in her portmanteau and then hastily undressed and got into bed.

A short time later she heard her aunt come along the hall on her way to her own room. As Cecily had expected, she looked in to see if she was asleep, and, finding that she was not, came in for a few moments to talk to her. Cecily took advantage of the opportunity to tell her that she was quite worn to a thread, and would probably rise later than usual the next morning, and then, having kissed her aunt—for the last time, as she unhappily reflected—was left alone to perfect her plans.

These were not complicated, involving, as she had told Lord Neagle, merely a flight via stagecoach to London, where she was certain that she would be able to contact the Jillsons at the Running Boar. And then, she told herself, having contrived to place herself beyond the pale of respectability by her reappearance upon the stage, so that Mr. Ranleigh's chivalrous intentions toward her must certainly be abandoned, she would be free to reap all the rewards of fame and fortune offered her by a career in the theatre.

The very thought, paradoxically, was sufficient to induce her to give way to a hearty bout of tears—after which, having resolutely dried her eyes, she rose, attired herself in Lord Neagle's clothing, and prepared to set out on her journey.

CHAPTER TWENTY

On the following morning Lord Neagle had the forethought to remind his uncle that he had promised to take him out in his curricle that day for a driving lesson, and successfully managed, by various stratagems, to keep him away from the house until shortly after noon.

They returned to find that Cecily's disappearance had been discovered. In point of fact, Lady Frederick and Miss Dowie were in the Small Saloon, distractedly poring over the note that Cecily had left behind her, when Mr. Ranleigh walked in with his nephew, and both ladies at once pounced upon him with demands for counsel.

'Disappeared?' Mr. Ranleigh said in an incredulous voice, as he endeavoured to sort out the facts of what had occurred from the spate of agitated words hurled at him. 'Nonsense! You must be mistaking the matter!'

He stretched out his hand for Cecily's note, which Miss Dowie immediately surrendered to him. It was, he found, quite brief.

'Dearest Aunt,' it read, 'I am very sorry indeed to give you Pain, but I think it will be much, much Better if I do not cause any more Trouble to Lady Frederick in trying to establish me Respectably, since I am quite old enough to decide my own Future now. Please do not try to find out where I have gone.' There were a few splotches on the page which might have been caused by tears, and the note concluded with the signature: 'Your loving Niece, Cecily.'

Mr. Ranleigh looked up, his face suddenly gone quite white

about the mouth. 'What in God's name does this mean, ma'am?' he demanded of Miss Dowie. 'Have you any notion?'

She shook her head numbly. 'No, sir, not the least in the world! The child was out of spirits yesterday and went up early to her bed. And when I looked in on her, she said that she was tired and would sleep late this morning—so that we thought nothing of it when she did not appear at breakfast. But half an hour ago, when I went up to her bedchamber, she was not there, and I found—that.'

She nodded toward the sheet of notepaper which he still held in his hand.

Lady Frederick put in, importunately, 'Where *can* she have gone, Robert? She cannot have thought of returning to the Bonshawes in this clandestine way—it is too absurd! And *why* should she have taken it into her head that I should not wish to do anything more for her?'

'Well, as to *that*, my lady,' Miss Dowie said rather sharply, 'I am sure I should not blame her for thinking such a thing, when you pressed it upon her so strongly yesterday that she ought to marry Mr. Goodgame!'

Mr. Ranleigh, who had seemed to be immersed in his own thoughts, interrupted at this point to address a trenchant question to his mother.

'What? Is this true, ma'am?'

'Well, I am sure you need not wonder if it is!' Lady Frederick said. 'Certainly it would be the height of absurdity for a girl in her position to think of refusing a respectable offer of marriage, merely because she had not yet had the opportunity of becoming well acquainted with the young man!'

An expression of hard anger that Lady Frederick had not often been called upon to face appeared in her son's grey eyes.

'I see!' he said curtly. 'So you too, ma'am, were endeavouring to coerce her into this marriage! Has Mr. Goodgame been accurately described to you, I wonder? If he has, it should not surprise you, I believe, that Miss Hadley preferred to leave this house rather than to be obliged to fear that she would be importuned to wed him!'

'But this is nonsense, Robert!' Lady Frederick said, with some spirit. 'Surely the child knew she would not be *forced* into a marriage that was genuinely distasteful to her! What motive could I have for doing anything so cruel?'

Mr. Ranleigh eyed her grimly. 'A motive, ma'am,' he returned, 'which I believe I was singularly foolish to have provided you with last evening when I . . .' He broke off, becoming conscious that Lord Neagle was still a highly interested spectator of the scene. 'Charlie, go to your room,' he said, in a voice that brooked no opposition. Lord Neagle reluctantly retired, and Mr. Ranleigh, closing the door behind him, continued to Lady Frederick, '. . . when I signified to you that it might be my intention to offer for Miss Hadley's hand myself.'

A vivid and unaccustomed flush overspread Lady Frederick's face. 'But, Robert,' she protested, 'surely you cannot be surprised that I do not wish you to sacrifice yourself to some over-nice notions of propriety! If *that* is my fault . . .'

But she got no further, for Mr. Ranleigh interrupted her with an odd, harsh laugh.

'Notions of propriety!' he exclaimed. 'My dear ma'am, has it never entered your mind that my feelings might be involved in the matter?'

'Your *feelings*!'

Lady Frederick repeated the words incredulously, while Miss Dowie, her own face showing equal amounts of surprise and disapproval, said stiffly, 'If this is some jest, sir . . .'

'A jest?' he said sardonically. 'Oh no, it is quite true! Apparently, however, I was as overcome as my mother appears to be by the possibility that I might actually have condescended to conceive a *tendre* for your niece, for certainly I said nothing to her of the matter. But I am wasting time,' he added in an altered, but still exceedingly hard, voice. 'If she has left this house, she may have been seen on the road, or they may have news of her at the coach-office in Cuckfield.'

He left the room as he spoke and walked rapidly into the hall, where they heard him ordering Welbore to send to the stables at once and have the bays put to and his curricle brought round again. Lady Frederick and Miss Dowie sat staring at each other in dismayed conjecture.

'Good heavens!' Lady Frederick said faintly. 'I had no idea! To be sure, I *did* think once—but that has been months ago, and I made certain it was only because he was angry with Tony for behaving so badly . . .'

Miss Dowie, however, was too much taken up with her anxiety over Cecily to spend more than a few moments on thoughts of anything else. She said it would be time enough when they had found Cecily to think about such matters, and thereupon went back to trying to puzzle out the reason for her niece's departure from Hillcourt.

'She cannot have wished to return to Timothy,' she said, 'though, indeed, if she *had*, she might well have hesitated to tell me of it, knowing how I should dislike it. But she seemed so greatly relieved to be able to leave there yesterday . . .'

Lady Frederick shook her head. 'It is quite beyond my comprehension,' she said. 'If it was my urging her to accept Mr. Goodgame's offer that made her run off, as Robert appears to believe, it would not at all have served her purpose to return to your brother's house. Yet it seems equally unlikely that she has gone to the Bonshawes . . .' She broke off as another thought entered her mind. 'Brackenridge!' she exclaimed, in accents of dismay. 'Good God, my dear, do you think it is possible . . . ?'

'That she has run off to go to him? No, I do not!' Miss Dowie said roundly. 'I shall never believe such a thing of her!'

Lady Frederick, seeing her kindling eyes, refrained from saying any more on the subject; but she could not rid her mind so easily of the idea. As the afternoon hours slipped by and nothing was heard from Mr. Ranleigh, neither she nor Miss Dowie could prevent herself from sinking into blacker and blacker gloom. Miss Dowie at last, feeling that she could no longer endure to sit idly waiting, went upstairs, where she conceived the idea of searching her niece's bedchamber for anything that might give her a clue as to where she had gone.

The results of this endeavour sent her downstairs again to Lady Frederick within ten minutes with a small jeweller's box clasped in her right hand, and with her face almost as white as her tucker.

'My lady,' she said, walking into the Small Saloon and interrupting Lady Frederick's game of Patience without ceremony, 'do but look at this! I found it at the back of one of Cecily's bureau drawers. Oh, my lady, does it mean—must it mean . . . ?'

She could not go on, but drew out her handkerchief and wiped her eyes, while Lady Frederick, lifting the lid of the box that had been offered her, sat staring at the diamond ear-drops Brackenridge had forced upon Cecily in the shrubbery at Inglesant.

'Bless—my—soul!' she ejaculated. 'I should not have believed it! My poor dear friend . . .'

'There is some explanation! There must be!' Miss Dowie, recovering herself, said fiercely. 'She left them behind her— did she not? *Why* should she have done so if she has gone to that man? And why should she have fled to Timothy's house to escape him, if she had already consented to allow him to buy her virtue with such baubles! I will not believe it of her!'

Lady Frederick, who did not know how to reply to her, was spared the necessity of doing so by her housekeeper, Mrs. Keaton, who appeared at the door at that moment, begging the favour of a word with her.

'It's about his lordship, my lady,' she said, in a voice that was big with importance. 'That is, it's about his clothes, and I *did* think you might wish to know . . .'

Lady Frederick, who was aware that Cecily's abrupt disappearance could not have escaped the observation of her household, did not fail to gather that the communication Mrs. Keaton desired to make to her had something to do with that event; but she was at a loss to understand the connexion.

'Yes?' she inquired. 'What is it, Mrs. Keaton?'

'Why, my lady, I shouldn't think to come worrying you with such a thing, except that it seemed—well, downright queer to me,' the housekeeper said, apologetically. 'The fact is, Alice tells me one of his lordship's jackets is missing from his wardrobe, and he has no notion how to account for it. *And* it seems there's other things gone as well . . .'

'What sort of things?' Lady Frederick interrupted. 'Speak up, woman! Other articles of clothing?'

'Yes, indeed, my lady—for she says it's a pair of his breeches too, and the half-boots his lordship likes to wear when he goes out shooting—*and* a hat . . .'

She broke off in dismay at sight of the forbidding expression that had appeared on her mistress's face.

'Would you be so good, Mrs. Keaton,' Lady Frederick said, deliberately, 'as to send to tell Lord Neagle that I should like to see him at once? *At once*—do you understand?'

The housekeeper dropped a curtsey and hurried off to execute the command, while Lady Frederick, relieved of the necessity of concealing her emotions that had been imposed by her presence, turned a harassed face toward Miss Dowie.

'Is it possible,' she demanded, 'that that abominable boy can have had anything to do with this? My dear Miss Dowie, my head is in a whirl! Gone off dressed as a boy! Good heavens, I have never heard of anything so improper!'

Miss Dowie, too, looked as if she found this latest possibility too much to support, and could scarcely summon up the spirits even to discuss it during the few minutes that elapsed before Lord Neagle himself appeared in the doorway. He was looking a trifle scared and more than a little defiant, and, on being taxed by his grandmother to tell her immediately what he had done with his missing clothing, set the tone of the ensuing conversation by declaring in a tone of obstinate martyrdom that wild horses would be unable to drag any explanations from his lips.

It appeared, in the course of the half hour that followed, that he had meant exactly what he said. None of the threats, pleas, imprecations, or cajoleries that descended upon him was able in the slightest degree to alter his determination. He drove the two ladies into a state of such frustrated fury that Lady Frederick, hearing at last the sound of carriage wheels on the drive outside, followed by her son's voice in the hall, was goaded to say in accents of grim triumph, 'Very well, my lad! We shall see what your uncle has to say to this! I daresay *he* will know how to deal with you! Unless he has succeeded in finding Cecily...'

One glance at her son's set face as he walked into the room, however, was sufficient to tell her that that happy event had not occurred. Mr. Ranleigh, in answer to the eager inquiries directed to him by Miss Dowie and his mother, said curtly that his efforts had met with no success whatever: not the slightest trace had he been able to find of Cecily.

'Yes, I can well believe it,' Lady Frederick said, 'for it would appear that you have been led quite off the scent, Robert! *I* have not been able to obtain the truth of the matter from Charlie, but I trust that *you* will. It seems that certain articles of his clothing are missing, and I cannot think there is any other explanation of the matter than that Cecily has gone off dressed as a boy!'

Mr. Ranleigh received this piece of information with no visible manifestation of either surprise or anger, but the light in his grey eyes as he swung round to face his nephew was so menacing that that young gentleman quailed beneath it.

'Well, Charlie?' Mr. Ranleigh asked, ominously.

His lordship swallowed convulsively. 'I—I can't tell you, sir,' he managed to stammer out, at last. 'Honestly I can't! I gave her my word, you see!'

Mr. Ranleigh appeared to consider the matter. 'Yes, I see,' he said after a moment, in a somewhat less formidable tone. 'You do not wish to betray her confidence. But you are old enough to understand, Charlie, that you may be doing her a far greater disservice by keeping silent than by speaking out now. A girl of her age wandering about the world entirely unprotected—even you must be able to see the danger of that!'

'Yes, but she will not be unprotected for long, sir!' Lord Neagle urged, looking relieved by the more reasonable tone in which his uncle had addressed him. 'I mean to say—I'm *sure* she knows just what she is doing, and if I was you I should simply stop looking for her, for she don't care to have you marry her, you know, and it will be *much* better if you let her go off and do as she chooses.'

To say that this statement produced a sensation among his auditors would scarcely be an exaggeration. Lady Frederick exclaimed, in tones of the utmost astonishment, 'Good heavens, how came she to know anything of *that*!' and Miss Dowie, in complete bewilderment, declared that she did not believe a word of it.

'It is quite out of the question that she said any such thing!' she said. 'It is Mr. Goodgame whom she does not wish to marry!'

'Well, she don't wish to marry him, either, ma'am,' Lord Neagle conceded. 'And I do not see why she need do so, after all, for there is another . . .' He halted abruptly. 'I shan't tell you any more,' he said, the obstinate look returning to his face. 'I promised her I shouldn't—and if you've told me once, sir, you've told me a dozen times: a gentleman never breaks his word!'

Mr. Ranleigh, who had had a very odd expression on his face ever since his nephew had informed him of Cecily's aversion to marrying him, did not appear to have paid a great deal of attention to the remarks that had followed. He said now briefly, to Lord Neagle, 'Go to your room, Charlie. I shall come up to you if I wish to speak to you again.'

His nephew needed no second invitation to depart. He took himself thankfully out of the room, and Mr. Ranleigh, closing the door behind him, turned to Lady Frederick with a sardonic expression in his eyes.

'Well, ma'am?' he said. 'Can you explain to me by what means Miss Hadley could have learned that there was any possibility of her being obliged to receive my—as I must gather—highly unwelcome addresses?'

'Robert, I swear to you that she did not hear of it from me!' Lady Frederick cried, looking upset and indignant at her son's tone. 'How can you think I should have done such a thing?—unless,' she added suddenly, as a new thought struck her, 'unless—oh, my dear Miss Dowie,' she exclaimed, turning to her, 'is it possible that she could have overheard our conversation last evening? You remember, I had been speaking of it just before she came into the room with my shawl.'

Miss Dowie said hollowly that she did indeed remember, but that it did not signify in the least.

'It must be that man, Brackenridge,' she said, in a despairing voice. 'Oh, Mr. Ranleigh, *pray* do not be angry with the child and give over your efforts to find her now, for I am persuaded that he has come round her—*how*, I cannot tell, for I am sure when she came away from Inglesant she had not the slightest wish to have further dealings with him. But he has contrived somehow to give her *these*'—and she held out the jeweller's box containing the diamond ear-drops to him—'and must, I am persuaded, have offered her marriage as well, or she would never have fled to his protection! But *will* he marry her, knowing of her what he does?'

Mr. Ranleigh, the lines about his mouth and jaw suddenly very marked, was looking at the winking baubles in the box.

'No, he will not marry her,' he said levelly. 'But if he has harmed her in any way, you have my word that he will answer to me for it, ma'am.'

'Fustian!' Lady Frederick cried. 'Robert, *do* but consider a moment—if you call him out, you may very well kill him, and what possible good can that do the girl? And then *you* will be obliged to leave the country . . . Oh, heavens, was there ever such a muddle! There must be some rational way out of it!'

Mr. Ranleigh, however, did not stay to discuss the matter. He said briefly to his mother that he believed it was probable that he would be leaving Hillcourt within the hour, and that he would be pleased to partake of anything in the way of a cold repast that could be set before him without delay, and thereupon walked upstairs to his nephew's bedchamber.

Lord Neagle looked up apprehensively as his uncle entered.

'Now, Charlie,' Mr. Ranleigh said, in a voice that set that young gentleman's heart to thudding uncomfortably against his ribs, 'I am going to ask you these questions only once. It is possible that Miss Hadley is in serious trouble, and under the circumstances you need not scruple to tell me the truth. Do you know where she went when she left this house?'

Lord Neagle looked imploringly at him. 'Oh, sir, really— *must* I tell you?'

'You must,' Mr. Ranleigh said, inexorably. 'Cut line, Charlie! To London—was it not?'

His lordship capitulated. 'Y-yes, sir.'

'By private chaise? Or by stage?'

'By private chaise? Oh no, sir, no one was to take her up. She said she should walk in to Cuckfield and take the stage there.'

'Dressed in your clothes?'

'Yes, sir.'

'I see. And what did she intend to do when she reached London?'

Lord Neagle, grasping at the last shreds of his code of honour, muttered that he did not know. He consoled himself, under his uncle's hard gaze, with the thought that he really did *not* know what Cecily's movements might be when she reached the city, for she had told him no more than that she meant to find Mr. Jillson, and he had not the least notion of how she intended to go about doing that.

Mr. Ranleigh, however, was not to be led off the subject so easily, and persisted in inquiring if Cecily had mentioned the name of any gentleman in connexion with her flight.

'Well, she mentioned *yours*,' Lord Neagle said hopefully.

'Yes, you have already told me that. *And* Mr. Goodgame's. Anyone else?'

Lord Neagle searched his memory desperately. 'Brackenridge,' he said after a moment, inspirationally.

His uncle's eyes narrowed. 'Yes? In what connexion?'

'Oh, lord, sir—I don't know exactly,' his lordship said, floundering on. 'To tell you the truth, I was devilish sleepy when she explained it to me . . .' Prompted by the look in his uncle's eyes, he went on hastily, 'Well, it had something to do with her not being able to obtain a respectable position any more, and not wishing to marry you, or that fellow she met in Hampshire, either—in fact, she said she would rather die than do *that* . . .'

He broke off doubtfully, for it occurred to him that his uncle was looking rather formidably grim—a not surprising fact, for Mr. Ranleigh was indeed feeling grim. It now seemed highly possible to him that Cecily, finding insuperable difficulties cast in the way of her career as a governess, and faced with the suits of two gentlemen, neither of whom she wished to marry, had impulsively determined to accept the offer of a man who—however much Mr. Ranleigh might dislike him personally—he admitted knew well how to ingratiate himself with the female sex.

That that offer had meant marriage to *her* mind, he had not the least doubt. That it had meant it to Brackenridge's was another matter altogether. He himself did not for a moment believe that it did, but he was well prepared to believe that Brackenridge, having by some means learned that Cecily had returned to Hillcourt, had managed to convey a message to her that had given her the assurance that she would be safe in throwing herself upon his protection.

If this were so, he had no time to waste. Whether Brackenridge was in London or not he did not know, but Lord Neagle had indicated that that was where Cecily had gone, and it seemed most probable that it was there that he might obtain news of her. He therefore told his nephew briefly that he would deal with him on his return and walked out of the room—leaving that young gentleman to breathe a sigh of immense relief over his having succeeded in preserving at least the core of the secret that Cecily had entrusted to him.

CHAPTER TWENTY-ONE

Mr. Ranleigh, driving his own curricle, arrived in London shortly before eleven o'clock that night, and went at once, without stopping at his own house, to Sir Harry Brackenridge's in Half Moon Street. A sleepy porter, looking more than a little surprised at the appearance of a caller at this time of night—and one, moreover, whose dress proclaimed that he had but just driven into town—informed him uncommunicatively that Sir Harry was gone out. However, the feel of a handsome gratuity slipped into his hand caused him to recollect that his master had announced his intention of attending an evening party at Lord Comerford's house in Curzon Street—a piece of information which, Mr. Ranleigh felt, must do much to relieve his immediate anxieties. If Cecily had indeed arrived in London that day and put herself under Brackenridge's protection, it seemed highly unlikely that that gentleman would be spending the evening at the Comerfords'.

He had no intention, however, of waiting until the morning to go into the matter further, and accordingly drove at once to his own house in Mount Street, where he changed his travelling dress for the knee breeches, silk stockings, and longtailed coat suitable for making an appearance at the Comerfords' party. He was aware that he had sent Lady Comerford his regrets on receiving her card of invitation for this event, since he had expected to be at Hillcourt, but she was all cordiality on seeing him enter her saloon at an hour far past that at which she had anticipated the arrival of any further guests, and accepted with complaisance his explanation that, urgent business having brought him back to town, he could not resist looking in on her party.

A quick glance over the crowded rooms, however, failed to give him a sight of Brackenridge. Coming across his uncle, Mr. Albion Wymberly, just emerging from the supper-room, he stopped him and put a question to him as to whether he had seen Sir Harry that evening.

Mr. Wymberly, whose face bore a satisfied smile which could only mean that the lobster patties had been to his liking and the champagne excellent, stared at him.

'Brackenridge?' he repeated. 'What the deuce do you want with him? Thought you didn't like the fellow.'

'I don't,' Mr. Ranleigh said briefly. 'Has he been here to-night?'

Mr. Wymberly considered. 'Must have been,' he decided after a moment, 'for he's always at these affairs of the Comerfords' unless he's out of town—which he ain't. Ran into him in Bond Street this afternoon. *Was* out of town,' he went on meticulously, seeing the attention with which Mr. Ranleigh had heard this statement, and improving on it with the notion of turning him up sweet, so that he might be in the proper mood when next approached for a small loan. 'Daresay you may have heard of it yourself—visiting an aunt in Somerset. Gave out that was what he was doing, at any rate. Shouldn't be surprised if the affair was actually a bit more interesting—after one of those prime little ladybirds he's always coming up with. Heard some rumours to that effect . . .'

He broke off, dismayed to find that, far from appearing grateful for this news, Mr. Ranleigh was wearing an air of thunderous calm.

'Yes?' he said levally. 'Go on, Albion. You have heard rumours . . . ?'

'Better ask Tony,' Mr. Wymberly said hastily, seeing Lord Portandrew bearing down upon them. '*He* knows Brackenridge better than I do—not in my set, you know . . .'

He took himself off, and Mr. Ranleigh turned to confront

his cousin, who came up, exclaiming in some surprise, 'Here, I thought you was going down to Hillcourt! What are you doing in town?'

'As you see, I have come back,' Mr. Ranleigh said, grasping his cousin's arm and impelling him toward the door of a small anteroom. 'Come along, Tony; I want to talk to you. Have you seen Brackenridge here tonight?'

Lord Portandrew blinked. 'Why, yes,' he said. 'But what's it to do with you?'

'Albion says he's just come back from Somerset, and that there have been rumours concerning a young woman . . .'

Lord Portandrew's brow darkened. 'Oh—that!' he said. 'Yes. Meaning to bring that up the next time I saw you. Came back to town yesterday—no, Wednesday, it must have been—and has been hinting we may expect to see him parading *Miss Daingerfield-Nelson* on his arm soon. What do you know about that, Robert? Has he found out where she is?'

'Yes,' Mr. Ranleigh said shortly. 'And I should like very much at the present moment to find out where *he* is.'

'Oh, well, as to that—nothing easier,' Lord Portandrew assured him. 'Said he was going to look in at that new gaming-hell in Pickering Place—can't have been more than half an hour ago. Ten to one you'll find him still there.' He added, as his cousin uttered a brief acknowledgement and turned away, 'Here! Wait a minute! I'll go with you. They won't let you in unless you have a card. Devilish discreet sort of place.'

'I imagine I shall have no difficulty,' Mr. Ranleigh said coolly. 'If it is the sort of house that has been described to me, you may be sure they are already well acquainted with the size of my purse and my value as a bird for their plucking.'

He did not remain in Curzon Street longer than was required to drink a glass of wine with Lord Comerford, who seized upon him as he was parting from Lord Portandrew, but walked downstairs at once and strolled around to Pickering Place. As he had predicted to his cousin, a brief conversation held with the individual who guarded the door from behind an iron grille quickly secured him the entrée to an elegantly furnished hall, from which he was invited to walk upstairs to the gaming saloons.

As he entered the first of these, an apartment given over to French hazard, he was greeted by several gentlemen of his acquaintance and invited to join them. A brief survey of the room informing him that Brackenridge was not among their number, however, he declined the invitation and moved on into the next room, where a faro-bank was in full swing. Here Brackenridge's brassy-yellow head at once caught his eye. Mr. Ranleigh, having exchanged a bill for several twenty-guinea rouleaus, strolled over to take a seat at the table beside his young friend, Lord Heseltine, who greeted him affably and remarked that the play was devilish dull that night. Brackenridge, who was seated across the table, glanced up and favoured Mr. Ranleigh with a look of slightly mocking surprise.

'Isn't this rather out of your line, Robert?' he inquired. 'I thought you seldom strayed from Watier's, or White's.'

'Oh, I have no objection to being fleeced in a good cause,' Mr. Ranleigh said, imperturbably placing his bet. 'I came, you see, for a word with you.'

Sir Harry's brows went up. 'With me? You surprise me!'

'No, I don't think I do,' Mr. Ranleigh said, as calmly as before. 'I should rather imagine, on the contrary, that you had been expecting something of the sort ever since you returned from Somerset.'

Lord Heseltine glanced acutely from Ranleigh to Brackenridge, opened his mouth to say something, thought better of it, and shut it again. Sir Harry laughed softly.

'I see,' he said. 'So you have not lost interest in that game as yet.'

'No, I have not,' Mr. Ranleigh said. 'May I suggest, however, that we refrain from discussing the matter until you have finished your play here?'

Lord Heseltine, an amiable young man, who stood somewhat in awe of the pair of noted amateurs of the Fancy who, he uneasily felt, were sparring in a considerably more deadly manner than that customarily seen within the confines of Jackson's Boxing Saloon, cleared his throat and ventured a soothing remark to the effect that the room was deuced hot.

'Quite insupportable,' Brackenridge agreed blandly. 'How very right you are, Heseltine! Do you know, I rather fancy that I should benefit by a little fresh air?' He gathered up his winnings in a leisurely manner and rose from the table. 'Are you coming, Robert? It is too bad to draw you away when you have scarcely arrived, but I have the feeling that your heart is not really in the play tonight.'

Mr. Ranleigh did not vouchsafe a reply to this remark, but nodded a good night to Lord Heseltine and walked downstairs with Sir Harry. The two, having received hats and cloaks in the hall, left the house together and strolled, on Mr. Ranleigh's invitation, in the direction of his house in Mount Street.

'Not,' Brackenridge said, 'that I should not appreciate a glass of your excellent Madeira, Robert, but I believe we may very easily conclude this conversation before we arrive in Mount Street. You wish to speak to me on the subject of—er —Miss Hadley, I believe she now calls herself. Do you not?'

Mr. Ranleigh gave him a brief, measuring glance. 'Exactly,' he said. 'How acute of you to guess!'

'Not at all!' Brackenridge demurred. 'I must confess, when I first heard that she had descended to the post of governess in some appallingly vulgar household, I was rather of the opinion that you had found that you really did not care to burden yourself any longer with her affairs and had therefore—er— left the coast clear for me. But Miss Hadley herself, when I had the pleasure of renewing our acquaintance in Somerset, rather gave me the impression that the situation was not precisely as I had been fancying it. By the bye, you *did* know that I had seen her in Somerset—did you not?'

'I did,' Mr. Ranleigh said evenly. 'What I do *not* know is how you can reconcile it with what I can only suppose you call your honour as a gentleman to pursue an obviously innocent girl for purposes that quite evidently have nothing whatever to do with marriage.'

The torch of a passing linkboy escorting a belated reveller home lit Brackenridge's face momentarily, and Mr. Ranleigh saw that it had reddened slightly. Sir Harry laughed with a forced hint of derision, however, as he countered, '*Is* she so innocent, then? I find that rather difficult to credit, after she has passed through *your* hands.' Mr. Ranleigh halted suddenly, and Brackenridge went on, with an unpleasant smile, 'You may force a quarrel upon me if you choose, Robert—but pray consider, before you do, the consequences to the *innocent* Miss Hadley. She seems anxious, for some odd reason, to maintain at least an appearance of respectability—which I daresay must become quite impossible if it is noised about that she has been the object of a brawl between us. Or were you thinking of pistols?'

'If you like,' Mr. Ranleigh said, without the least trace of emotion in his voice. 'At the present time, however, I should like merely to give you a warning. If I find that you are speaking to others of Miss Hadley in the tone in which you have just spoken of her to me, I shall not send you a cartel; I shall use my whip. Miss Hadley is under my protection—not in the way you imagine, but as a connexion of my family.'

'Indeed!' Sir Harry said, angered this time in earnest, it appeared, by Mr. Ranleigh's blunt words. 'And what of old Dowie, her uncle—who is at the present moment, I gather, dying of a quite fictitious apoplexy in Hampshire? If the chit, as you claim, looks to *you* for protection, why then has she ran off to *him* now?'

He paused, seeing that a very odd expression had suddenly appeared upon Mr. Ranleigh's face. In point of fact, Mr. Ranleigh was feeling very odd: he had the strangest sensation that a crushing weight had all at once been lifted from his heart. For Sir Harry's words could have only one meaning, and that was that he believed Cecily to be still with her uncle in Hampshire. And if this were so, he could have had no hand in her decision to leave Hillcourt, since it must appear that he was not even aware that she had left Dowie House and returned there. It seemed clear, therefore, either that Lord Neagle had been telling a deliberate untruth when he had said that she had set out for London, or that she had had some other scheme in mind in doing so.

Once he had arrived at this conclusion, his chief concern was to rid himself of Brackenridge's company, for if the latter really was ignorant of Cecily's flight it was in the highest degree desirable that he remain so. This he found singularly easy to do; Sir Harry, though evidently puzzled by the sudden alteration in his companion's mood, had no wish to continue a conversation which was not only unprofitable to him, but which seemed in a way to becoming positively dangerous. He was far from being a coward—indeed, he had called his man out on at least two occasions—but he was not fond of entering upon such affairs unless he was certain that his own skill must make it extremely probable that he would come off the victor.

And in Ranleigh's case there was no such probability. He knew him to be a dead shot, and one, moreover, whose coolness could not be expected to desert him when he was facing a loaded pistol aimed at him across a dozen yards of greensward in early morning light.

He therefore made no attempt to prolong the conversation when Mr. Ranleigh showed signs of wishing to conclude it, and soon parted from him, without accompanying him as far as his house in Mount Street.

As for Mr. Ranleigh, on reaching that imposing domicile, he went inside to issue several trenchant orders to his sleepy staff concerning the coming morning, and then repaired to his own bedchamber for a few hours of needed slumber. With Brackenridge eliminated as a factor in Cecily's plans, there appeared to remain only three likely places where she might have gone—to Dowie House, to Inglesant, or, if she had indeed come up to London, to seek out some acquaintance she had made during her brief career in the theatre there.

The last possibility seemed the most remote, but, since he was already in London, he decided to try first to obtain news of the runaway at the Running Boar. If this approach failed, as he feared it would, there would then be nothing for it but to set off for Hampshire and, if need be, for Somerset, to learn if Sir Timothy or the Bonshawes could shed any light on the matter of Cecily's disappearance.

CHAPTER TWENTY-TWO

These events occurred on a Friday. On Monday Mr. Ranleigh, having obtained no news of Miss Hadley at the Running Boar, and having then pursued his search for that elusive young lady in both Hampshire and Somerset without the least success, arrived back in town to find a note from Lord Portandrew awaiting him at his house in Mount Street. It informed him, in an agitated scrawl, that the newspapers were puffing the forthcoming appearance of *Miss Daingerfield-Nelson* that very evening in a performance of *The Beaux' Stratagem* at the Surrey Theatre, and urgently requested him to use his best efforts to prevent such an occurrence from coming to pass.

On perusing this missive, Mr. Ranleigh, although not addicted to violent language, was overheard by his butler to utter an oath worthy—as that shocked individual later averred—of a jarvey, after which he gave a curt command for his evening dress to be laid out immediately and disappeared into the library. Here he dashed off a pair of lines to Miss Dowie at Hillcourt, which he gave orders to be dispatched at once by private messenger, and then ran upstairs and rapidly changed his travel-stained buckskins and riding-coat for correct evening attire.

A glance at his watch had already informed him that he could not possibly reach the theatre until the play was nearing its conclusion, and, in fact, when he arrived there the robbery scene was already in progress, and Miss Daingerfield-Nelson, wearing a nightdress under a diaphanous dressing-gown trimmed with puffs of satin ribbon, with her dark ringlets straying in enchanting disorder from beneath a fetching nightcap of muslin and lace, was being dragged onstage with her mother, Lady Bountiful, by the two rogues, Hounslow and Bagshot. The attendant who showed Mr. Ranleigh to his place heard him utter a heartfelt, 'Oh, my God!' and, believing he had misunderstood him, said, 'Beg pardon, sir?'

He received no answer. Mr. Ranleigh's eyes were fixed upon the stage, where Miss Daingerfield-Nelson, seeing her lover, Aimwell, burst onstage to her rescue with drawn sword and engage both villains, was exclaiming, 'O Madam, had I but a sword to help the brave man!' in tones thrilling enough to evoke a storm of applause from an audience that included half the Bloods in London.

This audience, as Mr. Ranleigh guessed—or the anticipation of it, at any rate—had been responsible for Miss Daingerfield-Nelson's name's having been so abruptly inserted in the Surrey's playbill. In point of fact, Cecily, having arrived in London via the medium of a large green-and-gold Accommodation coach, in which she had played with great success the role of a young gentleman of some sixteen years called from school to attend the bedside of a desperately ill parent in the metropolis, had had not the slightest difficulty in attaining her goal of a rapid appearance upon the London stage. Mr. Jillson, readily located by a visit to the Running Boar, had taken her at once to see the managers of the Surrey Theatre, where he was himself engaged, and these gentlemen, as he had confidently predicted, were found to be not only willing, but eager, to employ the services of a young lady whose disappearance had been one of the *on-dits* of the town a few months before, and whose reappearance upon the Surrey's boards could be guaranteed to draw the male members of the *ton* in droves to their door.

The problem of the choice of a vehicle in which to present Miss Daingerfield-Nelson to this fashionable audience was solved without difficulty. She had been coached by Jillson, during her earlier brief theatrical career, in the leading feminine romantic role of Dorinda in Farquhar's comedy, *The Beaux' Stratagem* and, although the legal prohibition against legitimate dramas being presented at the minor London theatres was still in force, the recasting of the traditional five acts to three and the addition of a few songs was sufficient to allow any drama to be performed in these houses in almost unaltered form, under the guise of a burletta.

The Beaux' Stratagem, as it happened, was already in the Surrey's repertory, and Cecily was therefore at once put into rehearsal as the lively, innocent Dorinda, who is courted and deceived by the penniless Aimwell only to discover, at the play's end, that her fortune-hunting suitor is not only genuinely in love with her but is actually Viscount Aimwell as well. To give her added assurance in the part, Mrs. Jillson was cast in the role of Dorinda's more sophisticated sister-in-law, Mrs. Sullen, with whom many of Dorinda's scenes were to be played, and Jillson himself as the French officer, Count Bellair.

It was scarcely surprising that Cecily, thus pitchforked into a hectic round of rehearsals and fittings, should have had little opportunity either to consider the results of her decision to leave Hillcourt or to repine over them. In point of fact, she had no wish to do either. If she was to become Miss Daingerfield-Nelson in good earnest, she told herself, Hillcourt and its inhabitants must lapse into the dead past for her, and it therefore behooved her to put them firmly from her mind and immerse herself completely in her new life.

This she proceeded to do, discovering almost at once that the task was made a good deal easier by the novel enjoyments that the new life offered her. It was certainly agreeable, for example, to find herself suddenly an object of interest and attention to everyone with whom she came into contact, and she had not become so inured to the glamour of the theatrical world by her previous brief taste of it that the experience of acting one of the principal roles in a gay comedy did not seem a giddily exciting one to her.

She even flirted a little, demurely—perhaps inspired by the character she was impersonating—with the young actor playing opposite her in the role of Aimwell, with the result that he had tumbled half into love with her before they had so much as completed their first rehearsal together. In fact, he and the even younger Thespian who played Archer, his friend, were soon locked in a fierce competition for her attention, and constituted themselves a faithful bodyguard to escort her back and forth from the theatre to the Running Boar, both of them too jealous to be willing to trust the other out of his sight when he was in her company.

This devotion did not escape the observation of the buxom Mrs. Jillson, who advised her, in a feeling aside during a late rehearsal, not to allow herself to become entangled with actors —'for you see what it's led *me* to, love,' she said, casting a somewhat jaundiced eye upon her spouse, 'and, if I *do* say it myself, I might have caught a baronet on my hook if I had taken the proper advantage of my opportunities. And there's no telling what *you* might achieve, if you was to set your mind to it, for Jillson says he expects the house will be as full of lords as it can hold when we open, and all of them will be come to see you.'

These expectations, as Mr. Ranleigh's first glance over the theatre on that Monday evening had informed him, had not been vain, for the Surrey's managers indeed had the satisfaction of beholding quite as many peers as might have made up a respectably full session of the House of Lords enter their doors before the curtain rose on the first act of *The Beaux' Stratagem*. Cecily, to whom this fact was duly reported during the early scenes of the play, received the news with proper gratification; but when, at the conclusion of the robbery scene, Mr. Jillson informed her that Mr. Robert Ranleigh was now said to be a member of the audience as well she turned such an appalled face upon him that Mr. Jillson instinctively said, 'Good God!' in the tones usually reserved for his purely professional dramatic moments, and inquired what the matter was.

'N-nothing!' Cecily faltered. 'Nothing at all! Are you *quite* sure?'

'Quite sure? About what?'

'About Mr. Ranleigh! Perhaps it is—might it not be someone who resembles him?'

Mr. Jillson began to be conscious of a dubious feeling, somewhat akin to alarm, rising in his own breast. He had had the forethought, upon Cecily's arrival in London, to leave instructions at the Running Boar that on no account were either his own or Cecily's whereabouts to be disclosed to any inquirer—an action which had been responsible for Mr. Ranleigh's failure to obtain any trace of her there.

But the inquirer he had had in mind had been Miss Dowie, whose wrath he had counted on being able to allay more easily once Cecily had actually returned to the stage and it was to be seen how successful her career there now promised to be. He had had no thought whatever of Mr. Ranleigh's still being interested enough in her activities to cast the powerful shadow of his disapproval over them, and, being a prudent man, he found the possibility an alarming one.

An attempt to ascertain from Miss Hadley herself how matters stood between her and the Nonpareil gained him little, however. Cecily, recovering from the first shock of learning that Mr. Ranleigh was actually a member of the audience, merely informed him, in a brief and highly unconvincing statement, that that gentleman's approval or disapproval of her present occupation meant nothing at all to her—an announcement which Mr. Jillson received without noticeable gratification.

'The question is,' he persisted, 'does it mean anything to *him?*'

'Good gracious, no! Why should it?' Cecily said brightly, wishing that the unaccountable lump in her throat would go away. 'If you must know the truth, he is probably very *happy* and—and *relieved* to be rid of me!'

Mr. Jillson eyed her uneasily. 'Well, I hope you are right, my dear,' he said frankly, 'for my own brief acquaintance with him has led me to the unalterable conviction that he is *not* a man I should care to have as an enemy. But I daresay I shall have the chance to see for myself how the matters stand, for I have a disagreeable notion that he has not taken the trouble to come to the theatre at this hour without the intention of turning up in the Greenroom after the performance.'

'That,' said Cecily, tilting up her chin, 'is no concern of mine, for *I* shall not be there.'

'Oh yes, you will,' Mr. Jillson retorted with unaccustomed bluntness, 'or we shall risk having the theatre pulled down about our ears! I have been talking to the managers, and they tell me that the only way they have been able to keep the peace here tonight has been by faithfully promising any number of your admirers that you will put in an appearance there as soon as ever the performance has ended.'

Nothing that Cecily could say could alter this dictum on the part of her mentors, and she was obliged to bow to the prospect of meeting Mr. Ranleigh face to face within the space of the ensuing hour. It was an event that she could not look forward to with equanimity; in fact, stark panic, which almost sent her fleeing out of the theatre, held her in its grip for several minutes. Fortunately, she was soon obliged to go onstage again, and the concentration required to carry her through her role gave her no further opportunity to dwell upon the dismaying scene to be enacted in the Greenroom upon the play's conclusion.

Mr. Ranleigh, meanwhile, sat through the remainder of the performance with an impassivity which could only be considered as praiseworthy, in view of the severe exercise of self-restraint it involved. At its conclusion he was accosted by Lord Portandrew, who demanded at once, in fulminating tones, to know why he had not put a stop to Cecily's reappearance upon the London theatrical scene.

'My dear fellow, I am not her guardian!' Mr. Ranleigh said brusquely, the ordinary pleasant drawl quite gone from his voice.

'Well, you dashed well acted as if you was when I was at Hillcourt!' his lordship retorted. 'And you told me she was gone for a governess! What's she doing here? How did she get here? Has it anything to do with Brackenridge? *He's* here tonight, you know, and looking deuced up in the world over something!'

'So I have observed,' said Mr. Ranleigh, who had, in fact, not failed to note Brackenridge's presence in the theatre and the spirits in which that gentleman appeared to be that evening—

spirits which had evidently been improved by his having wined and dined very well before the performance. 'However, I am hardly in a position to answer your questions,' he went on, 'for I have just returned from several highly unprofitable days spent searching for Miss Hadley over half of England, my imagination unfortunately boggling at the idea that she would be birdwitted enough to thrust herself into such a situation as this.'

'Oh! You have?' said Lord Portandrew, digesting this somewhat bitter statement, but rising at once to Cecily's defence. 'Well, she has been driven to it, I expect! Dashed uncomfortable business, being a governess, I daresay!' He added urgently, as Mr. Ranleigh began to move away from him, 'What are you going to do now? Can't leave her in *this* fix!'

'If she wishes to remain in it, it is hardly in my power to compel her to do otherwise.'

'No, but . . .'

'I have sent off a message to her aunt at Hillcourt,' Mr. Ranleigh said, with admirable but somewhat ominous patience. 'Until she arrives in town, neither you nor I can do more than try the effect of persuasion—which, if I know Miss Hadley, means that we shall succeed in making no impression upon her at all!'

And he thereupon walked off toward the Greenroom, leaving his cousin to follow him if he chose.

The Greenroom had already been invaded by more than a score of Miss Daingerfield-Nelson's admirers by the time they entered it, and in a few moments that young lady herself, accompanied by Mr. Jillson, made her appearance. She was still clad in the dashing gown of jonquil crape, cut somewhat indecorously low over the bosom, in which she had just left the stage, and, as she had not had time to wash the rouge from her face, presented the picture of spurious sophistication which she had once so much desired to exhibit before Mr. Ranleigh.

Not entirely to her surprise, however, she found—as her eyes immediately singled out his tall figure in the thronged room— that the picture was not one that met with his approval. As a matter of fact, he looked uncompromisingly *dis*approving—an attitude which, although she could scarcely say she had not expected it, brought a look of distinct challenge into her eyes.

Very well! she thought. If he was determined to despise her, he should have good reason! She turned a warm smile impartially upon the dozen or more gentlemen who immediately flocked to her side, receiving their compliments with an encouraging aplomb that sent Lord Portandrew struggling in dismay through the press to her.

'No, really, Miss Ha—*Daingerfield-Nelson*!' he exclaimed. 'Not at all the thing! Shouldn't be here in the first place, you know! Best let me take you home!'

'Oh—Lord Portandrew! Did *you* come to view the performance tonight? How very nice to see you again!' Cecily said, pertinaciously ignoring his protest and extending her hand to him in a friendly manner. 'I hope I find you well?'

'Yes, yes—but . . .'

'And Mr. Ranleigh?' Cecily persisted, feeling herself buoyed up by the excitement of the evening sufficiently to be able to cast a pensively provocative glance in that gentleman's direction. 'Dear me, he does not appear so! What can have occurred, I wonder, to make him look so—so very *forbidding* tonight?'

To her considerable chagrin, Mr. Ranleigh did not rise to the bait, but continued to keep his distance from the eager circle about her, regarding her much with the air of a man permitting a troublesome child to go its length in folly before taking steps at the proper moment to remove it unobtrusively from the scene. A flare of stubborn anger rose in her breast, but she continued to flirt her fan with the coquetry well practised for her role in *The Beaux' Stratagem*, attending, with what she hoped was a cool unconsciousness of Mr. Ranleigh's hard gaze, to the various gallant protests directed at her for sparing a moment of her attention to such a fellow as Portandrew.

But her poise was overset completely, within a very few instants, by the sight of Sir Harry Brackenridge strolling into the room and approaching the group around her. *His* presence in the house had not been mentioned to her, and, though she had realised, when she had first conceived the idea of returning to the theatre, that her appearance upon the stage must inevitably bring her once more to his notice, she had consoled herself with the thought that, since she now had no reason to fear his disclosures concerning her theatrical career, he could no longer be a threat to her peace.

But one glance at those cold blue eyes and lazily smiling lips assured her that she had been far too hasty in dismissing him as an important factor in her life. He came up and, bowing over her hand, lifted it gently to his lips.

'My very dear Miss—er—Daingerfield-Nelson!' he said. 'So we meet again! I gather that your uncle's health has improved sufficiently for you to leave his bedside?'

Cecily, burningly conscious under his mocking gaze of her rouged face and revealing gown, stammered some disjointed reply, endeavouring at the same time to draw away her hand. He did not immediately release it, however, and was at once challenged rather suspiciously by Lord Portandrew, who demanded to know by what right he claimed such close acquaintance with Miss Daingerfield-Nelson.

'Oh, Miss Daingerfield-Nelson and I are old friends,' Brackenridge said, his eyes quizzing her mercilessly. 'Are we not, my dear? Let me see: it has been no longer ago than a fortnight—has it?—since we had the pleasure of a most interesting tête-à-tête in Somerset.'

Cecily gave him a trapped, imploring look. She saw now that he was quite as capable of making use of his knowledge of her employment at Inglesant, with all its connotations of her relationship with the Ranleighs, to his own advantage as he had been of using his knowledge of her career in the theatre, and endeavoured helplessly to think of a way to still his tongue.

It was unnecessary. She was aware suddenly that Mr. Ranleigh, observing her embarrassment, had moved quietly across the room and was himself now addressing Brackenridge.

'Playing off your tricks, Harry?' he inquired evenly. 'Miss Hadley is an unworthy opponent for you, I fear. Had you not rather cross swords with me?'

Cecily, who had grown rather pale on perceiving his approach, gave a gasp at the sound of her true name on his lips, and turned a startled gaze upon him. He was not looking at her, however; his eyes were fixed on Brackenridge. Sir Harry, as surprised as the others—though for a different reason—to hear her addressed as Miss Hadley, laughed rather uncertainly and said, 'I wasn't aware that you considered yourself Miss Hadley's champion, Robert! But your solicitude is superfluous, I assure you. Miss Hadley need fear no tricks from *me*.'

A dozen voices interrupted to inquire why Miss Daingerfield-Nelson had suddenly acquired a new cognomen, and Cecily was appalled to hear Mr. Ranleigh say, in tones as cool as if he had been uttering the merest commonplace, 'Miss Hadley is a young relation of mine who has been foolish enough to enter upon this adventure entirely against the advice of her friends. May I be permitted to escort you home, Miss Hadley? Your aunt will be in London in a day or two, and I believe you will make her much more comfortable if you will put an end to your little performance here at once.'

Cecily, gazing up into his eyes, felt as if the blood had quite left her heart. There was nothing to be read in them but a well-controlled anger, but she could not but wonder how much it had cost his pride to make such an acknowledgement before his friends.

That he had had little choice in doing so, she could not doubt. Sir Harry's remarks had plainly shown that he would not scruple to make use of his knowledge of her background to embarrass either her or Mr. Ranleigh; and it must therefore only have been a matter of time until the information contained in Mr. Ranleigh's announcement became public property.

She swallowed a constriction in her throat and said, with determined equanimity, 'Thank you, but Mr. Jillson will see me home, Mr. Ranleigh. I should not dream of putting you to so much trouble.'

'It would be not the least trouble for *me*, my dear,' Sir Harry said. Unlike the rest of the company, who had been so startled by Mr. Ranleigh's announcement that they seemed unable to decide what tone they were now to take with her, he appeared entirely to have recovered his sang-froid, and went on to say to Mr. Ranleigh, in his languid voice, 'My dear fellow, you have done your part now: you must see that you have quite frightened off all Miss Hadley's admirers. Really, it is hardly sporting of you; you have had your chance, and should have the good grace to step aside and leave the field to others.'

He reached out and audaciously took Cecily's hand in his as he concluded—a gesture which so surprised her that for a moment she did not move, but allowed it to rest there, while her eyes flew to Mr. Ranleigh's, watching her. The expression she saw there made her colour vividly; she gave an exclamation and snatched her hand away, saying vehemently to Brackenridge, 'I do not *wish* you to take me home! I do not wish *any* of you to take me home!' She looked around, saw Mr. Jillson hovering nearby, and, feeling that the last vestiges of her self-composure were deserting her, said to him in an unsteady voice, 'If you do not take me away this instant, Mr. Jillson, I shall walk home alone, for I mean to leave here at once, whatever *you* do!'

Mr. Jillson, attempting a few hasty apologies, hurried after her as she swept from the room. He was, on the whole, inclined to believe that it was as well for both him and Miss Hadley to retreat from the scene at this point, for he had a well-developed sense of self-preservation and it appeared to him—though he had been unable to overhear the conversation in which she had been engaged—that the atmosphere was beginning to grow ominous. Sir Harry, if his experienced eye was any judge of the matter, had had just enough to drink to make him reckless without making him tipsy, and Mr. Ranleigh bore all the signs of a man who was keeping so hard a rein upon his temper that it would be wonderful if it did not make a bolt for it and escape him entirely.

Such a combination, he felt, was likely to end in an explosion in which innocent—or nearly innocent—bystanders might well be singed, and he therefore made no objection to Cecily's desire to leave the premises at once, following her out of the room with an alacrity that even that overwrought young lady found satisfactory.

CHAPTER TWENTY-THREE

Mr. Jillson's forebodings turned out to be quite correct. At eleven o'clock on the following morning, while breakfasting at the Running Boar, he received a visit from one of his colleagues at the Surrey Theatre, who had come to tell him of certain events that had taken place the night before. This communication had the effect of sending him upstairs at once to Cecily's little parlour for an interview which he prefaced with the ominous statement that the fat was now fairly in the fire.

'Good gracious, why?' Cecily asked, instantly taking alarm, and putting down the card that had accompanied the third handsome bouquet of flowers that had arrived for her that morning, each bearing the compliments of one of her noble admirers. 'Has my aunt arrived in town?'

Mr. Jillson dismissed Miss Dowie with an impatient wave of his hand. 'My good child,' he said, 'I am perfectly capable of dealing with your aunt! Mr. Ranleigh, however, is quite another matter.'

'Mr. Ranleigh?' Cecily turned rather pale. 'Why, what in the world has *he* done?'

'What he has done,' Mr. Jillson said with some asperity, 'has been to feel himself obliged to resent certain highly injudicious remarks which I am told were made by Sir Harry Brackenridge at Watier's last evening—resent them, I may say, to the extent of throwing a glass of wine into Sir Harry's face in full view of at least a dozen of his acquaintances!'

'Oh, dear!' Cecily said in a small voice. 'Were the—were the remarks about me, Mr. Jillson?'

'As I understand it—though my information, I must admit, comes to me at third hand—they were.'

'And—and what happened then?'

'What happened then, my dear young lady, was that Sir Harry called Mr. Ranleigh out!'

'Called him out! You mean—they are to fight a duel?'

'Precisely. And I should like very much to know, if you do not mind telling me—in fact, I should dashed well like to know even if you do mind!—on exactly what footing you stand with Mr. Robert Ranleigh. I thought you gave me to understand last evening that any—er—intimate connexion there might have been between you was at an end.'

Cecily's cheeks flew scarlet in a moment. 'I never gave you to understand any such thing!' she denied. 'That is—I mean— there never *was* any such connexion between us as you appear to think! I am a distant relation of his, and he and his mother were kind enough to interest themselves in finding suitable employment for me. And I should never, never have run away from them,' she added feelingly, 'if I had had the least notion that anything like *this* would happen, for I quite see now that if he and Sir Harry are to fight a duel and he is hurt, it will be all my fault.'

Mr. Jillson, considering the matter fair-mindedly, said that he could himself not quite see *that*, but added that he wished she had favoured him with a more exact account of the state of her affairs when she had first arrived in London. It was apparent that his chief concern at the moment was over whether Mr. Ranleigh's interest in his young relation would lead him to resent the part he—Jillson—had played in her return to the theatre as violently as he had taken exception to Brackenridge's remarks, and he could be brought to give little attention to Cecily's anxious questions as to what might be done to halt the projected duel beyond assuring her that such a matter was quite out of the power of either of them to arrange.

Cecily, however, could not agree to this. The shock of Mr. Jillson's announcement had left her feeling little better than a murderess, for her imagination found no difficulty in leaping forward to picture Mr. Ranleigh's lifeless body lying on the greensward, with Brackenridge standing triumphantly over him, a smoking pistol in his hand.

Casting about in her mind, when Mr. Jillson had left her, for steps she might take to avert this appalling tragedy, and rejecting as useless the notion of going at once to Mount Street and imploring Mr. Ranleigh not to meet Sir Harry, she bethought herself of Lord Portandrew. She was not inclined to be hopeful as to the quality of the advice she might receive from him, but it would be better than no advice at all, and she accordingly sat down and scribbled an urgent note to him, begging him to come round to the Running Boar at once. This she dispatched by the hand of the landlady's eldest son, a lad of thirteen, and then sat down hopefully to await Lord Portandrew's arrival.

He was not long in coming. Within the hour he was ushered up to her little parlour, looking torn between gratification at her having sent for him and rather guiltily self-conscious over what he suspected had been her motive in doing so. He made a valiant attempt at first to convince her that he knew nothing about the projected duel, but she cut him short by advising him impatiently not to take her for a perfect ninny.

'Mr. Jillson has heard of it, and if *he* has, I am sure *you* must have, as well,' she said. 'Why did Mr. Ranleigh quarrel with that odious man? Was it because of something he said about me? Mr. Jillson says he believes it was.'

'Well, as a matter of fact—he's right,' his lordship admitted reluctantly. 'Harry was a trifle foxed last night, you know—nothing you might have noticed, for he has a devilish hard head —but it made him gudgeon enough to say in Robert's hearing that he believed you was holding out for a wedding ring, but he was willing to lay a monkey he would be able to . . . Well, never mind about that!' he concluded hastily. 'And that was when Robert dashed the burgundy in his face. Already in the deuce of a temper last night, you know; Harry ought to've known better than to set his back up. Didn't like it above half, your turning up here in the theatre after he'd been chasing about after you for days on end!'

'Oh—d-did he do that?' Cecily faltered, sunk more than ever into a dismal sense of the enormity of the amount of trouble she had caused. 'I daresay he *was* dreadfully vexed . . .'

'Well—stands to reason,' Lord Portandrew said judicially. 'Very upsetting sort of thing, careering all over England looking for a girl and then coming slap on her in a theatre full of people.' He fixed her with a gaze of some severity. 'Shouldn't have done that, you know,' he said. 'Not at all the thing! If you didn't like that governess place, you'd better have married me. Don't say you might have liked that much, either, but, dash it, it'd be better than *this*!'

'No, no! Indeed, I could not!' Cecily interrupted in a stifled voice. 'I mean—of course it is very kind of you to offer, but I should not think of d-disgracing you by accepting, for I am a n-notorious woman now—oh, yes! you must know yourself that I am,' she reiterated mournfully. 'No gentleman of fashion could possibly wish to ally himself with me now!'

'Well, dash it, I don't see *that*!' Lord Portandrew objected. 'I don't say you ain't kicked up a pretty row with this notion of yours to go back on the stage, but people ain't so gothic nowadays as to expect you need have as prim a reputation as some governess in a curst dull, respectable household to marry a man of *ton*!'

She shook her head, quite unconvinced. 'But *that* does not matter now,' she went on, in determinedly steadier tones. 'My only concern now is to stop Mr. Ranleigh from meeting Sir Harry.'

'Shouldn't think you could do *that*,' his lordship said decidedly. 'Deuced stiff-necked, all the Ranleighs; not at all likely Robert will apologise to Brackenridge. Very bad *ton* to try to avoid a challenge, at any rate. Shouldn't think he'd care to show his face in town if he did.'

'But Sir Harry?' Cecily inquired anxiously. 'Could not he withdraw? If he issued the challenge . . .'

'Daresay there's nothing he'd like better, but he won't,' his lordship said promptly. 'Thing is, he's mad as fire, and he won't have time to cool down before the whole affair's over and done with. Fixed for tomorrow morning at Paddington Green, you see.'

'Tomorrow morning!' Cecily looked at him distractedly. 'Oh, I did not know it would be so soon! Do you think, perhaps, if *I* were to ask Sir Harry . . . ?'

'No!' his lordship said, a horrified expression appearing upon his face at the very thought of such an impropriety. 'Good God, you ought to know nothing about it! Besides, he's a Bad Man, Harry; likely to take any sort of advantage of you if you so much as went near him with such a cork-brained idea!' He fixed an unwontedly stern eye upon her. 'You'd best promise me you'll give *that* notion up,' he said. 'Wouldn't have a minute's peace if I went away from here thinking you still had it in your head!'

Cecily looked recalcitrant for a moment, but eventually gave in, seeing that Lord Portandrew was alarmed enough to remain indefinitely in argument with her on the subject, and agreed reluctantly that she would not attempt to approach Sir Harry.

As it developed, however, there was no need for her to do so, for Lord Portandrew had scarcely left the house before one of Sir Harry's footmen arrived with a graceful note for her from his master. He was sorry, Sir Harry wrote, that he had had to part from her in such an unsatisfactory manner on the previous evening, having been able to say nothing to her of the matter that was uppermost in his mind and heart, and he hoped she would give him the opportunity of a private conversation with her that day before she went to the theatre. The note ended with a scarcely veiled hint that she had quite mistaken the character of his present intentions, serious reflection over the past few weeks having caused him to recognise the *permanent and sacred* (the words heavily underscored) nature of his attachment to her.

For several minutes after she had perused this missive Cecily was at a loss to understand its meaning. If it had come from any man but Brackenridge, she must have believed that his intention in seeking this interview was to offer her marriage; but she could not credit such a motive in him. Far from expecting that the weeks that had passed since she had seen him at Inglesant would have caused him to form such a plan concerning her, she would rather have expected him to have spent that time in concocting some scheme to pay her out for the disappointment she had visited upon him by running off from him.

Still it was possible, she thought doubtfully, remembering Lord Portandrew's reference to Brackenridge's belief that a wedding ring was her goal, that Sir Harry was by this time so obsessed with the desire to best Mr. Ranleigh by his success with her that he might even be prepared to offer her marriage to attain his end. At any rate, the opportunity his letter held out to her to try to persuade him not to go through with his duel with Mr. Ranleigh seemed much too good to be neglected, and she therefore sat down and dashed off a reply to it, in which she merely stated that she was at home and would be happy to see him at his earliest convenience. This she sent round to him by the footman, and then sat down in considerable agitation to await his arrival.

Her agitation was not decreased by the appearance at the Running Boar, some half hour later, not of Brackenridge but of Mr. Ranleigh. She was gazing out from the parlour window, which overlooked the inn-yard, when his curricle drew up below, and, perceiving his tall figure springing down from it and striding toward the door, she at once shrank back and ran to tell the landlady to deny that she was in. Mr. Jillson, whom she encountered in the passage as she hurried back to her room, halted her to ask what all the bustle was about, and was instantly required in the most distracted of whispers to be silent.

'It is Mr. Ranleigh!' she hissed. 'He *must* be got rid of at once, before Sir Harry arrives, for if they meet here they may quarrel again, and then *nothing* can prevent them from fighting that dreadful duel!'

'I should think nothing would prevent them even if they don't meet,' Mr. Jillson said candidly. 'But what are you up to, my dear? Brackenridge coming here, you say? Why, if I may make bold to inquire, should he come?'

'Oh, hush, *pray!*' Cecily implored, listening tensely to discover if the landlady's representations would satisfy Mr. Ranleigh that she was indeed not in the house. She could not distinguish what was being said below, but a few minutes later the front door closed and she heard the landlady's heavy tread on the stairs.

She was the bearer of a note from Mr. Ranleigh. Cecily, unfolding it, saw at a glance that it was both businesslike and brief. 'Miss Hadley,' it read: 'I am in expectation of Miss Dowie's arrival in Mount Street by tomorrow morning. She will call upon you here immediately, and will hope to find you in. I have just come from seeing the managers of the Surrey Theatre, and may inform you that your engagement there has been terminated. Yours, etc., Ranleigh.'

This last sentence drew an indignant gasp from her. 'Oh!' she exclaimed, colour flying into her cheeks. 'Of all the abominable, highhanded . . . !'

'What's he done?' Mr. Jillson inquired forebodingly, taking the precaution of dismissing the landlady as he did so.

'He says he has seen the managers of the theatre and I am not to be employed there any longer!' Cecily said, with strong feeling. 'It is exactly like him—but he need not think he can order my life as if I were a child, merely because I am related to him! I daresay the Surrey is not the only theatre in London, and even if he is so odious as to make it impossible for me to obtain an engagement here, *you* will be able to inform me how I must go about it to find employment in some theatre outside of London!'

Mr. Jillson, who was beginning to give the impression of a man with an unhappy conviction that he had been drawn unawares into a situation presenting a considerably greater number of dangerous pitfalls than he had ever bargained for, opined tentatively that, if a gentleman as rich and influential as Mr. Ranleigh had a mind to look after her affairs—without, he added obliquely, making those demands upon her which a gentleman might well insist on in such a case—she was a fool not to allow him to do so.

'Demands!' Cecily repeated wrathfully. 'But of course he will make demands! He wishes to marry me!'

Mr. Jillson turned a positively thunderstruck countenance upon her. 'Marry you!' he exclaimed. 'Ranleigh wishes to marry you? And you're thinking of refusing him? If you will pardon my speaking frankly, my dear, in that case you *are* a fool! Why, you would be rich and important beyond your wildest dreams...'

'He doesn't care for me in the least,' Cecily said in a small, gruff voice, her anger cooling as she considered the dismal realities of the situation. 'And, besides, it is very likely that I am mistaken about his wishing to marry me *now*, after what happened last night, and all he means to do is to remove me from a position of notoriety and provide for me in some—some retired place where I will not be an embarrassment to him any longer.'

She found this such a depressing prospect that for a few moments she failed to realise that voices were again emanating from the hall below, and came to herself with a start only at the sound of tones that were unmistakably Brackenridge's.

'Oh! It is Sir Harry!' she said, in a flurry. 'You *will* leave us alone, won't you, Mr. Jillson? For I *may* be able to persuade him...'

'If you believe he'll heed any tears or prayers of *yours*, you are fair and far out!' Mr. Jillson said bluntly. 'Take my advice, my dear, and have nothing to do with him.'

'Oh, *pray*!' Cecily interrupted, hearing Brackenridge's step upon the stairs. 'I *must* speak to him; it's of the greatest importance! Don't you see?'

Mr. Jillson did not seem to see in the least, but, as he appeared to have certain matters upon his own mind that required immediate and serious cogitation, he withdrew in the face of Cecily's pleas, leaving that young lady to whisk herself into her room and the next moment, at the sound of a knock upon the door, turn with a start and utter a rather breathless, 'Come in!'

CHAPTER TWENTY-FOUR

Brackenridge entered the room at once. He found Cecily seated primly in the chair into which she had flung herself the moment before, regarding him with a somewhat fluctuating smile.

'Oh! Sir Harry!' she said, allowing him to take her hand and watching rather warily as he smilingly bent to kiss it. 'How —how very kind of you to have come so quickly!'

'But what else could I do, when I was so fortunate as to receive an invitation from you?' Brackenridge said lightly, searching her face with a quizzing glance, as if he hoped to read in it the reason for this new complaisance in her manner toward him. She blushed—a sign of confusion that appeared to satisfy him. She saw quite clearly, from the cynical light in his eye, that he believed it was the hint of marriage in his note that had caused her to agree to see him, and had to grit her teeth against the desire to inform him just how mistaken he was in this belief.

She invited him to sit down, however, with as much cordiality as she could command, attempting to conceal her discomposure when he at once drew up a chair quite close to her own and calmly possessed himself of both her hands.

'Now, my dear,' he said, 'shall we come to an understanding? —for I believe it was for that purpose that you agreed to see me, and it is certainly for that purpose that I have come here. You find yourself—do you not?—in the awkward position of a young woman whose relations do not at all see eye to eye with her as to her future course in life. If it were not so, I should not presume to address you in this sudden manner . . .'

He broke off as Cecily, showing more than a little discomposure at this very direct approach, drew her hands away and jumped up, retreating to the window.

'Indeed, I do not know what you are talking of, sir!' she said, sparring for time. 'My—my relations? Do you mean my aunt?'

'I have not the pleasure of that lady's acquaintance,' Brackenridge said, watching her flurried countenance with his usual air of rather mocking composure, 'but let us include her in the list, if you like. I was speaking more particularly, however, of Robert Ranleigh.'

'Mr. Ranleigh? Oh—yes, of course!' Cecily drew a deep breath and decided, in the absence of the appearance of any inclination on Brackenridge's part to be diverted from his main purpose, to employ an equivalent directness. 'That—that is exactly what I should like to speak to you about, sir!' she declared. 'That is—what I mean to say is—Sir Harry, *must* you fight that horrid duel with him?'

A somewhat arrested expression suddenly appeared upon Brackenridge's face. 'How came you to know of that?' he inquired abruptly.

'I—someone told me. It does not matter.' She hurried on, throwing caution and truthfulness alike to the winds, 'Of course it was quite odious of him to do what he did, but—but he is said to be a dead shot, and I cannot bear to think that you should expose yourself . . .'

Sir Harry, digesting with difficulty, it appeared, this evidence of concern for his welfare, gave her another rather hard glance, but could read nothing in her face but the real distress she could not keep from appearing there.

'Why,' he said slowly, after a moment, 'that is not a matter that need trouble you, my dear.'

'Yes, but it does!' Cecily interrupted fervently. 'Indeed I shall never be able to forgive myself if anything dreadful comes of it! I am sure Mr. Ranleigh can be the most disagreeable man alive when it pleases him to be, but I daresay it was not entirely his fault that he was out of temper last night, for he had been searching everywhere for me for days, it seems, and—and I expect it was really *me* he would have liked to do something horrid to, only he could not, and so it happened to be you instead.'

She paused hopefully, for a sudden laugh had escaped Sir Harry, erasing the wary expression his face had worn.

'Searching for you for days!' he repeated. 'So that was it, was it? Let me tell you, my dear, that Robert Ranleigh is not at all accustomed to finding females fleeing from him! I daresay it must have been quite a new experience for him. What had he done to make you run away?'

'N-nothing! Only—I did not at all care to see him . . .'

'Well, you need trouble yourself over him no further, I assure you! From now on it will be my pleasure to guard you from his importunities.'

'But you will not be able to guard me if he shoots you,' Cecily pointed out urgently. 'Indeed, I think it will be much, much better if you will go to see him and tell him that you understand now that it was quite my fault that he behaved toward you as he did last night, and so he need not fight a duel with you, after all.'

'What! Cry craven to him? No, I think not!' Brackenridge said, with a rather ugly little laugh. He approached her and, taking one of her hands in his, imprinted a light kiss upon it. 'I am touched, however, by your solicitude!' he said. 'May I hope it portends that you will look favourably on what I am about to propose to you? No, don't give me your answer yet!' he said, halting her as she was about to open her lips to utter a hasty demur. 'Let me explain. Your situation is such that the usual courses to be followed in such a case as this cannot apply. You are, as I have said, in the hands of your relations, and I fear that, especially after what occurred last evening, Ranleigh at least will never agree to a closer connexion between us. It would be useless for me to speak of my feeling for you to him—and *his* influence, I must believe, will be paramount in any decision that is made concerning your future. That is why I must propose to you that you take your destiny into your own hands and fly with me . . .'

He paused, seeing that the expression on her face had altered suddenly. She was no longer looking at him with an air of obstinate alarm, but on the contrary appeared quite dazedly happy.

'Fly with you!' she repeated, her air that of a young lady who had suddenly been presented with her dearest wish .'Why, yes! Of course! The very thing!'

'Do you think so?' Sir Harry inquired, looking rather stunned himself at the enthusiasm with which his suggestion had been received.

Cecily turned a dazzling smile upon him. 'Oh, yes! I should like it above all things!' she assured him. 'Only it must be to-night, you know, for I dare not wait . . .'

'My dear girl,' Sir Harry interrupted her indulgently, 'you have made me the happiest of men, but surely there is no need for quite so much haste! You may have forgotten that I have a most urgent appointment tomorrow morning.'

'Yes, but there *is* need!' Cecily protested, calling up an expression of histrionic disappointment to her face that would have gladdened Mr. Jillson's heart. 'My aunt, you see, is to arrive in town in the morning, and if she finds me here she will take me away and then I shall never see you again! We *must* leave tonight!'

Sir Harry, who had not bargained for such ardour on Miss Hadley's part, looked thoughtful. An experienced man, something warned him against accepting it at face value; a cynical one, his scepticism as to the genuineness of her sudden affection for him merely assured him that it had been caused by the fact that the chit was grasping at the idea of becoming Lady Brackenridge. That he had adroitly contrived to give her the impression that she was to receive that title through lawful matrimony without committing himself to the least promise to that effect he considered one of the minor triumphs of his amatory career, and he was, in fact, so much pleased by his success that his usual cold judgment was somewhat led astray.

Also, her desire that their elopement be carried out at once had much to recommend it in his eyes. Only the wine-induced recklessness Mr. Jillson had noted on the previous night, coupled with the insulting provocation with which Mr. Ranleigh had countered his remarks concerning Cecily, had been able to overcome his customary prudent rule against entering upon an affair of honour in which his own safety would be in jeopardy. He had issued his challenge to Ranleigh in the white heat of anger, and ever since that anger had had time to cool had been casting about in his mind for some reason he could allege for withdrawing from the affair without becoming an object of opprobrium or ridicule to his acquaintance.

And now Cecily's suggestion of an immediate flight appeared to offer him that reason. Say that, he argued to himself, he carried the girl off to France and installed her as his mistress there: while he sojourned pleasantly in Paris with her, he might be assured that the news of his having boldly snatched her away from under Ranleigh's nose would turn the tide of ridicule so sharply against his rival that the fact that he himself had failed to appear upon the field of honour might be all but overlooked. The whole town knew that their dispute had been over Miss Hadley, and his emerging the victor in this matter must certainly be taken into account in the town's tattle concerning the affair.

And then *this* solution to his problem had the inestimable advantage of offering him both the girl and the safety of his own skin—neither of which he could be sure of if he went through with his engagement on the following morning. If Ranleigh were even to succeed in wounding him, it would be impossible for him to make the least push to carry the girl off for days, perhaps for weeks, and in the meantime she would certainly be removed from London by her aunt and he would have the devil's own time of it to come at her again.

All in all, he decided abruptly, he would be a fool if he did not close with the opportunity that was being offered him. The chit was willing—or she was willing, at any rate, to go posting off to a Gretna Green marriage, which it would be time enough to explain to her was not what he had in mind when it was too late for her to turn back—and all that was needed to change the next twenty-four hours of his life from an appalling nightmare to a highly gratifying amorous adventure was his own resolution to carry the scheme through.

He accordingly informed Cecily in satisfactorily loverlike terms that her wish was his law: the elopement should take place that very night. Rapid plans were made: she could not leave the Running Boar, she told him, until after the Jillsons had left for the theatre that evening, for she did not doubt that they would try to stop her if they knew of her purpose; and Brackenridge agreed that it would be more prudent for them to wait until darkness had fallen before setting out. A hired post-chaise, he added, rather than his own travelling-carriage, would take her up at the appointed time, so that his connexion with her flight would not be evident, and he would accompany the chaise on horseback for the first stage, rather than riding with her in it, as an added precaution against their being seen together in town.

He then took his leave, having possessed himself in parting of a kiss which Cecily, for all her desire to appear properly eager, could bring herself to receive only with excessive reluctance, and left her to face with some misgiving the consequences of the imbroglio into which she had so impulsively flung herself.

She had indeed, on first hearing Sir Harry's proposal that she elope with him, thought of nothing but the fact that here, come miraculously to her hand, was a way for her to get him out of town and so prevent his duel with Mr. Ranleigh on the following morning. Every other consideration had, for the moment, appeared of no consequence beside the paramount one of saving Mr. Ranleigh from injury and perhaps even from death, and it did not fully occur to her in just how awkward a situation she had placed herself until she was able to sit down and consider the matter quietly.

At the least, she realised then, she must engage to spend the better part of the night in apparent acquiescence with Sir Harry's plan to carry her off to Scotland—for she never doubted that Gretna Green was to be their destination—before she could risk telling him that she had no wish to become his wife: otherwise it would be possible for him to retrace his course in time to carry out his engagement to meet Mr. Ranleigh at Paddington Green. That such a deception would strain her histrionic powers to the utmost, she could not doubt. But worse than that was the misgiving she felt as to Sir Harry's reaction when he learned the truth. He would be very angry, of course—but, after all, she told herself, plucking up her courage, he could not force her to accompany him against her will on a lengthy journey, most of it to be accomplished in the full light of day on public roads. She must surely be able to induce him to allow her to return to London, however enraged he might become at her sudden change of heart.

What she would do when she did reach London again she had no idea, nor had she the leisure to examine that problem at the moment. If her aunt were to seek her out in the morning, as Mr. Ranleigh had informed her that she would, she must, of course, act as she bid her; if, on the other hand, Miss Dowie did not appear, doubtless the Jillsons would assist her in finding some new employment in the theatre.

But at least, she told herself, with a sudden lump rising in her throat, no one would any longer see marriage with Mr. Ranleigh as the solution to her problem, once she had disgraced herself not only by a notorious reappearance on the London stage, but also by spending the better part of a night travelling in company with Sir Harry Brackenridge.

CHAPTER TWENTY-FIVE

Nine o'clock, the hour appointed for her to leave the house, seemed to her to arrive with fatal swiftness. She had half-hoped, half-dreaded that a return visit from Mr. Ranleigh, or perhaps the reappearance of Mr. Jillson with some new plan to propose for the continuance of her theatrical career, might make it impossible for her to go through with the elopement; but neither of these events had occurred. Mr. Jillson, in fact, did not turn up at the Running Boar even when the dinner hour had arrived, and as for Mr. Ranleigh, he had no hope that any interference of his, before Miss Dowie's arrival, would have the slightest effect in diverting Miss Hadley's resolution to engage in any harebrained schemes she might be concocting for the future.

Cecily was therefore quite at liberty at nine o'clock, after having partaken of dinner with Mrs. Jillson, before the latter left for the theatre, and parried as well as she could her curious questions concerning Mr. Ranleigh's interference in her theatrical career, to let herself out the front door, portmanteau in hand, and walk from the inn-yard toward the post-chaise discreetly waiting just beyond.

Her resolution came close to failing, however, when she saw the mounted figure beside it, and only by calling up once more that vivid mental picture of Mr. Ranleigh lying wounded or dying on Paddington Green could she steel herself to continuing on down the street and entering the chaise.

It was of some assistance to her resolution that Brackenridge himself did not dismount to hand her in, but remained at a little distance. But she could not hope that this arrangement would continue beyond their first halt, and for some minutes, as the chaise jolted over the cobblestoned streets, she strove to gather her disordered thoughts and plan what her behaviour toward him would be when he came to ride beside her.

As she was quite unfamiliar with the intricacies of the London streets, she at first paid little heed to the route the chaise took, merely assuming that it was heading in the direction of the Great North Road, which she knew they must traverse on their journey to Scotland. But presently, rousing herself to peer from the window, she was astonished to see the gleam of water beneath and to find that they were crossing a wide bridge. It was the Thames that lay below—there could be no doubt of that—and even in her ignorance of London she was aware that they could not therefore be driving north. In fact, as she continued to gaze out the window in growing bewilderment, she recognised some of the landmarks she had seen when she had journeyed to and from Hillcourt, and she became convinced that they were taking the same road south that she had ridden over on those occasions.

For some time indignation superseded alarm in her mind. Even with her imperfect knowledge of the world, she knew that she, a minor, without the consent of her guardian, could not possibly be married in England, and that therefore, if Sir Harry indeed did not intend to take her north to Scotland, he could not have matrimony in mind.

But as the horses galloped on down the road, the chaise jolting and swaying with their speed as the city was left behind, she began to be more frightened. She had counted on Sir Harry's behaving with proper circumspection toward his future bride, which would have meant that she would have nothing to fear but a kiss or an embrace until sufficient time had elapsed for her to be able to tell him that she had changed her mind and wished to return to London. But if he did not intend marriage, her case was infinitely more serious. He might, in fact, she thought, have it in mind to take her to some secluded spot only a short distance from London, in which case not only would she have failed to help Mr. Ranleigh—since Brackenridge would then have ample time to return for his engagement at Paddington Green before morning—but she would herself face a far greater peril than she had ever bargained for.

What was she to do? If she were to jump out from the chaise at the first halt and demand to be taken back to London, she would have gained nothing by all she had risked; if, on the other hand, she remained silent, she might be plunging herself into the greatest danger. She was in a state of miserable indecision, and the result was that when the chaise had rattled into the courtyard of an inn which she recognised as the Greyhound at Croydon, where she and her aunt and Lady Frederick had changed horses on their journey to Hillcourt, she said nothing at all to Sir Harry when he opened the door of the chaise, but only regarded him with a highly unfriendly expression upon her face.

'My dear girl, you look deucedly upset!' Brackenridge said, smiling at her. 'What is the matter? Can I procure some refreshment for you? A glass of wine . . . ?'

'No, you cannot!' Cecily said, finding her tongue as she continued to regard him with a smouldering gaze. 'And you know very well what the matter is! You are not taking me to Scotland! This road goes south!'

'I am aware,' Brackenridge said composedly, getting into the chaise beside her and closing the door. 'However, I believe I did not mention Scotland to you, my sweet. I have a dislike to being married over the anvil—such a commonplace and even rather vulgar proceeding, don't you agree? They order—as Mr. Sterne puts it—this matter better in France.'

'In France!' Cecily's eyes flew wide. 'Is *that* where you are taking me?'

'Yes. Should you dislike it? Most girls would not, I feel sure. My yacht lies at Newhaven; we shall arrive there before morning, and then—a short voyage, a pleasant glimpse of the French countryside, and you will be in Paris, where we shall make it our first business to search the smartest shops for a wardrobe more fitting for your unusual beauty . . .'

'*I* should think you would make it your first business to find a clergyman who would agree to marry us—*if* there is such a one to be found!' Cecily said, quite unmollified by the alluring picture Sir Harry had drawn of the prospect before her. 'I don't believe you ever intended to marry me!'

Sir Harry smiled, but with a somewhat pained expression upon his face. 'My dear, pray acquit me . . .' he began, and possessed herself of one of her slender gloved hands, which she immediately snatched away.

'*Did* you?'

'My dear, really you must not be so blunt,' Sir Harry protested, looking amused. 'I assure you, it does not become you. Having cast yourself upon my protection, you are hardly in a position to be making peremptory demands, you know.'

He spoke lightly, but she saw his eyes through the half-darkness, and the expression in them was not one that gave her comfort. At the same instant the post-boy appeared at the carriage window to inform him that the change had been made and they were ready to start, and Sir Harry at once directed him to drive on. A moment later the chaise was rattling out of the inn-yard, and Cecily was left tête-à-tête with Sir Harry inside.

She turned to him, her eyes flashing indignantly. 'I have not said that you may take me any further, Sir Harry!' she said. 'I wish you will order the chaise to be stopped at once!'

Brackenridge shrugged. 'What? And expose ourselves to the curiosity of every gaping ostler and post-boy in the inn-yard? I think not, my dear. We shall be able to talk far more comfortably here.'

'I don't wish to talk to you! And I am *not* going to France with you!'

Mr. Ranleigh's claims on her were by this time quite forgotten; she was seriously alarmed, and if she could have done so without running the risk of breaking a leg, would have jumped from the chaise at that instant. But Brackenridge only laughed at the indignant expression upon her face.

'Oh, come!' he rallied her. 'It is not so bad as that, you know. I daresay we shall deal famously together. I am a generous fellow when my heart is touched—which I am sure you will know how to do, my dear—and when you have once lost this foolish fancy for what the world calls respectability, you will see that your position is really not an unenviable one. Marriage would be a very dull ending for such a creature as you . . .'

'Well, there is one thing you had as well know, and that is that I would rather marry a *toad* than marry *you*,' Cecily declared, goaded beyond endurance by his complacent air. 'But I never dreamed that was not what you had in mind when you asked me to come away with you—never!—and if you believe now that you can offer me a *carte blanche* . . .'

'One moment!' Sir Harry's face, which had darkened slightly at her declaration, came closer to hers as he gripped her wrist and bent his head the better to read her countenance. 'I think you had best explain yourself, my girl!' he said rather harshly. 'You had no idea of marrying me when you came away with me? How is this?'

Cecily, appalled by her indiscretion in having so nearly given away the true reason for her pretended elopement, reconsidered hastily. 'Yes—no!' she said disjointedly. 'It does not signify! I do not wish to marry you *now*, at any rate!'

'On the contrary, I think it signifies a great deal,' Sir Harry said, still scrutinising her averted face, while his grasp tightened even more securely upon her wrist. 'What kind of game are you playing with me, my pet? You don't wish to be my wife, you say—or my mistress, either—and yet you have come away with me . . .'

'I—I have changed my mind!' Cecily said desperately. 'Perhaps I *did*—wish to marry you—before . . .'

Brackenridge gave a short laugh. 'And it had to be tonight that we left London—did it not?' he said. 'Now I wonder why you found such haste necessary?' He suddenly released her wrist and both his hands came up ungently to grip her shoulders. 'Why, you little vixen!' he said, from between clenched teeth. 'You thought you would make a laughing-stock of me—did you? Lure me out of town so that I shouldn't be able to meet Ranleigh and then run off and leave me standing like a fool . . .'

'Let me go!' Cecily exclaimed, struggling to free herself from his grasp. 'You are—you are *quite* mistaken!'

'Oh, no!' Brackenridge said, with an unpleasant grin. '*You* are the one who is mistaken, my girl, to think you could gull me as easily as that! You have changed your mind, you say. Well, it seems that I have changed mine, too. I shall not take you to France, my sweet. We shall do very well for the night at an inn I know not five miles from here, where they are not fond of asking questions of the Quality, and which is not so far from Paddington Green that I shall not be able to keep my engagement in the morning . . . What the *devil* . . . !'

This last exclamation was caused by the sudden flashing by at breakneck speed outside the window of a curricle-and-four, followed immediately by a confusion of sounds—the swearing of post-boys, the terrified plunging of horses, and the harsh grating of wheels—and by the jolting halt of the vehicle in which they were riding. Cecily and Sir Harry were flung violently back into their seats as the chaise rocked on its protesting springs; before they had had time to recover themselves, the door was wrenched open and Mr. Ranleigh appeared in the aperture.

'I thought no one but you would be so imprudent as to spring hired horses in the dark in this neck-or-nothing fashion, Brackenridge!' he said in a voice of ominous calm. 'They told me at the Greyhound that you seemed to be in the devil of a hurry.'

'Mr. Ranleigh!' Cecily exclaimed, finding her voice before Brackenridge could recover his, and tumbling out of the chaise into her rescuer's arms without waiting for the steps to be let down. 'Oh, how *glad* I am to see you! *Pray* take me back to London with you! You would not *believe* what this horrid man intends . . .'

'On the contrary, I am quite certain that I *should* believe it,' Mr. Ranleigh said, depositing her safely upon the ground, his hands lingering upon her shoulders as he looked her over. She saw in some dismay that, in spite of the coolness of his manner, there was a fine-drawn look on his face and an oddly dangerous light in his eyes that she had never seen there before.

'I trust you have suffered no harm, Miss Hadley?' he inquired.

'Oh, no! Only it turns out he never meant in the least to take me to Gretna Green—and he said first that he intended to carry me off to France and then that he would take me to an inn near here . . .' Cecily explained, incoherently. She added darkly, 'Not that I ever intended to marry *him*, for a more odious, *scheming* person . . .'

'If we are to talk of schemes, my dear,' Brackenridge interrupted in a chill voice, as he in turn descended from the chaise, 'I believe *you* must carry off the honours. Tell me, was it your own idea to lure me off so that I should not be able to keep my engagement at Paddington Green in the morning, or were you handsomely paid for playing your little game? You will pardon me, Robert,' he went on, turning sardonically to Mr. Ranleigh, 'for having the bad taste to imply that it can scarcely have been chance alone that led you here. But has not your arrival come a trifle prematurely? You should have waited until you were quite certain I should not be able to meet you at Paddington before you came so nobly to Miss Hadley's rescue.'

He broke off, observing that the two post-boys, having succeeded in quieting the frightened horses, and Mr. Ranleigh's groom, Sivil, standing at the heads of his master's own team, were all three highly interested spectators to the scene going forward in the road. This circumstance, however, appeared to mean nothing to Cecily, for she said at once, indignantly, 'Indeed you are quite mistaken! Mr. Ranleigh knew nothing of what I intended to do!' She turned to Mr. Ranleigh, puzzlement in her eyes. 'But how *did* you find us here?' she asked.

'Your friend Jillson was good enough to give me a hint of what he suspected was going forward,' Mr. Ranleigh said, his eyes never leaving Brackenridge's face. 'He seems to have a healthy respect for the influence he believes me capable of exerting against him if any harm were to come to you, to say nothing of an unalterable attachment to what is vulgarly known as hard cash.'

'Yes, but I still do not see . . . *He* did not know where Sir Harry was taking me.'

228

'No, he did not,' Mr. Ranleigh said. 'However, after he had left me, I took the precaution of setting Sivil on the watch in Half Moon Street, and when he found Sir Harry hiring a post-chaise-and-four, and learned that the post-boys had been hired as far as Newhaven, he brought me word. Fortunately, I keep my own horses stabled on the Brighton post-road, so I had little doubt I should be able to overtake hired cattle.' He added, with such obvious contempt in his voice that Brackenridge stiffened under the words as perceptibly as if he had been struck, 'I must say, Harry, that you surprised me. I had not seriously believed that you would run from our engagement or I should have taken more certain precautions against your being able to carry Miss Hadley off.'

Sir Harry forced a laugh. 'I have not run yet!' he said insultingly. 'The jade has her own tale of Gretna Green, but she knew as well as I, when she embarked on this adventure, that what I had in mind was no more than a night's pleasure at an inn very near here . . .'

He got no further, for Mr. Ranleigh, with a useful right to the jaw, sent him sprawling into the middle of the road, and then proceeded to stand over him with the air of a man having every intention of concluding the business he had begun by the administration of a sound thrashing as soon as Sir Harry should have regained his feet. Cecily jumped and clapped her hands, and the post-boys, setting up a cheer at the prospect of a mill, slid from their horses for a better view of the proceedings.

It was too much for Sir Harry. He had been gulled by a chit of a girl into leaving London on a wild-goose chase that threatened not only to tarnish his reputation but to give him no opportunity of turning the situation into ridicule against his opponent by carrying off the girl who had been the cause of the quarrel between them. He had been knocked down by Mr. Ranleigh in full view of several interested spectators, and it was quite apparent that he would not be allowed to depart now without further punishments being visited upon him. Staring up into his rival's face from his humiliatingly recumbent position on the ground, Sir Harry lost his head completely, and, before anyone had the least idea of what he was about to do, he had struggled to a sitting position, pulled a silver-mounted pistol from his coat, and discharged it pointblank at Mr. Ranleigh.

Fortunately his hasty aim, from such a position, was far from perfect. Cecily, starting violently at the deafening report, closed her eyes for a panic-stricken moment; when she opened them again she saw, with overwhelming relief, that Mr. Ranleigh was still standing on his feet, looking down curiously at his right sleeve.

'Well, I'm damned!' he remarked, softly and reflectively.

Sivil, hastily confiding his team to the care of one of the post-boys, came running up, wrath and concern on his face.

'Mr. Robert, Mr. Robert—are you hurt?' he cried.

'No, no—the ball merely grazed me,' Mr. Ranleigh replied. He was looking at Brackenridge, who, his face livid in the pale light of the moon, had picked himself up and was regarding him with an expression of mingled hatred and apprehension in his eyes. 'You really are a paltry creature, Harry,' Mr. Ranleigh said to him, in a gently contemptuous voice. 'Odd—I never knew quite how paltry until this very moment.'

The post-boy standing at his horses' heads gave it as his opinion that coves as shot off pistols at other coves ought to be taken up by the constable, and announced his entire willingness to ride back to Croydon for the purpose of procuring the services of one of those useful individuals at once. Mr. Ranleigh, however, did not encourage him in this undertaking. He had drawn a handkerchief from his pocket and, handing it to Sivil, requested him to tie it about his arm.

'Oh, you *are* hurt!' Cecily cried. She turned to Brackenridge, her face kindling. 'You are no better than a murderer, to shoot an unarmed man!' she accused him. 'The post-boy is quite right! You *should* be brought before a magistrate at once, and all of us here will give evidence against you . . .'

'I think,' Mr. Ranleigh interrupted, addressing Brackenridge in the same cool, dispassionate voice, 'yes, I *really* think you had best carry out your plan to go to France, Harry. As you see, you may find England rather uncomfortable for some time to come, for I fear you cannot completely rely on the discretion of all the persons who have witnessed this little affair.' Sir Harry attempted to speak, but Mr. Ranleigh, his voice hardening slightly, cut him off. 'I am in earnest; you had best go,' he said shortly. 'You flatter me if you believe that *my* temper may not lead me to commit actions quite as imprudent as yours if you remain in my sight for another thirty seconds. If you can prevail on these fellows to take you up again and to bear still tongues in their heads about what has happened here, you will have done as much as you are able for yourself, I believe.'

Cecily, watching him in some awe, saw that, behind the calm with which he had accepted Brackenridge's foolhardy action, the dangerous look that had been upon his face when he had first halted the chaise was rising again. Brackenridge, too, appeared to sense the fact that he had best leave the scene while it was still possible for him to do so with a comparatively whole skin, and, with an oath, turned and mounted into the chaise. At this point the scene achieved an absurd anticlimax when Cecily, suddenly realising that her portmanteau was still in that vehicle, halted his departure by demanding its retrieval. When this had been accomplished, and Sir Harry had convinced the still re- luctant post-boys, by dint of flinging a couple of guineas at them, that they should mount their horses once more, the door of the chaise was closed upon him and the horses were finally set in motion.

Meanwhile, Sivil, who had taken the curricle in charge once more, had drawn it to the side of the road and stood waiting at the leaders' heads. Cecily was left standing alone with Mr. Ranleigh. She turned to him remorsefully.

'I am afraid it was quite all my fault,' she said, 'but indeed I meant it only for the best! I did not want Sir Harry to shoot you—and now he has done it anyway, and without giving you the least chance to defend yourself! Had you not best go to some inn at once, where you can have your wound dressed?'

Mr. Ranleigh, however, assured her that this was not neces- sary. It seemed to her that there was an unusual constraint in his manner toward her; she felt that her apology had been rebuffed, and was beginning in some mortification to move toward the curricle when he halted her by saying abruptly, 'One moment, Miss Hadley. There is something I wish you will oblige me by telling me. You said, I believe, that you had no intention of marrying Brackenridge when you set off with him this evening. What then was your reason for going with him?'

His eyes were searching her face so keenly that she did not know how to answer him. She began to speak, faltered, and was dismayed to see his face harden suddenly as he said rather roughly, 'I see. You need not answer me, of course, if it embarrasses you to do so. I should not have believed, though, that even a girl as inexperienced as you are would have been so foolish as to stake her reputation on the promises of a man like Brackenridge . . .'

'Oh!' Cecily said, finding her tongue and her indignation at the same moment. 'As if I should ever, for a single moment, have thought of marrying him! Or of—of going off with him without marrying him! If it had not been for that horrid duel, I should never have agreed even to *see* him again!'

Mr. Ranleigh had turned away, but his eyes, as she spoke, again went quickly to her face. What he saw there appeared suddenly to lift the cloud that had darkened his own countenance, but he said to her in the same hard tone, as if he did not trust himself to abandon it as yet, 'You would have me believe, then, that it was as Harry said, and your only intention was to lure him out of town in concern for my safety? Or am I perhaps flattering myself, and it was for *his* safety that you feared?'

Her eyes flashed at him through the darkness. 'If you dare to say such a thing to me again, I shall hit you!' she declared. 'He is the most odious, abominable . . .'

'And yet you have accepted expensive gifts from him, it appears.'

She gasped. '*What!* Oh—the diamond ear-drops! I do not know how you came to know about *that*, but he forced them upon me at Inglesant—he said that if I did not take them, he would let them fall to the ground for anyone to discover, and that then there must be explanations . . .' She paused, looking at him ominously. 'I *am* going to hit you!' she announced. 'You don't believe me!'

A smile suddenly lit his eyes. 'Oh yes, I believe you!' he said ruefully. 'If it were not true, I am sure you would have concocted a far more plausible tale to tell me—something of the sort that you devised to lead Harry off on this wild-goose chase tonight! Give me leave to tell you, Miss Hadley, that you are an unprincipled, meddlesome brat, and if you had come by your deserts you would even now be reaping the consequences of your harebrained interference in a matter that was no concern of yours. And, to crown it all, I daresay you consider I should be grateful to you, after you have put me through as anxious a pair of hours tonight as any I have yet been obliged to experience!'

'I do not consider that at all,' she said stiffly, trying to hold back the rush of tears that his words had unaccountably called up. 'I—I am aware that I have been very troublesome to you, but I *could* not wish you to be killed . . . And now I am tired to death,' she ended, on a note of desperation, 'and I do not at all care to talk any more about it tonight! *Pray* let us go back to London!'

She saw that he was looking down at her with an expression upon his face which she had never seen there before, and which for some reason made her heart jump in her breast in such a very odd manner that she felt for the moment quite unable to breathe. But, to her immense relief, he only said after a moment, in a much more cheerful voice, 'Very well. It will not do for us to remain standing here in the road, at any rate.' He added, as he escorted her to the curricle, 'I am taking you to Mount Street, by the way. Your aunt arrived there this evening with my mother, shortly before I set out; they will both be anxious to see you.'

This information was not calculated to soothe her already much tried nerves, but she felt there was nothing she could say that would have the least effect upon his decision, and therefore allowed herself to be handed up into the curricle in silence. He mounted up beside her and took the reins, his injury apparently being slight enough not to prevent him from driving, and Sivil, letting go the leaders' heads, expertly swung himself up behind as the curricle started forward.

Fortunately, in Sivil's presence Mr. Ranleigh did not seem disposed to enter into any further conversation on the events of the evening, and when they arrived in Croydon shortly afterward his regard for the impropriety of her driving alone in a gentleman's company in an open carriage at that time of night led him to halt at the Greyhound and hire a post-chaise there to carry her the remainder of the way to London. Shut up in this vehicle in solitary state, with Mr. Ranleigh driving his curricle behind her, she then had ample opportunity to consider the dismal state of her affairs, with her employment gone, her reputation in shreds, and her aunt and Lady Frederick doubtlessly awaiting her in Mount Street in highly justifiable indignation.

But, strangely enough, it was none of these matters that occupied her thoughts most disturbingly during the remainder of her journey. Rather, it was that disquieting look in Mr. Ranleigh's eyes as he had stood gazing down at her on the dark road.

What that look portended she could only conjecture, but those conjectures were enough to bring the warm blood to her face and the unnerving suspicion to her mind that, in spite of everything she had done to put herself beyond any gentleman's feeling obliged to consider himself the guardian of her reputation, he might still not have relinquished the plans concerning her future that had sent her fleeing from Hillcourt.

This suspicion was strengthened when, on their arriving in Mount Street, he brushed aside all the importunate questions and expressions of concern for his injury with which he was greeted by Miss Dowie and Lady Frederick, and, tarrying only for the briefest of explanations to them, swept her off into the library and closed the door decisively behind him. Cecily found herself, in a highly flushed and discomposed state, confronting a gentleman with a most disturbing glint in his eyes, who stood with his back resting against the door in a manner which suggested that he had no intention of allowing her egress from it until he had said all that he had to say to her.

234

She put up her chin in a rather forlorn attempt at defiance.

'This is quite—*quite* unnecessary, sir!' she said. 'I have nothing at all to say to you—and I beg you will not feel obliged to say anything to me that we shall both regret. I am sure Sir Harry will never trouble me again . . .' She paused, looking at him hopefully, but he only remained standing with folded arms, his shoulders propped against the door, courteously waiting for her to finish a speech which she felt herself quite unable to go on with. 'Oh!' she said indignantly. 'You *know* very well what I mean to say! It is quite *odious* of you to stand there looking at me like that!'

'Oh, no—would you say *odious*?' murmured Mr. Ranleigh provocatively, the glint even more pronounced in his grey eyes. 'Perhaps *uncooperative* . . .'

'Yes, that is exactly what I mean! You *know* that it is unnecessary for you to offer for me now, for Sir Harry can do me no further harm, and I assure you I have no wish to be—to be made respectable . . .'

Somewhat to her surprise, Mr. Ranleigh immediately agreed to this. 'Oh, quite unnecessary!' he said affably. 'I should not dream of making you an offer upon *that* account. As a matter of fact,' he added reflectively, 'I never did.'

'You—you didn't?' Cecily faltered, taken aback.

'No, you absurd infant, I did not. It did occur to me, however—before you deprived me of the opportunity of laying the matter before you by running away from Hillcourt—that, since I had fallen in love with you, the only course that appeared likely to offer me the slightest degree of future happiness lay in asking you to marry me. Which,' he added scrupulously, 'I hereby do.'

Cecily's hands flew to her burning cheeks. 'Oh, no, you cannot mean it!' she exclaimed. 'You cannot wish to marry me after I have behaved so *very* improperly!'

'You are mistaken. It is exactly what I wish,' said Mr. Ranleigh, unfolding his arms, pushing his shoulders away from the door, and advancing on her in an alarmingly purposeful manner.

Cecily, attempting to preserve the last remnants of rationality, found it next to impossible with Mr. Ranleigh's arms securely about her and her breast pressed tightly against the front of his impeccably tailored coat. She had the oddest sensation that it was beyond her power to prevent herself from flinging her arms about his neck, and succeeded in overcoming this disastrous impulse only by the strongest exertion of will.

'Oh!' she said, in a stifled voice. 'It is not at all k-kind of you to take such an advantage of me, Mr. Ranleigh!'

'Do you not think, my darling,' Mr. Ranleigh inquired, bending to drop a kiss lightly upon the tip of her nose and then looking down at her with the unmistakable air of a man proposing to repeat this reprehensible action within the space of a few moments, 'that, under the circumstances, you might contrive to call me Robert?'

'Under the circumstances . . . ? You cannot mean that you *do* wish to marry me! Oh, no—it is *quite* impossible. That is the reason I ran away from Hillcourt, you know—because I overheard Lady Frederick say that you felt bound in honour to offer for me, even though it was not at all your inclination. And —and Charlie told me that you did not even *l-like* me . . .'

'You see now what comes of listening to the conversations of persons who know nothing whatever of the subject they are discussing,' he said, adding firmly, as she opened her lips to speak again, 'I wish you will stop arguing over the matter, for I have not the slightest desire to hear any more objections. Ever since you succeeded in convincing me that you did not really wish to run off with Harry, I have realised that any representations you have made of being indifferent to me were wholly without foundation for nothing but a most unalterable attachment could have induced even you to embark upon such an outrageous adventure.'

'It was *not* outrageous!' she objected, stung into remonstrance. 'It might have succeeded very well if Sir Harry had not been so wickedly underhanded as not to intend to carry me to Gretna Green, after all!'

'Damn Sir Harry!' said Mr. Ranleigh. 'Let us forget him.'

He looked with disfavour at her bonnet. 'Must you continue to wear this abominable creation on your head?' he demanded. 'I cannot contrive to kiss you properly while you do so.'

She gazed up at him, still with great misgiving, but docilely permitted him to untie her bonnet-strings and remove the offending article from her head.

'Yes, but—are you *quite* sure?' she inquired anxiously. 'Because you know I *might* wish to marry you only because you are very rich . . .'

'Exactly as you wished to marry Tony,' he agreed.

'But I didn't . . .'

'Just so,' he said. 'Have I not told you, my incorrigible little love, that I wish to hear no more objections from you?'

'Yes, you have,' she confessed, breathlessly. 'Only, Mr. Ran . . .'

'Robert,' he said ruthlessly, taking her into his arms once more.

'Oh, very well!' she said, flinging caution to the winds and making no further attempt to resist the pressing impulse to throw her arms about his neck. 'It seems *very* odd of you to wish to marry me, but if you are quite sure . . . *Oh!*' It was some moments before she emerged, very much shaken and a little awed, from an embrace that had threatened to crush all the breath from her body. 'Oh, I *really* believe you do!' she said radiantly. 'It is very unlikely, but I am so happy! Are you going to kiss me again? I wish you will! Oh, Robert—Robert—Robert— *Robert*!'

STAR Books are obtainable from many booksellers and newsagents. If you have any difficulty please send purchase price plus postage on the scale below to:

> **Star Cash Sales**
> **P.O. Box 11**
> **Falmouth**
> **Cornwall**
> OR
> **Star Book Service,**
> **G.P.O. Box 29,**
> **Douglas,**
> **Isle of Man,**
> **British Isles.**

While every effort is made to keep prices low, it is sometimes necessary to increase prices at short notice. Star Books reserve the right to show new retail prices on covers which may differ from those advertised in the text or elsewhere.

Postage and Packing Rate
UK: 40p for the first book, 18p for the second book and 13p for each additional book ordered to a maximum charge of £1·49p. BFPO and EIRE: 40p for the first book, 18p for the second book, 13p per copy for the next 7 books, thereafter 7p per book. Overseas: 60p for the first book and 18p per copy for each additional book.